"Are you real?" she whispered.

His mouth traveled across her jaw and nuzzled her neck in the tender spot just below her ear. "You tell me. Does this feel real?"

He nipped lightly at the junction of her neck and shoulder, and a jolt of lust shot through her loins. She squeezed her thighs together, which turned out to be a mistake, because she'd managed to catch the bulge of his erection between the tops of her thighs in the process, and Bass groaned in response.

She shocked herself by sliding her hand down the indentation of his spine to his impressive glutes and gave a tug, pulling his hips even closer to hers.

"Carrie," he muttered warningly. "I'm a gentleman, but I have my limits."

"I'm a lady, but that doesn't mean I don't like busting through limits."

* * *

Code: Warrior SEALs—Meet these fierce warriors who take on the most dangerous secret missions around the world!

* * *

If you're on Twitter, tell us what you think of Harlequin Romantic Suspense! #harlequinromsuspense

Dear Reader,

I'm so delighted to share with you the final installment of my Code: Warrior SEALs series. I have really enjoyed returning to my writing roots and creating stories for a team of smoking-hot Navy SEALs and the smart, sexy women who love them.

This series has been especially meaningful to me because writing it spanned my fight with and ultimate conquering of cancer. In a way, the bad guys my SEALs defeated became symbolic to me of my own health struggles and victory in the end.

Writing this series has served as a rich reminder to me that we all have our own uphill battles to face in life, and that reading books is a vital escape from those. I would like to think romance novels also remind us that, at the end of the day, love can overcome every obstacle placed before it.

From the bottom of my heart, I hope this book gives you a needed escape from whatever challenges you face in your life, and I hope it helps you remember love is, indeed, the most powerful force in the universe. Love conquers all. For real.

All my best and happy reading!

Warmly,

Cindy

NAVY SEAL COP

Cindy Dees

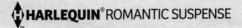

HARLEQUIN® ROMANTIC SUSPENSE

Recycling programs
for this product may
not exist in your area.

ISBN-13: 978-1-335-45652-6

Navy SEAL Cop

Copyright © 2018 by Cynthia Dees

This edition published by arrangement with Harlequin Books S.A.

For questions and comments about the quality of this book, please contact us at CustomerService@Harlequin.com.

® and TM are trademarks of Harlequin Enterprises Limited or its corporate affiliates. Trademarks indicated with ® are registered in the United States Patent and Trademark Office, the Canadian Intellectual Property Office and in other countries.

Printed in U.S.A.

New York Times and *USA TODAY* bestselling author **Cindy Dees** is the author of more than fifty novels. She draws upon her experience as a US Air Force pilot to write romantic suspense. She's a two-time winner of the prestigious RITA® Award for romance fiction, a two-time winner of the RT Reviewers' Choice Best Book Award for Romantic Suspense and an *RT Book Reviews* Career Achievement Best Author Award nominee. She loves to hear from readers at www.cindydees.com.

Books by Cindy Dees

Harlequin Romantic Suspense

Code: Warrior SEALs

Undercover with a SEAL
Her Secret Spy
Her Mission with a SEAL
Navy SEAL Cop

The Prescott Bachelors

High-Stakes Bachelor
High-Stakes Playboy

Soldier's Last Stand
The Spy's Secret Family
Captain's Call of Duty
Soldier's Rescue Mission
Her Hero After Dark
Breathless Encounter
Flash of Death
Deadly Sight
A Billionaire's Redemption

HQN Books

Take the Bait
Close Pursuit
Hot Intent

Visit Cindy's Author Profile page at
Harlequin.com for more titles!

Chapter 1

Deserted alley in the middle of the night when all sensible people were in bed? Check.

Famously haunted and badly lit location? Check.

Ground fog swirling thickly enough to create a spooky-as-heck mood and obscure everything? Check.

Either she was ready to start shooting the next episode of the popular television show *America's Ghosts*, or she was about to commit a homicide.

Of course, if the show's host didn't quit trying to tell her how to do her job filming him, there might just be a murder out here tonight.

Carrie Price stared through the viewfinder of her digital movie camera at her boss and renowned ghost hunter, Gary Hubbard. For tonight's episode he'd picked Pirate's Alley in New Orleans. The tourists and foot traffic were long gone, leaving just their footsteps to echo weirdly off the brick walls and their grotesquely elongated shadows to freak her out a little bit.

Bounded on one side by St. Anthony's Garden behind a tall, wrought-iron fence and on the other side by darkened shops with tightly closed wooden doors, the narrow alley was only lit by widely spaced cast-iron streetlamps, forming blue haloes of light in drifts of ground fog. The old bricks glistened with moisture and a damp chill hung in the air. She wouldn't have to apply any filters at all in post-production to achieve the show's signature gothic vibe.

Gary walked backward down the alley, narrating a story about the possibly haunted buildings now standing on the site of the Calabozo, a prison that once housed pirate Jean Lafitte and much of his crew. Then Gary spun a tale of a lost pirate treasure rumored to be hidden somewhere in New Orleans, known only to the city's ghosts. This season he'd branched out from strictly ghost hunting to include a treasure hunt in the show, a blatant publicity stunt to get *America's Ghosts* renewed for another season. It had been a good move. His ratings had gone through the roof as he churned out a plot line of convincing ghosts to lead him to a mythical treasure hoard.

She let Gary back away from her far enough that he became little more than a silhouette within the mysterious fog, his melodic baritone voice a disembodied entity floating out of the mists of time. She should get a freaking Emmy for this camera work!

Just starting to move forward and rejoin Gary for some close-ups of him looking tense and then excited as tonight's ghost "appeared" to him, she spied something dark moving out of the shadows behind Gary. Two dark somethings, in fact.

She jolted but kept the camera rolling. Gary hadn't told her he'd hired anyone to stage an apparition appearance. But these actors looked terrific. Clothed in black from head to foot, they'd even covered their faces with some kind of black cloth, which gave them an other-worldly eeriness as they crept up behind Gary.

He turned just as the pair of "ghosts" reached him. Uncharacteristically, Gary threw up his hands and stumbled as if he was frightened of these apparitions. Oh, God. This was going to make for a great episode. She would cut to commercial just after he threw his hands up and cried out in surprise. All of America would be on the edge of its La-Z-Boys waiting to see what happened after three minutes of sponsored ads.

The ghosts grabbed Gary and commenced dragging him down the alley away from her. He struggled, but the apparitions easily overpowered him. What was he doing? He never interacted physically with ghosts. Sure, he'd been going for over-the-top supernatural elements this season, but was he seriously staging a ghost abduction? Why hadn't he said something?

Whatever. It was his show. She was just the camera-woman.

Dammit, they were moving away from her too fast! Gary's silver hair was part of the white fog now. She was live recording audio, or else she would have shouted at them to slow down or maybe even to reset and redo the take. She would keep the footage of that first jolt of surprise from Gary, though. It had looked totally authentic even though he wasn't the world's greatest actor. She often had to coach him through multiple takes to get a decent look of surprise out of him.

She moved forward more quickly, hurrying between the soaring walls of St. Louis Cathedral on her left, and on her right, the Cabildo, once the seat of government in Louisiana and now a museum. Gary and the two ghosts were only vague shapes in the fog ahead of her. She was losing them!

They disappeared from sight entirely. An eerie cry drifted back to her, echoing off the walls and seeming to come from all around her. Pure audio gold.

She rushed forward and stopped abruptly as she popped out of the alley. Jackson Square stretched away across the street from her, obscured by the fog. She panned her camera left and right down Chartres Street. Where did they go?

"Gary!" she called out.

Nothing.

"Gary!" she shouted. "Where are you?"

Still nothing.

"This isn't funny. I need to reshoot your retreat into the fog. You guys moved too fast for me!"

What the heck? He *still* wasn't answering her. She retraced her steps into the alley. Had he and the ghosts turned down Cabildo Alley? She reached the narrow side street and peered down it. Only wisps of fog moved in a slow-motion ballet, pirouetting up into the night. But there was no sign of three men pulling a sophomoric prank on her.

Had she moved past them inadvertently? She strode all the way back to the north end of the six-hundred-foot-long alley and the van she worked out of. No sign of Gary and his hilarious buddies.

Enough of this. She pulled out her cell phone and angrily hit the speed dial button for Gary. She tapped an irritated foot as she waited for him to pick up. The phone rang. And rang again. And kept on ringing until it kicked over to voice mail.

Huh. If his phone was working, why hadn't he picked up? She walked from the show's van all the way to the far end of the alley and back, looking for anywhere the three men might have disappeared to. Knowing Gary, he'd ducked into some bar and was hoisting a few cold ones with his actor pals, laughing his ass off at the great joke they'd played on her. Jerk.

If that was how he wanted to play this game, then he could find his own damned way back to the lodgings the show had rented for their month of shooting in New Orleans. They were scheduled to film eight episodes here, and tonight was number three. Normally, Gary reserved his more juvenile pranks for the last shooting day in any location. He knew his stupid stunts annoyed the heck out of her and she usually needed a week or two to cool down before they worked together again.

He was old enough to be her father, for crying out loud. It was horrendously unprofessional to pull crap like this on set. She called him every name she knew as she drove the van back to their rented house, a narrow, shabby affair with a one-car garage downstairs and two apartments upstairs.

She took satisfaction in stomping all the way to her third-floor apartment. Still mad, she downloaded tonight's raw footage from her camera and played it back on the monitor of her computer.

On the larger screen, the alley looked even spookier than it had through her camera lens. Arms crossed in disgust, she watched the ghosts approach Gary, his turn, the look of surprise, and the brief struggle to follow. Hmm. Gary actually looked pretty darned convincing.

She backed up the tape and watched it again. Gary looked like he was genuinely trying to resist those guys.

A hum of alarm rumbled low in her gut. What if—

She played the tape a third time, and this time doubt poked her in the ribs. What if that was real? Not the ghosts, of course. In all the episodes of *America's Ghosts* she'd filmed, she'd never seen an actual ghost. Modern special effects were a marvelous thing.

But what if the abduction had been real?

She watched the tape several more times, torn by indecision. It was entirely possible that Gary had staged it, either because he thought it would make for good television or simply because he got a huge kick out of scaring the hell out of her. He knew she didn't believe in ghosts, and he was forever and always trying to convince her they were real by messing with her head.

If he really had been kidnapped, she needed to call the police right away. But if this was a joke and she called the cops, she would be embarrassed at best and charged with some crime at worst. And it wasn't like she had any reason to trust police after her past.

She tried calling Gary several more times on his cell phone, but she was sent to voice mail every time. A glance at the clock told her it was after 2:00 a.m., the traditional time for most bars to close down for the night. That was finally what decided it for her. Something was wrong if he wasn't answering her calls now.

Reluctantly, she Googled the phone number for the New Orleans Police Department. She hesitated, torn. If there was one thing in the world she hated worse than being jerked around by Gary, it was dealing with the police.

If only she had a friend on the show or knew someone who knew Gary. She could ask them to call the police and deal with all the questions and suspicion and recriminations. But no. She was even more antisocial than the ghosts Gary spent his life trying to capture.

Swearing under her breath, she punched in the stupid phone number.

"N'awlins Poh-lice. How may I help y'all?" a female voice drawled.

"I'd like to report a possible kidnapping." She winced as soon as she heard the words spoken aloud. She'd lost her mind. There had been no kidnapping.

"I'll connect y'all to the Missing Puh-sons Unit. One moment."

A male voice came on the line. "Detective LeBlanc." His voice, too, held a Southern drawl, but nothing like the previous cop's.

"Uhh, hi. My name's Carrie Price, and I think my boss may have been kidnapped."

"Why's that?"

"Umm, I filmed it."

"When did this happen?" The detective's voice was suddenly alert and interested.

"About two hours ago."

"And you're just now calling it in?"

Crapcrapcrapcrapcrap. She was in trouble for not calling sooner. "I thought it was a joke." She added in a rush, "And honestly, it may still turn out to be a joke. But he's not answering his phone, and the bars are shut down by now, aren't they?"

"Most of them, yes."

"I didn't want to bother you, but I keep watching the video, and he seems genuinely surprised and I think he's struggling for real against the ghosts."

"I beg your pardon?"

"Not actual ghosts, of course. Guys dressed up to look like ghosts."

"Riigghht. Where did this possible kidnapping happen?"

"Pirate's Alley."

"Of course." The detective's voice was dry now. Skeptical.

"Look. Can you just watch the video I filmed and tell me what you think of it?"

A sigh. "Sure. Do you want to come into the station?"

"It might be better if you came to my place. I have a high-resolution computer monitor and editing software that can enhance images, play video in slow motion, and do stop-action views."

"What's the address?"

She rattled it off and he responded, "I'll be there in fifteen minutes."

It turned out to be more like ten, and she worried the whole time that she was just playing into Gary's hands by calling the police. He was going to stumble in tomorrow morning, hung over as heck, and laugh his head off at her for panicking. And then she would have some tall explaining to do to the stern-sounding police officer.

When the door buzzer sounded, Carrie jogged downstairs to let in the cop…and stopped cold at the sight of the detective standing there. He was tall and would be good-looking with those lean cheeks and chiseled jaw if he wasn't also so dad-blamed scary looking. That stern frown of his made her want to confess to every petty wrong she'd ever committed. He wore civilian clothes, which surprised her, but he flashed his badge as she peered out the peephole.

She threw open the door and registered that he was close to a foot taller than her. She was only five foot three, so he wasn't a giant, but still. His waist was lean and his shoulders well-defined. Perhaps what struck her the most, though, were his piercing blue eyes. They were hard, exuding no-nonsense focus. Oh, God. He was everything she feared and loathed about police, and men in general.

"I'm Carrie Price. Thanks for coming." She held out her hand, unsure of how to act around a police officer who wasn't eyeing her with suspicion and wishing she wasn't making accusations of the most powerful man in town.

This cop briefly looked surprised, but then took her hand in his. It was warm. Firm. A thick callus at the base of his thumb abraded her skin. His fingers swallowed hers up, intimidating as heck. Sometimes she really hated being as tiny as she was.

"Bastien LeBlanc." In person, his Acadian drawl was more pronounced than over the phone.

She nodded, tongue-tied, and settled for turning and heading upstairs. She was vividly aware of him behind her, with a critical view of her rear end. Not that her behind was anything to write home about. She enjoyed running and tried to keep reasonably toned, but everything about her was small in scale. She could never compete with tall, voluptuous women with miles of curves.

Thankfully, she reached the third floor without falling on her face or otherwise humiliating herself. "Computer's over here." She headed for the kitchen table, which she had converted to a workspace. "Watch out for the power cords," she murmured, stepping over an orange extension cord.

"Roger," the scary detective replied.

That sounded more military than law enforcement. But then, he took the chair she indicated, and she reached over his shoulder to cue up the tape—and the scent of him knocked all rational thought right out of her head. He smelled like…warmth. His cologne was subtle and spicy and entirely edible. It totally didn't mesh in her mind with the frowning, badass cop.

"I'm the camera operator for a TV show called *America's Ghosts*, hosted by Gary Hubbard. I shot this footage of him earlier tonight."

Gary's deep voice filled the awkward silence and his image walked backward down the alley onscreen. She watched Detective LeBlanc from behind without comment, letting him form his own first impression.

The two men in black appeared, Gary turned around, and the men dragged him away. The whole incident took less than thirty seconds to play.

"Again," the detective ordered, his eyes never leaving the screen.

She leaned forward to restart the footage, and her arm brushed against his, her face coming dangerously close to his ear. She jumped, as alarmed as if she'd poked a bear. She might not take crap from Gary, but cops turned her into a terrified teen all over again.

While the detective watched the video, she furtively watched him, noting the tiny frown of concentration, and the way muscles in his jaw rippled as his face tensed. He must be watching the abduction bit now.

He glanced up and caught her blatantly scoping him out. She looked away hastily, her heart racing as if she'd just sprinted a mile. She felt her cheeks heating up. Sheesh, this man made her uncomfortable.

"You said you can do stop-action on this machine?"

"Yes."

"I need you to run the last part of the video, where the assailants grab Mr. Hubbard, frame by frame."

She almost said, "Yes, sir," but managed to mumble, "Coming up," instead. She had to reach past him again to operate her mouse, and her left breast brushed his right arm by accident. She sucked in a sharp breath and kept her horrified gaze locked on the computer screen. Thankfully, he just leaned forward to study the screen closely as she advanced the video one frame at a time, each frame progressing by one forty-eighth of a second.

"There. Stop," LeBlanc bit out, startling her. She stopped the video and stared at the image. The two black figures had a hold of Gary and appeared to be goose-stepping him away from her. She'd already seen it a dozen times.

LeBlanc poked at the screen. "Look at how this one is holding Mr. Hubbard's hand. He's twisting your boss's hand behind his back and forcing his forearm upward with the hold."

"And that's significant why?" she asked.

"It's a technique military members are taught for subduing prisoners."

She frowned. "Would police use the same grip?"

He grinned up at her briefly, and she gasped inwardly as his smile lit up the dingy apartment. "Naw. Cops use handcuffs."

"I'll bet that's what you say to all the girls," she shot back. The smart remark was out of her mouth before she could stop it. "Oh, crap. I'm sorry. I shouldn't have said that—"

"No worries. And no, that's not in my usual repertoire of pickup lines."

"You have a repertoire?" Darn it, she'd done it again! This guy was a *cop*, for crying out loud. Lord, he threw her off balance.

His mouth twitched, hopefully with humor. Great. At best, he thought she was ridiculous. At worst, he thought she was an annoying twit. Not that she could blame him. She was a hot mess tonight.

Frantic to distract him, she mumbled, "What does it mean that one of his captors used some special grip on him?"

The detective's muscular shoulder lifted in a shrug. "It's a detail we can use to help identify the assailants."

"You think that was a real abduction then?" she blurted.

"I do."

Panic erupted in her belly and promptly tried to claw its way out of her throat. Suddenly she felt light-headed and faintly nauseated. "But who...?" she gasped. "Why?"

The detective surged to his feet, looming over her. He grasped her upper arms in his powerful hands and guided her over to the sofa, where he sat her down. Which was probably wise. The room spun around her and lights danced before her eyes.

"Take a deep breath, Miss Price. Hold it for one, two, three. Now exhale slowly. Three. Two. One."

He talked her through several more breaths, and they helped her brain engage again. Still. She couldn't seem to keep her hands from fidgeting uncontrollably. She plucked at the seam in her jeans and then wrung her hands and tugged at her T-shirt. He sat down beside her and his hands closed over hers as she stared at him in anguish.

His gaze wasn't the least bit gentle. Thank God. She would've burst into tears then and there. But maybe that was a hint of sympathy lurking at the back of his deep blue eyes. Huh. The tough guy might just be human beneath that hard façade.

She wanted to crawl into bed, pull the covers up over her head, and curl up in a little ball with Mr. Paddles, her stuffed turtle. Which was weird if she stopped to think about it. She didn't revert to little girl behaviors, well, pretty much ever. Not since she'd run away from home all those years ago. She'd been barely more than a child then.

The detective spoke not exactly gently, but less harshly than before. "The New Orleans Police will do everything we can to find Mr. Hubbard as quickly as possible."

"You're sure it's not a prank?" she asked in a small voice.

"I don't think it is. Mr. Hubbard's body language in the video is consistent with genuine surprise and fear as he's being dragged away."

"I followed them down the alley. I couldn't run because the camera would jostle too much, but I walked at a good clip. It was under a minute until I reached the end of the alley. Where could they have gone in so little time? God, I'm such an idiot—" She broke off as it dawned on her she was babbling.

The detective snorted. "With a minute's head start, they could have thrown your boss into a vehicle and driven away without you ever seeing their taillights."

Her breathing started to speed up again, and the detective looked her in the eye, took a deep breath, held it, and then released it slowly. Staring at him, she followed along, matching her breaths to his. It was an intimate thing, breathing in concert with him. Their gazes locked—his focused and calm, and hers probably completely freaked out.

In any other circumstances, she would be wildly attracted to a man who looked like him. But as it was, she could hardly keep the panic at bay. And it wasn't just panic over Gary. Merely being in the presence of this man scared the heck out of her. And not only because he was a cop.

"Why Gary?"

"I don't know why Mr. Hubbard was a target," he said reasonably. "You tell me. Was he in any trouble? Did he have any enemies?"

She stared up at him in dismay. They were really going to do this? He was going to question her for real? Lord, she hated questions from police.

Her panic galloped away from her then, and her entire body shook with it. She'd been questioned like this once before, and look how that had turned out. Her best friend had died. Because of her. Because she'd gone to the police. Had she done it again? Had she just gotten Gary killed, too?

Chapter 2

Bastien stared down at the frightened young woman before him. She was a tiny little thing. And right now, scared out of her mind, she looked about twelve years old. Scratch that. She was too hot ever to be mistaken for a child. She was petite but she had curves in all the right places. Her hair was brown with gold streaks and currently pulled into a high ponytail that hung long and smooth down her back. Her eyes were big and dark, and her skin had a beautiful olive undertone. He'd place her ancestry as at least partially Mediterranean.

She was the kind of woman a man looked at twice. Maybe had some dirty dreams about. Had he met her in any other setting—at a bar or with a mutual acquaintance—he'd have done his damnedest to charm her into his bed.

Did she realize she was wringing her hands again? He really shouldn't stop her—they were a useful body language tell—but damned if he could stop himself from reaching out to take her hands once more, rescuing her reddened fingers from death by squeezing.

Thing was, he was no rookie. He knew better than to fall into the whole comfort-the-family-member thing. It wasn't his job and could end up being a giant distraction when it came to finding missing persons. He had become a cop to solve problems. To use his military training to catch bad guys. When he was on duty, he was all about the job. Put the pieces together. Solve the crime. Move on to the next case. He did his best to stay away from all the messy human emotions that came with his line of work. They were nothing but a distraction.

However, he wasn't entirely without basic human decency. And that forced him to feel at least a little sympathy for this young woman in the face of her fear. Still, this was work, and it was not his job to pat her hand and say, "There, there." It was his job to find the guy in the video.

And like it or not, he was sitting in front of his only currently identified suspect. She wasn't much of a suspect as they went. After all, she'd come forward to the police with direct video evidence of the crime. But, he couldn't rule her out, either. She was a known close associate of the missing person.

He prompted her, "Can you think of anyone who would want to do Mr. Hubbard harm?"

"That's a complicated question where Gary Hubbard is concerned," she finally offered up.

"Why's that?"

A sigh. "His television show has devoted fans and equally devoted haters. There's a whole group on social media devoted to debunking his ghost sightings."

Seriously? Ghosts? He schooled his face to give away nothing and nodded encouragingly.

Another sigh from the young woman. "Gary has a big personality. He likes to play jokes on people and delights in poking at people's most cherished beliefs. He's a bit of a curmudgeon in that regard."

"Give me an example."

"He tries to refute generally accepted versions of history using communication with ghosts to dispute commonly held understanding of famous historic events. He did a series of shows about the founding fathers and talked to ghosts of their slaves to prove what a good deal it was to be one of their slaves. Gary got hundreds of death threats over those shows."

"When did these episodes air?"

"At the end of his first season, six years ago. The public outcry was what got his show renewed, in fact."

Damn. It was old history, then. That didn't sound like a motive now for kidnapping and possibly worse. But he asked nonetheless, "What's the most recent scandal he's stirred up?"

"Well, this season, he's working on a treasure hunt having to do with the last French governor of Louisiana in 1803. The guy supposedly worked for Napoleon, but Gary got it in his head that this guy, Pierre Clément deLaussat, was a secret French royalist."

Still didn't sound like motive for kidnapping or worse. What was he missing? He prompted, "And this is controversial because…"

"Gary claims to have been approached by the ghost of deLaussat's mistress, who told him deLaussat was in possession of a great royal French secret that he hid in New Orleans."

"Are you kidding me?" Bastien blurted.

The young woman winced. "I wish I were."

"I hardly think the reputation of some guy who lived in the early 1800s is worth committing a felony over."

"You would think, wouldn't you?" she responded. "But Gary's detractors get wired way tight when he attempts to challenge history."

"If he's using conversations with ghosts as his rationale, I can see why they get up in arms."

She looked up at him, her chocolate eyes worried. "Enough to harm him?"

That was the question, wasn't it? He summarized: "So far, all we know is that two guys grabbed him and took him away from Pirate's Alley. Maybe they wanted to get more information from him. Or hell, I don't know, maybe they wanted him to perform a séance."

She snorted. "Gary wouldn't know how to do a real séance if a ghost jumped up and bit him in the butt."

"Duly noted," he replied dryly.

Her gaze snapped to his, and a moment of humor shone in her eyes. It lit her entire face, transforming her into a fey creature for an instant. Whoa. He could almost believe in ghosts and otherworldly beings when she looked at him like that.

Kidnapping. Investigation. Ask questions. He dragged his mind back to business and managed to come up with, "You said he's on a treasure hunt. For what? How valuable is it? Maybe someone snatched Hubbard to get at a rich treasure."

"I don't know what the treasure is. He won't say. He's releasing clues in each show this season and plans to do a big reveal in the season finale."

Bastien frowned. "How can you not know? Aren't you working closely with him on the television show?"

"You'd think." Bastien detected a hint of bitterness

in her voice. So. She wasn't happy that the boss was keeping secrets from her. Unhappy enough to provide a motive for kidnapping, maybe?

He asked, "Has Mr. Hubbard received any recent threats? Maybe letters or emails?"

"I don't know. He handles his own correspondence. I'm just the cameraperson, and I do the first post-shoot editing."

Did that mean she was responsible for dubbing in ghosts? He was tempted to ask, but he wasn't here to argue with a ghost hunter over the existence of ghosts. "Do you have access to Mr. Hubbard's email account?"

"No."

"Too bad. Normally, we have to wait until a subject has been missing for forty-eight hours before we can use police resources to begin searching for him."

She frowned. "I might be able to figure out his password. He's not the most creative or computer-savvy guy on the planet."

"It would be best if you leave his computer alone for now." Spotting the stubborn look that entered her eyes, he added, "If you do get into his account, give me a call immediately."

She nodded, a frankly adorable frown puckering her brow. And, she was back to looking like a nymphette. He would *not* look at her chest. At a glance it wasn't anything to write home about, but at a second glance, she was nicely endowed in proportion to her overall smallness. Dammit, he respected women, and he was not going to turn this interview into a leering session.

"Can you think of anything else that might help me find Mr. Hubbard?"

"He's a big beer drinker. Tends to hang out at microbreweries and in bars that serve artisanal beers."

That gave him a place to start. He could canvas the local bars. "Do you have a picture of Mr. Hubbard that I could have?"

"Of course." She moved over to the kitchen sink and lifted out a three-ring binder that she carried back to the sofa.

"You don't cook much?" he asked.

"What?" She glanced back at the sink and down at the binder. "Oh. No. I destroyed a pan once while trying to hard-boil eggs. And it was stainless steel."

"Impressive."

"Did you know eggs actually blow up?" she asked indignantly.

He bit back a snort of humor. "Can't say I did."

She sat down next to him, and he was abruptly aware again of how small she was. Her face was fine-boned and slightly heart-shaped, vaguely elfin in appearance and utterly lovely. "They make a god-awful mess when they do. Yolk goes everywhere, and it dries on stuff like paint."

His lips twitched in humor as she rifled through the binder.

"These are publicity photos he sends to fans. Would this work?" She pulled out an eight-by-eleven glossy head shot of Gary Hubbard.

He studied the professional picture critically. "That's arguably the best photo I've ever seen of a missing person. Hell, it's practically life-sized."

She smiled back at him. "Let's just say Gary is not a modest man and leave it at that."

"Tell me more about him."

"He's been a television personality for nearly thirty years. He hosted a string of failed game shows. Tried a talk show, but he wouldn't shut up and let his guests talk. That lasted only half a season. Then he landed the ghost-hunting gig. He's been doing *America's Ghosts* for six years."

"Wife? Kids? Business partners?"

"No to all three. He likes to be in control. He's got a crew back in New York, and they research locations, set up shoots, and help with post-production work, but on the road, it's just him and me."

That sent warning flags up in his mind. He asked, "How would you describe your relationship? Just co-workers? Friends? More?" He watched closely for tells of a lie. She was a lot younger than Hubbard and might not want to admit to an affair if there was one.

She startled him by laughing in genuine amusement at the question. "Me and Gary? Together? That's hilarious. No, it's a little sick, actually. We're definitely not more than friends and coworkers. Sheesh. He's older than my father."

Bastien was surprised by the relief that flooded his gut. It was none of his business who she slept with. Still. He was glad she wasn't involved with her boss.

"How did you come to be associated with the show? Were you assigned to it by the network?"

"No. Gary hired me. He told his bosses he wanted to work with me, and they reviewed my portfolio and agreed to hire me."

Huh. So she owed her job to him. Did that reduce her viability as a suspect? Or perhaps she resented him because of it. Aloud, he asked, "What all do you do for Mr. Hubbard…as his coworker?"

"I film the show and direct him from behind the camera. Then he and I do the initial post-production editing and cleanup."

She continued, "We shoot anywhere from three to

ten episodes in a single location, and then we usually return to New York. The editor there cuts together the shows and Gary records any voice-overs they require."

"How long have you two been in New Orleans?"

"About two weeks. We spent a week checking out spots to film, and the plan was to spend about three weeks filming for the show."

How had this glorious creature been in his city for two weeks without him knowing about her? His radar for beautiful women must be slipping. Usually he was the first to know and the first to make a move. Not that he was sleezy about it. He liked women, and they liked him. He just didn't like to get too deeply involved with any one woman.

Consciously suppressing his natural tendency to turn on the charm with the lovely Miss Price, Bastien asked, "While you were scouting locations, what did Mr. Hubbard say about this supposed treasure he's tracking?"

"Not a word. He's keeping whatever he knows about it completely to himself."

Too bad. A rich treasure would certainly constitute a motive for kidnapping or worse. "Has Mr. Hubbard suggested on the show that the treasure is valuable?"

"This season hasn't aired on television yet. But in the episodes we've already shot, he has indicated that the treasure is priceless."

"Who all has seen the footage shot so far?"

"Gary, me and the production crew in New York."

"I'll need names of everyone on the crew."

"Umm, okay. I can get that for you in the morning. I think I know everyone, but I may be missing someone who has access to the footage."

He nodded and then said, "So you'll be in town a few more weeks?"

"Assuming Gary shows up soon and we can resume filming on schedule."

"What if he doesn't show up?" he responded casually.

Horror filled her eyes, and then tears followed. He saw a lot of tears in his line of work and had become hardened to them long ago. But this woman's unshed tears brimming in her stricken eyes twisted his gut painfully. He bit back an urge to tell her not to worry. That he would find her boss for her and bring him back to her. But he knew better than to make promises he couldn't necessarily keep.

She choked out between sobbing gasps of air, "Gary's like a father to me. He can be a pain in the butt, but he has a good heart, and he looked out for me when I needed it—"

She broke off. An interesting choice of words. Had she been in some kind of trouble that Hubbard rescued her from?

On the weekends, Bastien pulled reserve duty in a Navy SEAL unit, and his teammates often accused him of being a suspicious bastard. He assured them it was merely his cop's instinct. And right now, that instinct was firing on all cylinders. There was a story behind this young woman. He would bet his police badge and his Budweiser—his SEAL insignia pin—that she had secrets to hide.

He asked, "Have you and Mr. Hubbard had any disagreements recently? Any falling-outs?"

She answered without hesitation, "We fight all the time. Gary always thinks he knows better than me how to stage and film the show. But he has no artist's eye whatsoever, not to mention no training as a camera operator."

Hmm. No evasion in her answer, but an admission

of friction. He couldn't take her off the suspect list yet. Too bad. His gut feeling was that she was not part of the kidnapping plot. But he only trusted gut feelings when they involved guns pointed at him or bad guys sneaking up behind him. In the world of law enforcement, it was all about evidence and cold, hard facts. Which was, of course, part of the allure of it to him. No need for messy things like emotions and relationships.

He stood up and fished a business card out of his wallet. "Here's my phone number. Call me if Mr. Hubbard shows up or contacts you. If you think of anything else that might help me locate him, call me any time, day or night."

"When do you sleep?" she asked.

One corner of his mouth curled sardonically. "I don't."

"You're a cyborg, then?"

"Something like that." He had to give her credit. She had a quick wit. When she wasn't hiding things or scared silly, she was probably an entertaining person to be around. "Don't worry about waking me up. If you hear from him or think of something, call me right away. Time is the enemy in missing persons cases."

She nodded her understanding and reached for his card. Their fingertips brushed and he caught her fast, light inhalation. Attracted to him, was she? *Aww, baby. It's totally mutual.*

An urge to reach out, cup the sweet curve of her cheek in his hand, to lean down and brush those berry lips with his, to whisper in her ear that he would make everything all right, nearly overcame him.

Damn, she was messing with his head! It must be the fact that he couldn't have her that was making her so completely irresistible. But he had a hard rule about not dating on the job, and he wasn't about to break it. Not for her. Not for any woman.

Not that he actually dated much at all. What with working long hours as a cop and longer hours on the weekends training SEALs, he didn't exactly have a thriving social life. Throw in the occasional deployment with the SEALs where he could be gone anywhere from a few days to weeks, and it wasn't worth the effort to try to sustain relationships in between the demands of his twin careers.

He supposed he technically could be accused of serial dating a long string of women. But he didn't engage in actual relationships with any of them. At best, a few of them rose to the status of friends with benefits. But he'd learned a long time ago never to give away his heart to anyone. He'd seen the devastation love wrought, and he wanted no part of it.

He followed Carrie out of her apartment and down to the second-floor landing. "Who lives in this apartment?" he asked, pointing at the locked door there.

"Gary. The show's producer rented this whole building for the month we'll be in town."

"Do you have a key to his place?"

"I do. He's forever misplacing his keys and locking himself out, so I'm the designated spare key lady."

Did she realize that having access to his home made her more of a suspect? It connoted more of a personal connection between them than she'd admitted to so far. The vast majority of abductions, and murders for that matter, were committed by people close to the victim.

He waited while she fumbled around in her fanny pack and found the spare key to Gary's apartment.

She reached out to unlock the door and he forestalled

her, grabbing her wrist quickly and saying sharply, "Let me do that."

"Why?"

"It's unlawful trespassing for you to enter without the owner's permission. I can legally enter to search the premises in an emergency. And given that we have film of the man being abducted by force, I'd say that qualifies."

In reality, he didn't want her tampering with any evidence that might incriminate her. Not to mention he wanted to make sure there were no hostiles lurking in the abducted victim's home.

He stepped in front of her and eased the key into the lock. He turned the knob silently and pushed the door open by slow degrees. No movement on the other side, no sound. No reaction at all. He eased the door further open.

He gestured for Carrie to stay back and slipped inside the darkened apartment, identical in layout to the one upstairs.

Hubbard's apartment smelled like beer and stale pizza and was beyond slovenly. The place looked like it had been tossed. Seat cushions were on the floor, the contents of drawers spilled out, and everything thrown off the shelves. Television was still here, so not a robbery.

If the place had been searched, it had been a hasty search. A quick once-through looking for something specific. Had whoever tossed it found what they were looking for? It did look like the whole place had been searched, which led him to believe the searcher had not found what he sought.

He hadn't sensed any stress at all in Carrie when she handed over the key. His gut was at it again, proclaiming loudly that she hadn't had anything to do with this ransacking. *Shut up, gut.*

It took him under a minute to clear the entire apartment, with just a main room, bedroom and bathroom to check out. It was empty.

He didn't spot any clothing, personal items or toiletries to indicate that Miss Price spent any time down here. Again, relief flowed through him. *Dammit.* He lectured himself forcefully. *Not. His. Business.*

He moved back to the entry door and switched on the lights. "He's not home."

"May I come in?"

"No. I don't want you to disturb the crime scene."

"Crime scene—" She rounded the corner to stand in the doorway and stared inside in dismay. "What happened? It looks like a tornado hit."

"I'd say someone searched the place. Could Mr. Hubbard have done this, or was it likely an intruder?"

"He's a slob, but he's not this bad."

"From where you're standing, can you identify any of your employer's possessions that are missing?"

She looked around helplessly. "I don't know."

"Okay. I'm coming out and I'll seal the door until the crime scene guys can get over here and have a look at the place. I'm going to ask them to lift fingerprints and do an inventory of possessions. Maybe they can identify who did this. It's likely whoever searched this place was involved in Mr. Hubbard's disappearance."

He jogged down to his car and brought back supplies. He pasted a red paper seal to the door and frame, so if anyone opened the door they would break the seal. Then he put a big yellow X of Crime Scene Do Not Cross tape over the entire entrance.

"I'm the only other person who lives in this building," she commented after he was done. "You could have just told me not to go inside."

Yes, but she was a suspect. He shrugged. "Gotta follow procedure."

She walked him down to the street-level exit. He turned to face her and her eyes were big and dark with worry, and maybe fear.

His gut twisted at the sight of her looking so lost and vulnerable, and he couldn't stop himself from saying, "Try to get at least a little sleep. You will need stamina over the next few days if Mr. Hubbard has, indeed, been kidnapped."

If possible, her eyes got even bigger and more worried looking.

"Call me if you hear anything at all tonight or if you remember something that might help me find your boss. Hell, call me if you're scared and can't sleep."

She nodded doubtfully.

"Promise?"

"I guess."

"Promise me," he repeated. He was making a mistake, to press her like this. He was skirting dangerously close to forming a personal connection with her.

"All right. I promise."

Why in the hell he'd felt compelled to extract that promise from her, he hadn't the slightest idea. And frankly, he had no desire to examine the impulse any more closely. There was something about her that made him want to protect her.

Weird. He'd never lived to protect women before. In fact, the women he worked with—attached as support staff to his SEAL unit—were badass in the extreme and fully capable of protecting themselves. They would laugh their heads off at him going all protect-the-little-lady on a crime suspect. Even if she was both little and a lady.

He desperately hoped she was actually a damsel-in-distress. But he feared Carrie Price was simply a talented con artist. God knew, he had plenty of experience with those.

Chapter 3

Carrie tried to sleep, but every time she dozed off she dreamed of men in black whisking her away and carrying her down into darkness cold enough to freeze her lungs. She woke up gasping for air, so terrified she pulled the covers all the way over her head and cowered under the blankets, clutching her stuffed turtle close like she had when she was a frightened child.

As dawn crept around the flimsy curtains and the city outside her window began to wake, she gave up on sleeping. She called Gary's phone, and when there was no answer, she went downstairs to check the seals on his door. *Please be home. Please be home.*

The red seal was still in place, the yellow crime scene tape undisturbed.

Damn.

Real dread for Gary's safety roared through her, and her legs barely supported her weight as she fought the urge to cry. This was her fault. If she'd realized the abduction was real she could have run forward, fought the attackers. Two on two, Gary might have stood a chance of escaping.

Who was she kidding? She barely weighed a hundred pounds soaking wet and didn't know the first thing about self-defense. And Gary was no spring chicken. Still. There had to have been something she could have done.

Heart heavy, she went upstairs and called the television show's executive producer. It was barely 7:00 a.m. in New York and the guy didn't pick up, so she left an urgent message that Gary was missing and appeared to have been kidnapped.

She played the videotape again, unable to watch it now without spotting that distinctive twist and lift move put on Gary's hand behind his back. She couldn't stop watching the tape. Over and over, she watched the black shapes appear, move in behind Gary, grab him, and rush away into the night. But no matter how many times she watched it, the outcome was the same. Gary was gone.

There had to be something useful she could do to find him or at least prove he was indeed missing.

Had he received threats he hadn't told her about? He had seemed distracted ever since they'd arrived in New Orleans. But she had put it down to his obsession with finding his lost treasure and proving that the last governor of Louisiana had been no friend of Napoleon's.

When critics lambasted him online for perpetrating a giant historical hoax, he'd muttered a few cryptic comments about having tangible proof this time. A few nights ago, when he'd come home late, more drunk than not, he'd even mumbled about being close to finding an incredible treasure while she'd taken off his shoes and tucked him into his bed.

What did you get yourself mixed up in, Gary?

She was choking down some dry toast when it belatedly dawned on her that Gary had put a duffel bag in their van yesterday as they'd left for the Pirate's Alley shoot. She raced downstairs to the garage and threw open the back of the van.

Opening the drab olive canvas duffel, she spied Gary's laptop sitting on top of a pile of his filming clothes—flowing artist's smock shirts with open collars that he thought were appropriate for a master ghost hunter. Personally, she thought they made him look like an old hippie.

She grabbed the laptop and headed back upstairs to try to break into it. Detective LeBlanc might have told her to leave it alone, but she had to do something to find her boss. She couldn't just sit back and wait for two days until the police got around to declaring him missing.

A computer hacker she was not. However, she knew Gary pretty well, and she doubted he was the kind of guy to get too creative with his passwords. How hard could it be to figure it out? She tried a dozen combinations of his birthday, address, and the name of his childhood pet, a mangy mutt he still talked about, forty years later.

Not that she could fault him for over-loving his dog. Her best friend, Shelly Baker, had often declared that the only reason she didn't kill herself was because her cat would miss her too much. If a pet was a kid's reason to live and sole source of love, Carrie supposed that was better than no love at all.

Her own parents and her older brother had been okay. They'd been average people with average expectations of her. As long as she passed her classes and didn't get into trouble, they didn't pay much attention to her comings and goings.

She'd tried to talk to them about Shelly when things had started getting bad at her friend's house, but they'd told her to keep her nose out of it and that how Shelly's mom and stepdad raised her wasn't anyone else's business.

She added Gary's agent's name to the mix of possible password combinations, and on about the sixth try, his computer popped open.

Yaaasss! She fist pumped the air.

The past several days' worth of emails didn't yield anything that screamed of threats from a potential kidnapper. Gary got several hundred emails a day, though, and it was going to take a while to read through his entire backlog of emails and deleted messages.

She pulled out her cell phone and Detective Leblanc's business card. Reluctance roared through her. He was an authority figure and scary to boot. But he'd been adamant that she call him if she found anything new and that he would be mad at her if she didn't call. It wasn't even 8:00 a.m., though, and he'd been at her place until after three. Maybe she should let him sleep?

No. He'd said to call any time.

She dialed the number before she could second-guess herself.

"Detective LeBlanc." He sounded alert and not half dead like she would if she were woken from a deep sleep.

"It's Carrie Price. I found Gary's computer and figured out his password. I'm into his email."

"I told you to stay out of his place."

"His laptop wasn't in his apartment. It was in our van."

"And you failed to mention this to me last night why?"

Crud. The detective sounded pissed. "I forgot," she confessed. "I didn't remember that Gary had put a duffel bag in the van yesterday until I was eating breakfast this morning."

"I need you to bring the laptop down to the station immediately."

She wasn't sure how she felt about the prospect of seeing the hot detective again. Particularly at a police station full of cops. He was definitely pretty to look at. *But. Cops. No bueno.*

"Umm, okay," she managed to mumble.

"I'll meet you there in half an hour," he declared.

She wrote down the address he gave her and left the house right away. She still didn't have the knack of navigating New Orleans's copious one-way streets, back alleys, dead ends, and random pedestrian-only streets thrown in for fun. Parking turned out to be a challenge, as well. But, she found a spot a block away, ran for the police station and, exactly thirty minutes after her call, careened into the precinct, red-faced and breathing hard. Her cotton blouse clung to her back.

"Can I help you?" a cop behind a tall desk asked her.

"I'm here to meet with Detective LeBlanc."

"Name?"

"Carrie Price. He's expecting me."

"Elevator to the second floor, turn right when you get out, last door on the left at the end of the hall."

She more or less caught her breath in the elevator, and then lost it again when she realized she was about to see the hot detective who smelled like heaven.

The panic ultimately won out, erasing all thoughts of hot guys from her mind. Gary was definitely in big trouble. He never spent the whole night out. He always crawled home, his back teeth awash in beer, and slept it off, snoring like a chainsaw. If she'd had any doubt last night about the authenticity of his kidnapping, that doubt was fully erased this morning.

She stepped into a loud, messy squad room with a dozen desks in it, all of them piled high with papers and manila folders. Men and women talked on phones or talked to each other, and zydeco music twanged from a low-quality radio somewhere.

A few men spotted her and eyed her up and down while she scanned the room nervously for Detective LeBlanc. She didn't see him, however.

But then a big hand cupped her elbow from behind and she jumped about a foot in the air.

"Easy, darlin'. It's just me," a familiar voice drawled behind her. Detective LeBlanc. "Let's go find ourselves a nice, quiet spot where we can talk without these guys ogling you like a bunch of Neanderthals."

The tone in his voice was fond. Affectionate, even. He liked his coworkers. Huh. So ice didn't run in his veins, after all. It was one of the first signs of genuine humanity she'd seen in him, other than his reluctant flashes of compassion last night.

Shouts and insults came back at LeBlanc in response to his remark, and he responded in kind. Then he shook his head, grinning, and guided her out of the squad room.

She liked this more relaxed version of the good detective, although she didn't know whether to be complimented or embarrassed that he'd pulled her away from the other officers.

He escorted her down the hall and opened an unmarked door, poked his head in, then stood back to open it fully for her. He slid a plastic sign that said In Use into a slot on the door, and ushered her inside.

It smelled like a urinal that had been cleaned with scented bleach in a failed effort to mask the underlying stench. The detective pulled out a metal chair for her and held it while she sat down. A metal bar stretched across the table in front of her. LeBlanc sat opposite her, and she set the computer on the table.

"What's that for?" she asked, gesturing at the bar.

"We handcuff violent suspects to it."

Oh, crap. Was she a suspect? Is that why he'd brought her into what was clearly some sort of interrogation room? It even had the big glass mirror on the wall that everyone knew was a one-way window. She glanced up, and sure enough, there was a camera in the corner near the ceiling.

"Why don't you show me the computer?" LeBlanc suggested.

Right. Gary's laptop. She opened the screen and quickly typed in the password. Then she handed the device over to him. He took it without comment and spent the next few minutes browsing through it. She thought she was going to explode with impatience before he finally looked up at her again. Surely there was some sort of clue on it that a detective could spot right away. They had to find Gary before something bad happened to him.

"You hungry?" he asked.

Food? He could think of *food* at a time like this? Heck, she could hardly remember to breathe. "Excuse me?" she mumbled.

"Are you hungry? You know. Desirous of partaking in food to break one's fast or to satiate hunger pains?"

She rolled her eyes at him, and then took personal

inventory. "I guess I could eat." She'd forgotten to do so last night after she'd gotten home, and a half slice of dry toast this morning hadn't done much to satiate her hunger pains. Gary's kidnapping had been a wee bit distracting.

"Lemme pass this laptop to the tech boys and then you and me, we're gonna go get some breakfast."

"I thought you said you couldn't use police resources to track down Gary for two days."

"I think we can make an exception given that we have actual film of the abduction. Which reminds me, I'll need a copy of that to pass to the forensics guys."

"I thought you might." She dug in her purse and came up with a thumb drive. "I copied the video footage onto that." She dug again. "And here's the list of people who work on the show in New York. I tried to call the producer a while ago, but he didn't pick up his phone. When I hear back from him, I'll check to make sure I didn't miss anyone."

"Perfect." He took everything from her and swung by the squad room to drop off the list. He handed it to an attractive female officer who made Carrie feel completely inadequate. The woman detective was tall, confident-looking, and curvy. All the things Carrie was not. The woman even joked around casually with Detective LeBlanc. If there was a nice big rock anywhere around here, Carrie would just go ahead and crawl under it now.

Unlike the female detective, she completely sucked at being around other people. Some people even accused her of being antisocial. She preferred to think of herself as a loner. Not that she'd always been that way, of course. She'd had lots of friends in high school. And she and Shelly had been inseparable—

LeBlanc touched her elbow again, and again, she

jumped. Lord, that man made her nervous. He ushered her upstairs to a lab of some kind. A harassed-looking guy jotted down Gary's password and took the laptop and thumb drive off the detective's hands with a promise to get to them as soon as possible.

LeBlanc placed a hand on the small of her back as he guided her into a crowded elevator, but she was prepared for the contact this time. It was nothing personal, of course. Surely a man like him would see nothing of interest in a shy, antisocial girl like her.

She did notice that he was using his big body to block her from the other riders in the elevator car. Was he protecting her, or was he subtly taking custody of her? It was hard to tell.

Darned if she could think of anything else but that big, warm palm resting lightly on the small of her back as they rode the elevator down to the first floor. Normally, she disliked men touching her. But this one's hand was sending all kinds of crazy responses through her body. And they weren't all bad. Which was a little shocking. Since when had she decided men—cops— were okay?

She breathed a sigh of relief when he guided her out of the crowded elevator and into the morning hustle and bustle of the French Quarter. His hand fell away from her, but the memory of it was still sending bolts of lightning zinging through her and still confusing her completely as to what it meant.

"I know a little joint around the corner that makes the best beignets in the Big Easy."

She normally didn't do dessert for breakfast, but this morning, she was all over the idea of a huge greasy donut doused in powdered sugar. "Lead on," she declared.

The "joint" turned out to be long and narrow, barely wider than its double front doors, as if it had once been a bar. The detective spotted two open, high swivel stools near the back and pushed through the crowd toward the seats. He took her hand and curled his arm behind his back, not releasing her hand as he towed her along behind him in his wake. Which was just as well. People never moved out of the way for her. She was about as intimidating as a baby bunny rabbit.

She perched on her stool beside him and jumped as the man behind the bar bellowed, "'Ey, Bass! Where ya been, man?"

"Here and there," LeBlanc said. "Saving the world. You know how it goes."

"That I do," the older man said shrewdly.

A portly tourist sat down on the stool beside hers, crowding her over toward LeBlanc. Her left thigh was forced into contact with his right leg, which felt like freshly forged steel pressed against hers. Their shoulders overlapped a little, although his were a hand span taller than hers.

His presence surrounded her, enveloped her. And, for the first time since the attack last night, she felt safe. Which was totally weird. Cops usually made her feel exactly the opposite. But this morning, in his presence, she could finally breathe normally again. She relished the easy slide of air in and out of her lungs.

She glanced up at him, vividly aware of the intimacy of their seating arrangement. "Bass? Is that what your friends call you?"

"That, or Catfish, which is a nickname from my work in the military."

"Hah! You *were* military!"

He blinked down at her, looking surprised. The

flecks of silver against a background of ocean blue fascinated her as they danced in his eyes. "I still am military, part-time. But how did you know?"

"You said, 'Roger' to me last night, and I figured you might have been a soldier."

He studied her keenly. "You're an observer of people, then?"

Swear to God, she was getting a little breathless sitting smashed against him like this. "It's my job to look at everyone through the lens of how my camera would see them. Details matter."

"Indeed they do. How long have you been working for Gary Hubbard?"

"Three seasons."

"Ahh. That explains the change in the quality of the show three years ago."

It was her turn to stare at him. "How do you know that?"

"Last night I watched a bunch of clips from *America's Ghosts*."

"Shouldn't you have been out looking for Gary?"

"The bars were all closed. And I took a walk through Pirate's Alley before I went home. I couldn't find any forensic evidence to help us identify his captors. Frankly, the best evidence we've got is your film of the incident. It's a rare thing to get actual high-quality video of a crime under investigation."

"Glad I could help," she replied wryly.

The coffee arrived in an old-fashioned chrome pot, and Bass poured her a cup of what turned out to be delicious chicory coffee, strong and aromatic. A moment later, a huge plate covered in fried, spiraling donut batter and powdered sugar was plunked down in front of her.

She took a bite of the hot, crispy pastry, tender and

moist on the inside, and groaned as her taste buds orgasmed. "Ohmigosh, this is fantastic."

Bass grinned, watching her as she took another bite…and groaned again. "You like it?" he drawled.

"God, yes."

"So you appreciate good food, but you don't cook."

She picked up a napkin to wipe away what had to be a confectioner's sugar mustache. "I like food too much to mangle it, so I let other people cook it."

"Cooking's not that hard. Someone just has to show you how, and then it takes a little practice."

"Do you cook?" she asked him curiously.

"I've been known to putter around a bit in a kitchen." He flashed her a thousand-watt smile that all but knocked her off her stool. Was he flirting with her? Surely not. But still. Dang, that man oozed charm. With difficulty, she recalled the general thread of their conversation.

The big bad detective was an amateur chef? Interesting. "Have you got a specialty?"

"Folks seem to like my jambalaya."

"That's some sort of stew, isn't it?"

He grabbed his chest theatrically, which made her grin. "Woman, you're killing me. Jambalaya is not just stew. It's seafood and sausage in a base of rice and vegetables in broth, the whole thing seasoned until your eyes water from how good it tastes."

She frowned. "I don't do spicy food. My eyes would water from the heat."

"Ahh well. A taste for heat can be learned."

His voice had a rough edge that shivered across her skin. Or maybe that was just her shivering in response to his double entendre. She glanced at him sidelong, and he was frowning down into his cup of coffee.

Her heart tumbled to the floor. He seemed annoyed with himself, maybe for making the inadvertently sexy comment. Drat. He wasn't attracted to her in the least. She looked away, more disappointed than made any sense to her at all.

"Where are you from that you don't know what jambalaya is and you don't like a little heat?" he asked, the sudden question startling her.

His expression was closed now. Stubborn. The man had no intention of flirting with her. At all. She mumbled, "I live in New York City. But I'm originally from upstate New York."

"Ahh. A Yankee. That explains a lot."

Nope. Not attracted to her at all. He was backing off that heat comment as fast as humanly possible. Well, hell.

"What does my being a Yankee explain?"

He merely shrugged and took a sip of hot coffee. They ate in silence for a moment, and then, in an abrupt change of subject, he said, "I put out a BOLO on your boss."

"What's a BOLO?"

"It stands for Be On the Look Out. The entire NOPD got copies of the picture you gave me and will be watching for him. If he's out and about anywhere in the city, we'll find him and bring him in."

"What if he doesn't turn up?" she asked, dread thick in her throat.

"Then we'll see what the forensics guys find in his computer. If that doesn't give us anything to work with, we'll pursue other leads until we find him. You haven't had any phone calls from anyone since last night, have you?" he asked.

"You mean like a ransom call?" she blurted, surprised.

"Correct."

"No"

"I'd like to stay with you through the day today. If there's going to be a ransom demand, it usually comes in the first twenty-four hours after an abduction."

"Do you want to hook up my phone to a machine that can trace the call?"

"Kidnappers worth their salt know how to disguise the location of calls these days. They use voice-over-Internet protocols and bounce the calls off a bunch of IP addresses. Long story short, we can't trace calls if the caller doesn't want to be traced."

"That sucks," she commented. "You'd think technology would help the police catch more criminals."

"What works for us works for them."

"Just a heads-up for you," she said reluctantly. "When word gets out that Gary's been kidnapped, it's likely to draw some media attention."

"How much media attention?"

"News crews, journalists, probably some tabloid photographers," she answered grimly. She would have to find a way to stay behind the scenes. Off camera. At all costs, her face could *not* be broadcast nationally.

Bass swore under his breath. "Look. I can't be put in front of cameras or have my picture taken. I may have to hand this case off to someone else—"

"No!" She interrupted him sharply, "I want you!"

His sapphire gaze snapped to hers, flashing blue fire, and for an instant, raw attraction flared between them. Then his expression shuttered once more, going implacably distant.

"You believed me last night and didn't wait to act,"

she babbled. "I trust you. And I don't usually trust police at all—" She broke off, appalled at oversharing like that.

"Why not?"

Well, fudge. She hadn't meant to blurt that out. "Umm. It's nothing. Never mind."

"No, I do mind. Why don't you trust cops?"

"It's an old story that should stay buried. I didn't break the law if that's what's worrying you. I just had…a bad experience."

"Not all cops are alike, you know. Take me, for example. I'm better looking than most."

She had to smile a little at that.

"What would Gary normally be doing today?" Bass asked, interrupting her turbulent emotions.

"He would sleep through the morning and wake up around noon. He putters around doing nothing all afternoon, goes out for supper, and then we head over to the next shooting location and set up for the night's shoot."

"And where is that scheduled to take place tonight?"

"An old house in the French Quarter that has been converted to a bed-and-breakfast. It's supposed to be haunted, of course."

He pounced on her choice of words. "You don't buy into the haunted bit?"

"I suspect the owner is mainly interested in getting free publicity for her business. I thought the legend of the ghost in her parlor that she submitted to the show was pretty thin. It felt made up to me when I first heard it, and our researcher in New York wasn't able to find any record of this supposed ghost anywhere else."

His mouth twitched, but he asked seriously enough, "Are some ghost stories *not* made up?"

She rolled her eyes. "Don't get me started. Gary is

a hard-core believer, but in my three years with him, I have yet to see a real ghost."

"Thank God," Bass muttered under his breath. She wasn't sure whether or not she was supposed to have heard that remark, but she responded to it anyway.

"You didn't think I actually believe in all this woo-woo stuff, did you?" She burst out laughing at the notion. "Filming *America's Ghosts* is just a job…in an industry where getting steady work is a rare gift."

He grinned. "You have no idea how glad I am to hear that." Their gazes met and the sparks exploded again. Lord, he was attractive. And this funny, friendly version of him was darned near irresistible. Men never flirted with her. She was the mousy one they looked past to find the hot girls.

"I thought folks in New Orleans were superstitious," she countered. "That they go for voodoo and fortune-tellers and ghosts."

"I'm not from New Orleans. I'm from the low country west of the city."

"As in bayous and alligators?" Her eyes went wide. *No thank you to either of those!*

He grinned broadly. "Everyone gets all hepped up about a few bitty ole' gators. You stay out of their way, they'll pretty much stay out of yours."

"They still scare me to death," she declared. "They eat people."

"Only the big ones actually eat people. The smaller ones might bite your leg off or take a chunk out of your side, but they can't swallow you whole."

She snorted. "If you're trying to make me feel better, you're failing spectacularly."

He shrugged. "Gators are primitive, and they are predators. But they're not completely stupid. And they perceive us as predators in return. They honestly do try to stay out of our way for the most part. Now, if you want to worry about critters where I come from, those would be snakes. We've got 'em all. Copperheads, cottonmouths, even rattlesnakes. Sometimes they're so thick you can't go thirty feet without seeing one."

"Nope. Nope, nope, nope, nope, nope. I do *not* do snakes."

He laughed. "City slicker."

"Guilty as charged. I'm a city girl all the way." She slugged down the last of her coffee and finished off her beignet with a lick of her fingers.

"What would you normally be doing at this time of day?" Bass inquired.

"Sleeping. We work late at night, and I often sleep till noon."

"God, that sounds decadent," he mumbled.

"It is. Then I get up, go for a run, eat, and spend the afternoon editing dailies."

"Dailies?"

"The raw footage I shot the night before. I do a rough cut and pull together all the best footage, then I send that video and the rest of the raw video to the post-production folks back in New York. They create the finished show."

"Do you want to go back to your place now and crawl into bed for a few hours?"

Her shocked gaze shot to his. She swore she caught a momentary glint of amusement behind those bright blue eyes, but she couldn't be sure. *Jeez, Carrie. Not everything the poor man says is an invitation to have sex.* She must be even more attracted to him than she realized—or admitted to herself.

"Umm, no. No time to sleep," she answered belatedly. "I'm going to have to reschedule tonight's show shoot until tomorrow and hope Gary turns up in the meantime. Besides, I'm too worried to sleep, and that cup of coffee's gonna keep me revved up for a few hours."

"Then how about we head back to Pirate's Alley? You can walk me through what happened."

Like she was going to refuse to cooperate with the police investigation? She followed in his wake as Bass elbowed his way through the morning coffee crush, and she breathed a sigh of relief as they stepped onto the sidewalk once more. Along with her fear of snakes, she wasn't a particular fan of being crushed in crowds. She supposed that came from being small and easy to overlook.

"Claustrophobic?" Bass murmured.

"How did you know?"

"The look of relief on your face when we made it out of that crowd."

Note to self: the cop is definitely as observant as I am.

"Jackson Square's not far from here," he said. "Are you up for a walk?"

Stretching her legs after all the stress of the past few hours, maybe burning off a little adrenaline, sounded great. She nodded and he headed out.

She was impressed that he shortened his stride so she could keep up. Thank God. She hated having to race-walk or half jog to keep up with people.

The pedestrians crowding the sidewalks all appeared to have places to go and things to do, ignoring each other and barely noticing the elegant old city they passed through. As for her, she couldn't keep her gaze from straying up to the wrought-iron balconies and tall, shuttered window casements. Goodness, this city was photogenic.

"Tell me about yourself," Bass asked.

"Not much to tell." She clammed up out of habit. Police were bad. Say nothing to them.

"Let me rephrase that. What's the research going to tell me when my people are done looking you up?"

"Why are you going to look me up?" she demanded. "That's an invasion of privacy!"

"This is a police investigation, Miss Price."

"Call me Carrie. Miss Price makes me sound like an old lady."

"Only if you'll call me Bastien. Or Bass."

She mumbled an affirmative. But it felt weird to think of calling this intimidating detective by his first name. The flirty guy had definitely given way to the cop as soon as they left the restaurant. His jaw had gone hard again, and he was back to asking her pointed questions and then staring a hole through her when she answered him.

"You're dodging my question, Carrie. Who are you?"

He was totally right, of course. She was dodging him. "What do you want to know about me?" she asked, feeling surly.

"Where are you from?"

"Born and raised in New York, north of Albany."

"Your whole life?"

"Yup."

"Do you like snow?"

"Hate it," she replied with genuine passion.

"Me too. Miserable stuff to crawl around in."

"When did you figure that out? And where? It's not like it snows around here very often."

"If I told you I'd have to kill you."

"Oh, puh-lease. That's such a tired line."

He flashed her a brief grin. "And yet, I stand by it."

He sounded serious behind that boyish smile of his. *Yikes.*

They arrived at the mouth of Pirate's Alley, but it looked completely different this morning. It was still narrow and historic looking, but the fog and mysterious darkness were gone, replaced by street artists setting up easels and clipping sketches to the wrought-iron fence of St. Anthony's Garden. A clerk was opening up a hat shop on the corner, and in the bright light of day, the alley looked completely harmless. A few pedestrians strode past, not meandering as if they were there to visit the alley, but passing through en route to somewhere else.

"Why isn't the alley blocked off with police tape? Isn't it a crime scene?" she asked.

"The NOPD can't officially investigate a kidnapping for forty-eight hours. A crime hasn't technically taken place yet. I'm going ahead with the preliminary work unofficially, based on that video of yours. Which the forensics guys haven't verified as being authentic, by the way."

"It's authentic!"

"I believe you," he said soothingly. "But you also have access to high-tech equipment that could doctor film images easily. The NOPD will have to verify that tape before they act on it."

She huffed, annoyed. She had no reason to fake Gary's kidnapping.

Bass was speaking again. "...besides, I went over every inch of the alley last night and didn't find any evidence whatsoever."

How could a crime have happened in this exact place

just last night? Life had gone on completely unaffected by Gary's abduction. It didn't seem fair, somehow.

"...and how deep in the alley were you when those men approached Gary?" Bass was asking.

"Oh. Uhh, down this way." She walked nearly half-way down the alley. Using lampposts as references, she estimated where Gary had been standing when the attack happened. "Gary was about here, and I was about twenty feet back that way." She pointed to where they'd come from.

"I'll pretend to be Gary, and you go stand where you were," Bass directed her. "I'm going to call your cell phone, and you talk me through what happened."

She backed away from him. Her cell phone rang, and Bass's voice caressed her ear. "Can you hear me?"

"Loud and clear," she managed to choke out. "Can you hear me?"

"I've got you five by five."

As she recalled, that was military speak for him hearing her just fine.

"Talk me through it," he murmured in her ear.

She gulped at his sexy drawl. "Umm, Gary was walking backward slowly. He got to where you are now and stopped to talk about the ghosts from the old prison. That's where they jumped him. Right where you are now."

Bass stopped moving. "Then what?"

"I stopped as well to film what I thought was a staged attack. When they grabbed him, they started moving away quickly. I couldn't run after them or my camera would jiggle too much. I wasn't using a steady cam rig last night."

"What's that?"

"It's a harness a cameraman wears. The camera's

mounted to it. The harness compensates for my movement or shaking in the camera to keep the filmed image perfectly steady. Hence the name."

Bass turned and started walking away from her swiftly. "Follow me at the speed you were walking last night. I want to time how much of a head start the kidnappers had on you."

She did as he ordered, dismayed at how rapidly he pulled away from her and disappeared around the corner at the far end of the alley. She started counting seconds in her head as she continued to walk at the speed she remembered moving last night. About here, she'd sped up some. Not too fast. About like that.

Fifty-five. Fifty-six. She reached the end of the alley and Bass stepped out from behind a building on the corner. "Almost a full minute," she said in dismay. "God, if only I'd known he was in real trouble, I could have run after them. Maybe seen a getaway car. Gotten a license plate."

"Don't beat yourself up over it," Bass replied. "You might have ended up kidnapped right along with your boss. Or, if you had caught up with them, even worse could have happened to you. For all you know, they were armed and dangerous. At least this way, you survived to report the crime."

"Aren't there traffic cameras or something you guys can pull footage from to find out where Gary went once he and his captors reached this street?"

"We've got partial closed circuit coverage of the city, but far from every block of it is covered. The cameras here point into Jackson Square, not up and down Chartres Street. I put in a request last night for the footage to be pulled, but I'm not hopeful it will help. Plus, it'll take a day or two to get it."

"Who on earth wants something from Gary? He's just a schlocky ghost hunter with a moderately successful TV show. It's not like he's rich or anything. He's perpetually broke, in fact."

"That's what I plan to figure out."

She stared up at him entreatingly. "You have to find him. He wouldn't hurt anyone."

"Tell me this, Carrie. Do you think you might be in danger, too?"

Shock passed through her body like a wave of icy water. "Me? Why me? I'm nobody."

"Are you sure the two of you didn't see something, maybe film something, that someone didn't want seen?"

"No, I'm not sure. We've been filming here and there around New Orleans. Background shots for filler during the show's voice-over narrations."

"I'm going to need to see that footage. All of it."

"Uhh, sure. It's back at my place."

"Then that's where you and I are headed next."

Chapter 4

Bass followed Carrie up the stairs to her apartment once more. The tush on that woman was literally making him sweat as he watched it twitch from side to side at eye level in front of him. She might be petite, but damn, she was put together. Her body was athletic, but she moved with grace. She was a runner, huh? Her thighs would be lean and strong, and her stamina better than most, both of which would be great in bed—

Stop. That.

Of course, she was also totally off limits. The list of ethics violations he would be charged with if he got involved with a suspect in an active investigation boggled his mind. As he'd hoped she would, when he got her out of the precinct and doing something social like sharing a meal, she had loosened up with him quite a bit. The girl definitely had some bad history with police going on.

He also hadn't failed to notice that she consistently dodged his questions when he asked for details about her personal life. No matter. His office's research assistant was top-notch, and she would find out everything there was to know about Carrie Price.

One other thing he'd noted at breakfast. Carrie wasn't showing any of the agitation of a criminal the police were closing in on nor was she showing him any blatant evasiveness. At least not where her boss was concerned.

He was increasingly convinced that Carrie herself hadn't kidnapped her boss. But that didn't mean she hadn't been a co-conspirator. She'd had access to her boss's computer for hours last night. She could have used the time to wipe away evidence. Indeed, he'd had a quiet word with the lab tech this morning and asked him specifically to look for evidence of tampering.

Maybe Carrie was angling to get her boss's job. Or maybe she had a personal beef with the guy. She certainly did have enough knowledge of Gary's schedule and movements to help set up a kidnapping.

As he passed the second floor en route to Carrie's apartment, Bass checked the seal he'd put on Gary's door last night. It was unbroken, and the yellow police tape still crisscrossed over the doorway. She hadn't lied to him about that, at any rate.

Carrie let him into her place, which had been straightened up since last night. Nervous energy? Or maybe a guilty conscience?

"It'll take me a minute to pull up all the tape we've shot since we got here," she said nervously.

Watching her closely, he dragged one of the other kitchen chairs around the table in front of the computer monitor. Why was she so jumpy? What was she hiding from him? His gut might be telling him she wasn't a felon, but it was damned well telling him she was keeping secrets from him, too.

He really wanted her not to be guilty of rubbing out her boss. But he'd learned long ago not to judge people by their appearances…or in this case, by the intensity of his attraction to her.

Carrie Price was hard to describe. Just when he settled on cute, she would go and do something sexy like smile sidelong at him with those captivating eyes of hers. Or she would pause for a millisecond when she was leaning past him, appearing to inhale the scent of him. He'd nearly turned to her last night when she did it the first time—to do what, exactly, he didn't know. Kiss her maybe. But then she'd stepped away and gone back to being as adorable as a feisty little kitten.

"Here's the footage we shot the first day. It's mostly long shots of approaching the city."

He glanced at the monitor and then glanced again, surprised. "Were you in a boat in Lake Pontchartrain when you shot that?"

"Gold star for the local boy knowing what his city looks like."

He snorted. "It's my job to know this town like the back of my hand."

"I've got nearly twenty hours of raw film. Do you want to watch it all, or just watch certain types of footage? Oh! Or I could run it at double or quadruple speed."

"I think we can safely skip the long shots. You weren't likely to catch enough detail in a shot like that to freak out a bad guy."

"Not to mention a bad guy probably wouldn't know I even shot the film. All of this stuff is shot through zoom lenses. In many cases, I'm standing off at a much greater distance than the shot would lead you to believe. Zoom lenses allow me to control what goes into my camera frame and what I cut out."

Her entire face lit up when she talked about her job. Obviously she was passionate about it.

They moved on to the film of the first show Gary had shot in New Orleans. He'd been chasing the ghost of Jean Lafitte. One of New Orleans's most famous residents, the pirate and his brother, Pierre, loomed large in the city's early history. The pair had smuggled in shiploads of luxury goods that had made New Orleans an attractive place for wealthy people to settle, in spite of the wretched climate, disease, floods and uncertain political future. The Lafittes were entirely obvious targets of a ghost-hunting show looking to romanticize New Orleans's history.

Carrie had a great eye, and he'd never seen the city look better than through the lens of her camera.

"You have a gift for avoiding shooting drunks, panhandlers and crazies," he commented.

Carrie replied, "People want to see the sanitized, magical version of the locations we shoot. Places where ghosts could plausibly exist. They don't want to see the ugly reality of the world."

That made sense. However, it meant the likelihood of Carrie having filmed someone or something that had caused her boss to be abducted were not good.

It took them several hours to go through all the pertinent raw film, and he saw nothing and no one that could have triggered an attack on Gary Hubbard. As much as he would enjoy continuing to sit next to the delectable Miss Price, he had a job to do. And the bars would be open by now. Time for him to pound the pavement and rule out Gary having gone on a bender last night. Local bartenders were pretty good about pouring drunk tourists into cabs and getting them back to their beds safely. Which was why he seriously doubted Gary was lying in an alley somewhere sleeping off a hard night of drinking.

Unfortunately, that left only Carrie Price as a viable suspect in the guy's disappearance at the moment. Surely there had to be somebody else. To that end, he asked her, "And you're positive Gary didn't meet with anyone outside the show since he arrived in New Orleans?"

"No, I'm not positive. I'm not his babysitter."

At least she was talking about the guy in the present tense. Murderers tended to shift to the past tense when they spoke of their victims.

Bass stood up to leave. "Don't worry, Carrie. The NOPD will figure this out." Problem was, he felt time slipping away from him. The first twenty-four hours of any abduction were crucial, and they had yet to receive any kind of communication from the kidnappers. He had no motive and no idea where the kidnappers might have taken Hubbard. He had no idea where to even begin looking for the guy. Which didn't bode well for Gary Hubbard. The only reason people kidnapped a person, if not for money, was usually to kill them.

He spent several fruitless hours combing the bars, brothels and flophouses within walking distance of Pirate's Alley, a photo of Gary Hubbard in hand. Nobody had seen the guy, nobody had heard any disturbances, nor had they seen anything out of the usual. Granted, the usual in New Orleans could be a little weird. But a kidnapping would have caught the attention of anyone who'd seen it.

He'd just returned to the office hot and sweaty and

thinking longing thoughts about a cold shower and a colder beer when his phone rang.

"Detective LeBlanc."

"Hey, Bass. Sandra Coleman in Traffic here. I got your request to review the closed circuit cameras in Jackson Square, and I checked every angle that might have caught someone near the exit from Pirate's Alley into the square. I struck out. No cameras caught any vehicles or people coming or going in that time frame."

"Bummer."

She continued, "I checked all the cameras around that area last night, and I didn't see any vehicles with three men, or any vans or trucks that might have been used in an abduction. I scoured everything. Good news is at that time of night, there's very little traffic."

"And you saw nothing at all?"

"Nope. And frankly, that's telling. Anyone who could totally avoid our cameras knows where they are. Which means you're likely looking at local talent being responsible for your guy's disappearance."

Bass hung up the phone thoughtfully. Locals, huh? Had Carrie had time to come to town, hook up with local thugs, and arrange for her boss's capture? He made another call and found out the warrant he'd filed overnight had been approved. He had permission to check into both Gary Hubbard and Carrie Price's bank accounts and credit card transactions.

He never failed to be surprised at how often solving a crime came down to the money trail. He opened up a search engine on his computer and entered the warrant number. Bank documents and credit card statements popped up on his screen for both victim and prime suspect. *Come to daddy.*

But an hour later, he pushed back from his desk in

frustration. There were no unusual expenditures to indicate that Carrie had paid for a hit, or that Gary was involved in anything shady. All he'd learned was that Gary couldn't manage money to save his life, and Carrie was seemingly frugal and careful with her modest finances.

He had to be missing something. But what?

Carrie tossed and turned in the dark, in spite of being exhausted. She was missing something. What on earth had Gary been involved in that had gotten him kidnapped? The only unusual thing he'd been talking about recently was his excitement over the idea of proving Napoleon's last governor of French Louisiana had secretly been a loyalist to the French monarchy. Where was the scandal in that? It was two hundred years ago, and who cared who the guy had been loyal to? He'd still handed New Orleans and the rest of Louisiana over to Thomas Jefferson when the time came.

She had no idea what time it was when she heard the bump downstairs. Was that Gary? She sat up in bed and listened hard. Had she imagined the sound?

Nope. There was another thud, this time of something heavy and hard hitting the floor.

She jumped out of bed in her flannel pants and junky T-shirt and ran barefoot out of her apartment and down the stairs. She was going to kill Gary. Flat-out wring his neck—

She froze in front of the door. The police seal, a red piece of sticky paper, was still in place. And the garish X of police tape was still there, too. How did Gary get into his apartment if not through the front door?

She looked down and noticed no light showed under

the door. Although, as she watched, a beam of light momentarily flashed under the door and then retreated.

Oh. My. God. That was *not* Gary in his apartment!

Her heart leaped into her throat and commenced beating like a hummingbird's wings. She tiptoed back away from the door, easing up to her apartment step by cautious step. She was light-headed with fear by the time she reached her own door, slipped inside, and carefully, quietly, bolted the locks. Continuing to move carefully, one foot at a time, lest the floor squeak and alert the intruder downstairs, she headed for the kitchen counter where her cell phone was recharging.

She dialed Bastien LeBlanc's phone number with clumsy fingers.

"Yo," he answered sleepily.

She whispered frantically, "It's me. Carrie. There's someone in Gary's apartment, and it's not Gary."

"Go into your bathroom and lock the door," Bastien ordered tersely, suddenly speaking with sharp clarity. "Hide as best you can. Climb in the tub and lie down. I'll call 911 for you so you don't have to speak aloud to them. Stay on this line with me. Don't hang up. I'll be there as fast as I can. You're going to hear sirens before I get there, most likely. Just stay put until I come for you. Got all that?"

"Yes," she breathed, already moving into her tiny bathroom. She did as Bastien had told her to and climbed into the big cast iron tub. Very, very carefully, she pulled the shower curtain shut around her, wincing as the curtain rings squeaked against the metal shower rod.

In her ear, she heard the sounds of shuffling, as if maybe Bastien was getting dressed. Then heavy breathing. He was running. A car engine gunned and tires squealed. Give the guy brownie points for coming to her as fast as he could.

Something scraped downstairs, like maybe a piece of furniture being moved. She jumped as something big crashed below. It sounded like a dresser had been tipped over. Whoever was in there was ransacking Gary's place and didn't give a damn if she heard it. Which meant that the intruder either didn't know she was up here or planned to come up here to search when he was done with Gary's apartment.

She'd been scared—really scared—a few times in her life, and she'd been worried sick the past twenty-four hours, but she'd only experienced true fight-or-flight panic like this once before. And it had not turned out well for her. At all.

It took every ounce of will she possessed to force her body to remain still and curled in a ball inside the tub. The urge to run for her life was overwhelming, and her limbs ached with adrenaline, begging to fly.

"Still with me?" Bastien asked.

"Yeah," she whispered.

"I know you want to do something, anything, rather than just hide in a bathroom, but trust me. You're in the safest place you can be. Hang in there."

Huh. He must've have been in a tight spot before to know what she was thinking and feeling so accurately.

"I'm about five minutes out. Any sirens yet?"

"No."

"Okay. I may beat the uniforms there, then." He swore at something having to do with clueless drivers and then came back on the line with her. "Can you still hear movement downstairs?"

"Yeah," she breathed.

"Can you tell if it's more than one person?"

"No idea."

"I'm going to come in hot, which means I'll have a gun out. Don't freak out if you happen to see me with it, okay?"

"Okay." She added, "Be careful. It's dark."

"No problem. I've been a Navy SEAL for ten years. I know my way around in the dark."

Wow. A SEAL? That was a relief. Maybe she did stand a chance of getting out of this bathroom alive, after all.

He was speaking again. "I'll clear Gary's place first and try to apprehend the intruder. There could be a ruckus downstairs when that happens, but stay where you are. That way I'll know you're clear of my field of fire and I won't mistake you for a hostile. After I'm done downstairs, I'll come up and get you. Just be patient."

She whispered, "Be careful."

He laughed a little. "Count on it, darlin'."

In spite of her breath-stealing panic, something warmed a little in her heart at him calling her darling. Down here in the South, it was no doubt a casual expression that meant nothing. But no one had ever called her by an endearment before. It was nice.

"I'm about a minute out, so I'm gonna go silent now. Don't say anything more to me or you might give away my position. But I'm gonna leave my phone on so you can hear me and know when I'm done mopping up downstairs."

She'd counted to thirty in her head when a faint sound of sirens became audible in the distance. They weren't an unusual sound in the city, but she prayed they were the ones coming for her. It was selfish, but she prayed the bad guy would flee before Bastien got here and engaged him in a potentially lethal confrontation.

Sure enough, the sirens got louder and closer. Oh, yeah. Those were her sirens. In fact, within a few more seconds, they were so loud she couldn't hear if the intruder downstairs fled or not. She could only assume the person had come in through a window. Would he or she go out the same way? Or would the intruder race up here to take a hostage? Point a gun at her and demand something?

Her imagination ran wild with awful possibilities until she put herself right into the middle of a full-blown panic attack. She was going to disappear just like Gary. Bastien would get here and find her gone as well. And there would be no clues. Heck, he might even think she'd fled the city and not look for her at all. Would the bad guys torture her? Assault her? Kill her?

A door crashed somewhere downstairs.

Oh, God. Was that the bad guy leaving or the good guys arriving?

The next few minutes took an eternity to pass while she waited in silence, hugging her knees and biting back moans of distress. Over the open phone line, she heard the occasional shuffle. But for the most part, Bastien was utterly silent.

Without warning, her bathroom door flew open. A big, dark shape loomed in the doorway, silhouetted through a crack in the shower curtains.

She lurched, terrified, biting off a scream so it came out as a squeak.

"Carrie? It's me."

Oh, thank God. All the tension went out of her body, and suddenly she was so weak she didn't have the strength in her legs to stand up.

The curtain tore back, and Bastien shoved a beefy handgun in the back waistband of his pants. He reached down and lifted her to her feet as if she weighed no more than a child. She flung herself at him and clung to him as if her life depended on it.

His strong, warm arms closed around her, and at long last, she let out a full breath. She was safe. And then the shaking started. Her entire body trembled violently, and she couldn't seem to control it.

"I'm s…sorry," she mumbled.

Bastien's arms tightened around her even more. "No worries. This is a perfectly normal reaction to fear."

She buried her face against his chest and unashamedly let him hold her until the worst of her shaking calmed. Eventually, it dawned on her to wonder how long it had been since anyone had held her like this. Even when she'd been a little girl and had nightmares, her parents had subscribed to the theory of "go back to bed and get over it. It's just a dream."

But Bastien scooped her up in his arms and carried her over to her sofa. Gently, he set her down. "Whatchya got there?" he asked.

"What?" She looked down at the scrap of ratty fur in her arms. "Oh. It's a stuffed sea turtle. His name is Mr. Paddles. I've had him since I was little. My parents weren't much for comforting me as a kid, so whenever I got scared, I hung onto him. He always kept me safe."

Blessedly, Bass didn't make fun of her for still having her childhood stuffed toy. All he said was, "I've got to go help the guys downstairs take a look at the crime scene. Will you two be okay here until I get back?"

She nodded, abruptly embarrassed at how she'd thrown herself at him and that she still had a comfort toy.

"I won't be long. I just have to check in with the uniforms in Gary's place and make sure they call for a crime scene unit. I want to lift more fingerprints and see if we can get an ID on who tossed Gary's apartment this time."

"Tossed?"

"Ransacked. Generally destroyed. Last night, someone searched the place. Tonight, someone trashed it."

She watched his powerful back and long stride as he left her living room. Obviously, someone was looking for something they thought Gary had. But what? The guy couldn't keep a few bucks in his wallet or a cent in his bank account to save his life. What else worth committing crimes over did the guy have?

She bloody well hoped this didn't come down to a ransom situation. Gary had no money, and she wasn't rich by any means. Would the television network pony up a fat ransom to get an aging ghost show host released? Somehow, she doubted it. Paying for Gary would set a bad precedent with future kidnappers, right?

Freezing cold, she reached for the crappy acrylic afghan on the back of the sofa and wrapped it around herself and Mr. Paddles. She pulled her knees to her chest and huddled in the corner of the sofa with her turtle until Bastien came back. He hadn't lied. It only took him a few minutes to do whatever he had to do downstairs.

"How are you feeling?" he asked her quietly.

"Cold. Numb. Scared."

"Mild shock. Totally normal. You'll get thirsty soon. Maybe get another round of the shakes, too."

"You sound like you've been through this before."

He shrugged. "I'm SEAL trained. We're taught to set aside emotions like fear and anger. They cloud the judgment. But I certainly know the symptoms of a good scare."

"You're right about the emotions clouding judgment

thing. I was so mad at Gary for playing another prank on me that I failed to notice he was actually being kidnapped right under my nose. This is all my fault."

Bastien stared at her for a moment. "No," he answered slowly, "I don't think it is."

"I beg your pardon?"

"No one can fake panic like I've seen from you a couple times, now. You were genuinely terrified."

She frowned. "Was that in any doubt?"

"Don't mind me. I'm just a suspicious SOB. Comes with the job."

"Which job? Being a SEAL or being a cop?"

"Both." He stood up. "Let's get you out of here. The crime scene guys are going to be banging around downstairs making a racket for hours. No way are you going back to sleep tonight if you stay here. Tomorrow morning will be soon enough for you to tell us if anything has gone missing from Gary's place."

"I'm not sure I'll be able to spot anything—"

"Don't think about it now. Don't worry about it. That's a job for tomorrow. Right now is about taking care of yourself."

He must have sensed her mind going blank on what that was supposed to mean, for he stood up and swiftly scooped her up into his arms, blanket and all. "C'mon," he growled. "Let's get out of here."

He paused long enough for her to grab her purse off the kitchen counter, but then he left her place swiftly.

"I hate being carried like this," she mumbled.

He paused in the middle of her staircase to stare at her. "Why?"

"It makes me feel like a child. My whole life, people have picked me up and tossed me around because they're bigger than me. Mr. Paddles notwithstanding, no one sees me as an actual adult woman."

Bastien set her down and snorted. "Honey, it's hard to miss that you're a woman."

He resumed heading downstairs without waiting for her response, which was just as well. Her jaw had mentally dropped so hard she wasn't sure she could speak if she tried.

He'd noticed her in the same way she'd noticed him? Never in a million years would she have guessed that. He was so serious and focused on business all the time.

All the way out to the car, she tried to think of a good reason why she shouldn't let him whisk her away from her place like this, but not a single decent argument came to mind. He opened the passenger door of a vintage muscle car that looked perfectly restored. She slid inside, noting that the leather seats even smelled new, and the dashboard practically glowed as if freshly polished.

He climbed into the driver's seat and the engine roared to life like some mythic beast preparing to devour any road put before it.

"Nice car," she murmured.

"Thanks. Took me two years to rebuild the engine and restore her."

"Her?"

"Sally Ann. Cars have names, you know."

"Indeed. All cars?"

"Yup. If you ask them and then listen real close, they'll tell you."

"I'll keep that in mind next time I own a car."

"You don't own a car?" Bastien asked, sounding aghast.

"I live in New York City. No need for one. Besides,

parking costs a fortune. The show owns the van Gary
and I road trip to shooting locations in."

"Blasphemy. I collect cars."

"How many?"

"You'll see in about ten minutes."

Her gaze snapped to him. He was taking her to his
place? What did that mean? Her curiosity was overwhelmed by a single stunned thought. *Ho. Lee. Cow.*
He must actually like her, as in *like* her. Why else would
he take her to his home for the night? He could just as
easily have deposited her at the nearest hotel.

He turned into a driveway in a semi-industrial area,
stopping before a steel gate leading to a lot surrounded
by a tall, solid fence made of vertical metal panels. He
punched a remote opener and the gate swung open.

She expected a pseudo junkyard with old cars parked
everywhere and rusted car parts strewn about. She was
wrong. The full moon illuminated a perfectly manicured lawn under sprawling trees leading up to a connected pair of large metal buildings that were neat as
a pin.

Bastien punched another remote opener and a huge
garage door slid upward. He drove into the barn-sized
building, and here were the cars in various stages of
repair and disrepair that she'd expected. But the shop
was as neat as the exterior. Every tool was in its place,
the gray-painted floor sparkled, and the entire atmo-
sphere was one of energetic order.

It was a revealing look into the man, himself. He
was clearly not fond of chaos. Believed in routine. She
could relate to both. And given how heavily fenced this
place was, she surmised he was a private man, as well.
She could totally relate to that.

Which made it even more surprising that he'd chosen to bring her to his home. He'd physically and meta-phorically allowed her to pass his defenses. She was a little staggered, truth be told.

A sleek, Italian sports car rested overhead on a lift, and a vintage pickup truck was parked beside it. She didn't recognize the other vehicles. But there were eight in all.

"Is this your collection?"

He laughed. "Naw, these are just the cars I'm work-ing on now. Through that big door on the right is where I keep my babies."

She smiled, amused at his open adoration for his cars.

He parked Sally Ann and came around to open her door for her. "Can you walk?"

She answered indignantly, "Of course I can!" But when she stepped out, clutching Mr. Paddles close, her knees were more wobbly than she cared to admit. Huh. This shock thing was a kick in the pants.

He moved ahead of her to a building within a build-ing that took up the whole far end of the large, metal-sided shop. It looked like a cabin that had been built inside this old warehouse. He punched a number into an alarm pad, then laid his palm on a flat screen above the numbers. The front door unlocked with a buzz, and he opened it, gesturing for her to go in front of him.

She slipped past him, surprised to see a comfort-able living room with a kitchen opening off to one side of it. The kitchen was nearly as big as the living room and decked out with the latest in appliances. A hallway opened off to her left, appearing to lead to a bedroom and likely a bathroom.

"Is this where you live?"

"Home sweet home, darlin'."

"It's nice."

He shrugged. "It serves my needs. Hungry?"

"Do you always think about food first?"

"After the killing's done, yeah. My mind naturally turns to food next."

"You didn't kill anyone in Gary's place, did you?" she asked in quick horror.

"Nah. Intruder fled before I got there. As sad as I am that I didn't get to nail the guy, I'm glad he left before he could hurt you."

She stared at Bastien's back as he pulled a pair of mugs from the cupboard and set them on the white quartz counter. He was more worried about her safety than he was about solving a crime? What did that mean?

If only she could interpret his behavior like she would if he were some normal guy. But he wasn't the least bit normal. In fact, she'd never met another man remotely like him. He seemed…larger than life. Like he lived bigger and more fully than the average Joe.

He fished a chocolate bar out of a cupboard and startled her by pulling out a big knife and cutting board. He chopped the chocolate with rapid-fire strokes of the knife under his hands like a chef, and in a matter of seconds was scooping up slivers of chocolate into the mugs using the flat of the knife blade.

"You're good with a knife," she commented.

"All SEALs are good with knives." He poured part milk and part cream into the mugs and popped them in the microwave. He turned to face her, flipping the butcher's knife up in the air end over end and catching it by the handle.

She gulped. It was a scary display and a vivid reminder that this man was fully as lethal as he looked.

"Did you find anything in Gary's apartment that might help you identify his kidnappers?"

He shook his head and dropped the knife in the sink. "They were looking for something specific, for sure. Assuming these were the same people who searched it the first time, they seem convinced it's hidden somewhere in Gary's apartment.

"Tonight they didn't just search. They ripped the place apart. Given the level of destruction, and that they stuck around until the cops were almost on top of them, I have to guess they didn't find what they were looking for."

"What could it be?" she asked in dismay.

"I was hoping you could tell me that."

"I have no idea what he's got himself tangled up in."

Bastien studied her intently, as if he was reading her mind. She wished he would. Maybe he would find something stashed away in some dark recess of her memory that she'd forgotten she knew, something that would help find Gary.

The microwave dinged, and he pulled out the steaming mugs. Using a small whisk, he whipped the melted chocolate and milk until a head of froth formed. "Try this. But be careful. It's hot."

She sipped the hot chocolate cautiously, and groaned out loud in delight. "I've never had anything this creamy and rich."

"Oh, baby. Then I've got a whole lot of good eating to show you."

Her gaze lifted to his over her mug. Did he mean that? Was he interested in a personal relationship with her outside of the search for Gary? Or was he just flirting unconsciously because it was how he acted with all women? He was certainly good-looking and charming enough to be prime ladies' man material.

He led her into the living room where he collapsed on the sofa, kicked off his shoes, and propped up his bare feet on the coffee table. He sipped his own hot chocolate appreciatively. There was something endearingly incongruous about the big, bad Navy SEAL barefoot, sipping hot chocolate. She perched on the far end of the sofa, eyeing him surreptitiously.

Eventually, he muttered, "Feel free to get comfortable. I'm not going to devour you."

"Sorry. I guess I'm still shook up from earlier."

"Totally understandable. Tell me everything you heard."

"It was just a bunch of scrapes and bumps and thuds. And then I called you and headed for the bathroom."

"Any voices?" he asked.

"None at all."

"Interesting."

"Why?" she asked.

"Because I expect we'll find at least two sets of prints in Gary's place. It takes time to wreak that much havoc on a home, and some big pieces of furniture were upended. Normally, when a pair of intruders is working together they call back and forth with things they've found or hiding places to check."

"If these intruders didn't talk at all, what does that say about them?"

"They're disciplined. Professional. Have worked together before."

"Why would people like that snag Gary? It makes no sense at all."

"My concern is that these guys are proceeding completely logically if they're hunting for some specific object or some piece of information." He ticked off on his fingers as he talked. "Grab the guy you think has it. If he doesn't cough it up, search his home. If you're convinced it's in his home, search again, but more aggressively. If that doesn't work, try his place of business. Then move on to his coworkers, family, and friends."

"So I'm next?" she asked in a small voice.

Bastien's relaxation fell away, revealing itself for the thin veneer it really was. In place of the kicked back dude, a cold, hard Special Forces operator abruptly stared back at her, his gaze focused. Unwavering.

"I promise you, Carrie, they'll have to go through me to get to you."

Gulp.

Chapter 5

Bass hated to terrify Carrie, but she had to know the danger she was in. And she looked plenty scared, all right, hugging that ridiculous stuffed turtle like it was her only armor against the world. She even abandoned her mug of hot chocolate on the coffee table and stared fixedly at his black television screen as if a show were playing on it. In his experience, if a woman abandoned even chocolate, she was upset, indeed.

His thoughts turned to sleeping arrangements for tonight. Too bad he'd converted his spare bedroom into an office a few months back. He pretty much never had houseguests, and if one of his SEAL teammates spent the night, they were just as happy on a mattress on the floor of the garage as in a real bed.

It was nearing 4:00 a.m., *again*. This woman was hell on his sleep schedule. At least she looked as ready to drop as he felt. Her eyelids drooped, and her whole body was drooping as well.

He murmured to his voice light controller to turn off the kitchen lights and dim the living room lights. As he expected, Carrie's eyes closed almost immediately, and she curled into a ball against the pillows at the far end of the sofa, hugging her turtle.

He watched her sleep, memorizing the gentle curve of her cheek, the sleek line of her neck, and the delicate grace of her fingers tucked sweetly under her chin. Right now she had no makeup on and was wearing sloppy pajamas, and she'd never looked more beautiful. Her skin was clear and soft and her features naturally lovely.

Good thing those big, dark eyes of hers were closed. They were murder on his self-control. He just wanted to sink into them and lose himself every time she gazed up at him as if he was some kind of conquering hero.

When he deemed that she'd had enough time to sink into a deep sleep, he moved quietly to his bedroom and pulled back the covers. Then he returned to the sofa and scooped her up in his arms.

She might hate being carried, but tonight she only murmured incoherently and snuggled closer against his chest as he carried her back to his bed.

He laid her down gently and drew the covers up over her. Something moved deep in his belly at the sight of her in his bed. It was as if she belonged there, as if he instinctively recognized his mate taking up residence.

Whoa. He had no plans to settle down with one woman. Ever. Love meant vulnerability and vulnerability meant pain.

His mother had never recovered when his father walked out on her and had ultimately turned into an angry, bitter woman who lived a deeply unhappy life. He was no stranger to loss, himself. He'd lost a few teammates over the years. The pain of losing one of his brothers-in-arms was every bit as bad as, at the ripe old age of eight, watching his father drive away and never look back.

He silently opened his closet and fished out a spare blanket, then retreated to the living room sofa. He'd been dozing for perhaps an hour when he heard a soft cry from Carrie. Barely awake, he was on his feet and moving swiftly.

She was twitching and tossing in her sleep. Nightmare, obviously. This was one of those moments when he regretted completely and totally sucking at the comforting thing.

Not that it was rocket science to offer simple comfort to another human being. Hell, all he had to do was wake her up. Although, she'd looked exhausted when he brought her into his house earlier. Poor kid probably hadn't really slept since Hubbard went missing two days ago. Mentally swearing, he stared down at her, willing her to settle back into untroubled sleep.

No such luck. She tossed and cried out again, her sleeping face contorted in fear.

Dammit. Knowing what he ought to do and convincing himself to do it turned out to be two different beasts. For a man who'd jumped in and out of the sack casually with dozens of women over the years, he was acting pretty damned ridiculous. *Just get in bed and hold her, you jackass.*

He moved around the far side of the bed. Easing beneath the covers, he slipped in beside her and very gently gathered her in his arms.

This was a mistake. He knew better than to cross this line from professional to personal with her. He could get into trouble. Worse, he could compromise an investigation. Bad idea. Bad, bad idea.

He had to keep his emotions out of this. He was a human being temporarily comforting another human being. Nothing more. He was smart and disciplined; he could climb out of this bed and resume his role as cop to her as a suspect, even if she wasn't much of a suspect.

Immediately, she burrowed against his chest and quieted as if she subconsciously recognized him. He lay very still, absorbing her trust in nothing short of shock. Huh. That actually felt really good.

He was used to his colleagues trusting him in combat situations. But this was a whole different kind of trust than that. It was…softer. Sweeter. Call him a caveman, but he kinda liked this feeling of being the big, strong man protecting a woman-in-need from harm. Not that he for a second believed that Carrie couldn't handle herself.

Gradually he relaxed, and eventually slipped into the sleep of a contented man.

Carrie woke up slowly, relishing the warm cocoon of blankets and smooth sheets covering her. She shifted slightly, and her pillow shifted as well, startling her to a higher level of consciousness. Her pillow was smooth, warm, and harder than feathers by a lot.

She slitted one eye and then both her eyes flew wide open. She was in bed with Bass! And her so-called pillow was his right pectoral muscle!

She shifted again, and a big hand tightened slightly against her back. His right arm was wrapped loosely around her. He sprawled on his back, and she'd sprawled on him, apparently. When had this happened?

She tried to reconstruct last night, and the last thing

she remembered was closing her eyes for a moment to ease their gritty fatigue while sitting on his sofa. She must have fallen asleep. But then...

He must have carried her in here and crawled in with her. Which was thrilling, in spite of it also being shockingly forward of him. But then, he struck her as the kind of man who went for what he wanted and didn't let anything stand in his way.

Off duty and away from police work, he was a pretty decent guy, warm and kind. And he'd been great with her on the phone when the intruder had been downstairs. Apparently, she'd just had to get past that initial crusty cop exterior to find the nice guy beneath.

She had no idea what time it was. His bedroom didn't have a window and was so dark she could barely make out Bass's sleeping features only inches away from her. She closed her eyes and drifted off to sleep again, satisfied that she was safe, and delighted that she was sprawled on top of possibly the hottest man she'd ever met.

When she woke again, it was because her human pillow was stretching languorously beneath her. It was wanton of her to do it but she stretched as well, straightening her arm out across his chest and stretching her leg across his thighs.

Everywhere her body rubbed against his, she encountered muscle and more muscle. His body was not particularly bulky, but lord, he was a hard man. Of course, being a SEAL, he likely took fitness to a whole new level of insane.

"Hey there, sleepyhead," Bass murmured. He turned on his side to face her and shocked her by pulling her close in a bear hug. Her hands ended up around his waist, their legs tangled together suggestively. Sure, she had on pajamas and he wore shorts of some kind, but still, a whole lot of skin-to-skin contact was going on. Her pulse leaped, and her awareness of him spiked even higher.

He smelled good, he felt good, and he made her feel feminine and sexy. *Best. Wake-up. Ever.*

If she wasn't mistaken, he'd just buried his nose in her hair and taken a long inhalation. And then, ohmigosh, his lips moved lightly against her temple as he murmured, "How'd you sleep?"

"Great, actually." She added shyly, "You?"

"Fantastic. Sorry for crawling in with you. But you were having a nightmare of some kind and I didn't want to wake you. I figured you could use a decent night's sleep after the excitement the past two nights."

She couldn't help herself. She rubbed her nose against his chest hairs a little, relishing the tickle of their silky spring. "Thanks," she mumbled.

"Do you want to sleep some more?" Bass murmured, his voice husky with sleep and sexier than ought to be legal.

"I think I'm good."

He chuckled quietly, "You're better than good, darlin'."

She tilted her chin to look up at him just as he tilted his chin down to look at her. Their lips brushed ever so lightly, and he inhaled as sharply as she did.

She froze.

He froze.

And then very slowly, as if trying—and failing—to resist, he closed the short space between them and kissed her again.

His warm mouth brushed across hers lightly, his lips firm and confident, and he coaxed her into the kiss with all the sexy Southern charm she associated with him. Her mouth opened beneath his, but he didn't rush the kiss, taking his time, adjusting his head to fit better to hers, his right hand sliding underneath her shoulders and up to cup the back of her head.

He lifted his mouth away and she followed him, kissing him this time. A hint of laughter rumbled in his chest, and he deepened the kiss, taking back control.

His tongue swept inside her mouth, and she met it with hers, tasting and testing the heat and slide of hot man flesh. It made her think of how good sex with him would be. *Hoo baby. Sign her up for some of that!*

Her body arched against his, loving the hard wall of him against her softness. For his part, Bass swept her against his body, urging her closer. She was happy to oblige and plaster her body against his. Her hands roamed across his back, relishing the deep ridges of muscle on either side of his spine that flexed as he moved restlessly against her.

What an athlete. Sex with him would be a demanding affair, no doubt. But ahh, the benefits would be amazing.

The junction of her thighs cradled the hard bulge of his arousal, making her breath hitch and her limbs go liquid with desire. Which startled her. She wasn't a limbs go liquid kind of girl most of the time.

Sure, she liked looking at a hot guy as much as the next woman, but she had never thought of herself as the sort who had any real shot at a man like Bass. He was smart and charming and so pretty he was almost hard to look at. And it wasn't like she ever stayed in one place long enough to form actual connections with much of anyone.

"Are you real?" she whispered.

His mouth traveled across her jaw and nuzzled her neck in the tender spot just below her ear. "You tell me. Does this feel real?"

He nipped lightly at the junction of her neck and shoulder, and a jolt of lust shot through her loins. She squeezed her thighs together, which turned out to be a mistake, because she'd managed to catch the bulge of his erection between the tops of her thighs in the process, and Bass groaned in response.

She shocked herself by sliding her hand down the indentation of his spine to his impressive glutes, and gave a tug, pulling his hips even closer to hers.

"Carrie," he muttered warningly. "I'm a gentleman, but I have my limits."

"I'm a lady, but that doesn't mean I don't like busting through limits."

He rolled her onto her back and loomed over her, propped on his elbows on either side of her head. Regret and a solid dose of stubborn entered his shadowed gaze. "Look. We shouldn't be doing this. And I don't get involved with women without their full consent. You didn't ask to sleep in my bed or have me comfort your nightmares."

As it so happened, she was prepared to give him her full consent. She opened her mouth to do so, but he interrupted her, saying, "Not to mention the ethical problems of me sleeping with you during an active investigation."

He said it like he was investigating her. Her heart dropped. Of course. She had to be a suspect in Gary's kidnapping. She was the person closest to him. Was all of this business of Bastien bringing her to his home and getting close to her simply him trying to figure out if she was a kidnapper or not?

She should have known better. Her burst of confidence that he actually found her attractive died on the vine all at once, wilting her self-esteem to approximately zero.

She gathered herself to apologize for throwing herself at him when a phone rang behind him, stopping her.

Bass cursed under his breath. "I've got to take that. It's my work phone."

He said that like he wouldn't have taken the call anyway. He was probably thrilled to dodge explaining that the real reason he didn't want to have sex with her was because he just wasn't that into her. Honestly. A hot player like him and mousy little her? He was totally out of her league.

He rolled away from her to pick up a cell phone off his nightstand, and she drew a shaky breath, feeling bereft. He had just dodged an epic mistake, and she had just missed a colossal opportunity. Even pity sex from him would have been better than outright rejection from him.

She was doomed never to have a decent love life. The combination of her travel schedule, weird work hours, and general shyness had made that an impossibility.

"Detective LeBlanc," he snapped.

He sounded annoyed. Was it possible he was irritated at being interrupted with her? Nah, no way. He'd been saved by the bell for sure.

Bass listened for a long time to whoever talked on the other end of the line, eventually saying, "Thanks. On my way."

He had to go, and they weren't going to resume their morning tryst.

She sighed mentally. He was no dummy. He would never let himself get maneuvered into a position like this again. It had been a great fantasy while it lasted to imagine having a relationship with him. Heck, she'd have been cool with just hooking up with him.

But she wasn't destined for a man like him. And she could tell Bastien LeBlanc wasn't the kind of man to let himself get trapped into pity sex twice.

She watched in disappointment as he rolled out of bed and moved over to the closet, pulling out slacks and a polo shirt and yanking them on with sharp precision.

He was going to go about his day's business and think better of a fling with some chick implicated in an active police investigation. And even if he was a little bit attracted to her, his highly developed sense of ethics would no doubt kick in. And that would be that. No more fling with the hot detective for her.

She climbed out of bed, and that was when it hit her that she had no clothes. She had come here last night in her pajamas. She didn't even have a toothbrush or a hairbrush. Staring around in dismay, she wasn't sure what to do next.

Bastien paused in the act of strapping on a leather shoulder holster. "What's wrong?"

"I don't have any clothes. I don't even have any shoes."

"No problem. That call was the robbery unit guys calling me from Gary's apartment. They've finished their examination of the place and want you to come over and see if you can spot anything missing. I'll drive you back."

Relieved, she headed for the bathroom and borrowed a comb she found in the medicine cabinet to semi-comb out her hair. She finally resorted to French braiding it and using a piece of dental floss to tie off the end.

By the time she stepped out, the nutty smell of high

quality coffee filled the air, and she groaned with delight.

"I take it by that moan of pleasure you'd like a cup of my world-famous fresh-ground coffee with cinnamon and whipped cream?" Bass asked drolly.

"Ohmigod. That sounds better than sex."

He shot back, "Then you haven't had sex with me, honey."

As soon as the words left his mouth, he glanced up at her in chagrin. He mumbled something that might have been an apology, but she was too miserable to hear it properly.

Of all guys to actually develop a crush on, why, oh why, did it have to be a cop? A drop-dead, do-me-now cop who was investigating her? Sometimes the universe had a really lousy sense of humor.

He handed her a steaming cup of coffee mounded with whipped cream. She took a sip and died a little right then and there. "Good lord, this is incredible."

Bastien muttered, "That's what all the ladies say."

She gave him a sidelong glance. She couldn't resist flirting, even though she knew it to be futile. "In bed or out?"

"Ahh, darlin'. That's for me to know and you to find out, now, ain't it?" His drawl was thick as molasses and gave the lie to his flirtatious response. He was treating her like he treated all the girls. It was nothing personal. At all.

"Too bad duty calls," she said. If only he would lift the mug out of her hands and set it aside before sweeping her up against him and kissing her until her knees wobbled like a toddler's. She would love to taste his world-famous coffee on his world-famous lips.

She would bet he'd kiss her until she felt drugged.

Yup, high on Bastien LeBlanc. There were worse fates in life. Too bad she wouldn't get to experience any of them.

"Do you need something more substantial to eat before we leave?" he murmured as he moved even further across the kitchen from her with a reluctant look on his face.

God. He must sense how pathetically needy she was and be repulsed by it. "No," she mumbled. "I've had enough."

"You don't know what you're missing, *chère*. I make the best omelet this side of the Mississippi."

"Oh, really?" She added halfheartedly, "I may have to test that claim sometime."

"It's a date." He scooped up a set of car keys from a board with two dozen sets of keys hanging from hooks on it.

She padded barefoot through the pristine workshop and into the second building, which turned out to be a storage garage at least as big as the shop. She gasped at the rows of gleaming cars and trucks parked side-by-side. He led her to a zippy looking little Aston Martin and held the passenger door for her. The car fit her petite frame to a tee, and she waited in anticipation to see how Bass would fold his big frame into the sports car. The seat looked pushed all the way back, and his shoulder nearly brushed hers, but he did, indeed, fit.

The small interior was intimate and sexy as the engine purred smoothly beneath her. If a girl sat just the right way, the seat would act like a vibrator against her nether regions. Crud. She clenched her butt cheeks and crossed her legs, denying herself the guilty pleasure.

Instead, she murmured, "Awesome car!" as he pulled out into the street and accelerated like velvet.

Bass grinned over at her, clearly pleased to show off his handiwork. "She's a classic."

"What's her name?"

"Carlotta."

"I thought Aston Martins were British."

He shrugged. "A car's allowed to have whatever name it wants."

Taking in the meticulous restoration of the interior, she said more sincerely, "Well, I approve of Carlotta. She's a beauty."

Carrie sat back and enjoyed the ride as Bass handled the sports car with smooth confidence.

"How do you split your time between being a police officer and being a SEAL?" she asked.

"With difficulty."

"Why?"

"SEAL missions don't always come with a neat beginning and end. I've gotten stuck out in the field a few times and not been able to get home in time to work my police shifts. And now the NOPD wants to promote me to a supervisory job. But I can't accept a management position and then run away to play soldier any time I'd like."

"What are you going to do?"

A troubled look came over his face. "I don't know. I love both jobs. But the day's coming when I'm going to have to choose."

She could see where two such demanding careers could come into conflict. Worse, though, it sounded as if the guy had no time at all for a personal life.

Disappointment speared through her—whoa. Wait. Why was she disappointed? It wasn't as if she planned to settle down and be someone's little Sally Homemaker. If she stopped moving, she would die. Literally.

They turned onto the street where she was staying, and Carrie gasped. "Why are there so many cop cars?"

Bass swore under his breath. "I was afraid of this," he said grimly.

"What's happened?"

"Gary's disappearance has started making waves and has become a high-profile investigation. Everyone wants to get his fingers into it."

Bass stopped among the cruisers that completely blocked the street. He contemplated the chaos in visible disgust while she wiggled her bare toes nervously, acutely aware of being in her ratty pajamas. She was going to have to walk through all of that to get to clothes. Well, crap on a cracker.

He pointed at an unmarked step van. "That dark blue van is the crime scene unit that's been going over Gary's place. That black sedan is the robbery unit guys. And the cop in that black-and-white is one of the other detectives from Missing Persons. Black Charger with the portable siren on top is my captain's car. He's here to make sure the rest of us don't mess up, and maybe to get some face time if the news channels show up. He's thinking about making a run at Police Commissioner."

"The news might be here?" Carrie asked.

"Well, yeah." Bass threw her a quizzical glance. "You're the one who warned me this case could get media attention."

"I can't end up on television!" she exclaimed, alarmed.

"Why not?"

Lonnie Grange was why not. She'd fled him years ago and had been hiding from him ever since.

She was able to avoid answering when Bass dived for a parking lot down the street as one of the neighbors pulled out of a legitimate parking space. He got distracted parallel parking, and she jumped out of Carlotta as soon as the vehicle was fully stopped.

Bass hurried to catch up to her as she padded down the cold cement sidewalk. "You okay?" he muttered as they approached a cluster of uniformed cops standing in front of her house.

Hell, no, she wasn't okay!

Dammit, he had to be all perceptive and aware of her moods, didn't he? "I'm fine," she lied.

She *really* didn't want to talk with him about why she hated the idea of being on TV. Not to mention, she wanted actual clothes, her toothbrush, a hairbrush, and some shoes, in that order.

"Hey, Bass. What's up?" one of the cops asked, looking back and forth between Bastien and Carrie. The guy clearly wanted an introduction, but thankfully, Bass merely placed a protective hand in the middle of her back and guided her through the crowd to her front door.

She paused on the second-floor landing to peer in through the open door to Gary's apartment. The place was completely wrecked. She stared in dismay at the smashed furniture, ripped-open cushions, and drawers lying upended on the floor.

She ran up the last flight of steps, abruptly eager to get far away from Gary's problems and save herself. It was selfish, and she truly was worried sick about him, but she also had no desire to get sucked into his drama and die. She hoped that didn't make her a bad person.

Bastien followed her into her place and she retreated to the bedroom to dress and freshen up. She took her time, putting on more makeup than she usually did, and braiding small pieces of hair from her temples and pulling them back behind her head in a cute style before she finally emerged again. She needed her full armor if she was going to face the day she knew lay ahead.

He was still sitting in her living room when she stepped out. *Note to self: I am a patient man.* He looked her up and down with a look of appreciation that made every second of primping worth it.

"Going someplace?" he asked.

"After I talk with the crime scene guys, I'm supposed to do the setup shots for the haunted bed-and-breakfast today. I thought I'd go ahead and film the location's background shots in hopes that Gary is found and can do the actual nighttime ghost shoot soon."

Bass's blue eyes darkened to the color of a nighttime sky. "I hope you're right."

"You don't sound convinced."

"I'm not in the business of giving family and friends false hope. I'm sorry, but with every day that passes, the odds of finding your boss go down."

A surge of fury rushed through her. "I don't understand why this is happening!"

He moved close and she held her breath, hopeful he would draw her into his arms. He didn't. Damn.

"Keep being strong for Gary. That's the most useful thing you can do right now. I'm here for you whenever you need someone to talk to."

If only she could, indeed, lean on him for support. This morning had been an anomaly, and he was already back to being the distant and professional cop. If only she could absorb a little of his calm assurance.

"Speaking of people to talk to," he added, "do you have any family members who can come down here and lend you some moral support?"

"Not hardly. When I left home to go to college, it

was with the understanding that I was on my own and wouldn't be back."

"Trouble at home?" he asked quietly.

Not the kind of trouble he was talking about. She shrugged. "My parents just felt as if they only owed me and my brother eighteen years. After that, they cut us off financially. And in my case, that meant I cut them off emotionally."

"Are you in touch with them at all?"

"We talk on birthdays and major holidays. They would probably welcome a visit from me, but I have no desire to go back."

"Why not? What aren't you telling me?"

Choosing her words carefully, she answered, "I left my hometown for personal reasons that had nothing to do with my family."

"What reasons?"

"Persistent, aren't you?"

He stared down at her expectantly. It was as if he was mentally compelling her to tell him the whole truth and nothing but the truth.

She stared back stubbornly, conveying her own mental response. *Not. Gonna. Happen.*

Their staring contest stretched out, and she sensed that he was never going to back down. She had to give him something or he wouldn't ever break this staring contest.

"Fine. If you insist," she huffed. "A friend of mine had a run-in with the law, and it didn't turn out well. I flung around some big accusations before I left my hometown that would make it difficult for me to go back now. Satisfied?" It wasn't a lie, but it was miles and miles from the full story.

Bass made a noncommittal sound like he still didn't

think he'd heard the truth. Of course, he hadn't. Not by a long shot.

She turned and fled her apartment. It wasn't noble or brave, but she simply didn't want to face any more of his questions.

She charged down the stairs and went outside—

And stopped cold as she was barraged by people shouting at her. Cameras and microphones were shoved in her face, and behind them, the avid faces of reporters and photographers stared at her. She recoiled violently. What on earth?

"What can you tell us about the disappearance of Gary Hubbard?"

"Has there been a ransom demand?"

"Do the police think he's dead?"

"When did he disappear?"

"Is it true you filmed his abduction?"

"Why didn't you call the police immediately?"

"Are you involved in the kidnapping?"

That last shouted question caught her attention. Right. Like she would tell them if she was in league with the kidnappers. What kind of idiot did they think she was?

"What the hell?" a deep voice said from the stairs behind her.

She turned to ask Bass for help in getting past the phalanx of aggressive reporters, but she caught a glimpse of his heels and no more as he retreated at high speed back up the stairs. In the blink of an eye he'd vanished. Gone. No sign of him. Wow. How did he do that so fast?

She kept her back resolutely to the cameras. She really, *really* couldn't afford to be splashed all over the news in conjunction with Gary's disappearance.

What to do? If she went back inside her apartment, the media would just camp outside her door until she was forced to come out. Better to make a break for it now, before she got trapped. She looked left and right, seeking an escape route. Damn. The only way out was through that gaggle of loud, nosy reporters.

A uniformed police officer stepped forward. "Y'all okay, ma'am?"

"I could use some help getting these folks to back up so I can get my van out of the garage."

The cop perused the crowd of reporters and photographers knowingly. "Only way y'all gonna git 'em ta move is ta run 'em over. Y'all just go on ahead and back on out of your garage, and they'll git the idea. They'll jump right spryly if you's gonna smash 'em flat."

She shook her head at the guy's thick Cajun patois but liked his thinking. Throwing her arm over her face, she dashed for the garage, shoved up the sliding door, climbed into the van, revved the engine, and backed it straight at the crowd of news people. *Please God, let this work.*

Chapter 6

Indeed, the reporters did jump right spryly to avoid getting run over. In fact, they scattered like bowling pins that had a strike ball thrown at them. It would have been deeply satisfying were she not so panicked at being filmed on some major news channel where lots of people might see.

Glancing in her rearview mirror, she winced to see reporters sprinting in various directions, no doubt racing for vehicles to follow her. She stomped on the accelerator and prayed no one would successfully manage that.

The "haunted" bed-and-breakfast she and Gary were supposed to film next wasn't in the best part of the French Quarter. But she did have to admit it had a deliciously spooky air about it. Overgrown vines crowded the iron gate that blocked the courtyard, and an air of neglect clung to the rusty second-floor ironwork and peeling paint. A pretty courtyard coated with green mildew and overgrown flower beds stretched away behind the gate.

She threw open the back of the van to grab her camera gear and, as she reached for it, spied Gary's duffel bag sitting on the ribbed metal floor. She probably ought to carry that into his place so its contents could be included in the police inventory of his personal possessions. Later. When the press wasn't stalking her and Bass wasn't playing invisible.

Grabbing her camera bag out of the back of the van, she knocked on the B&B's front door.

A woman who'd seen the back side of fifty but was attempting to hide it beneath garish makeup answered, gushing, "You must be the camerawoman from *America's Ghosts*. Carrie Something. I'm Amelie Reigneaux." She looked eagerly over Carrie's shoulder. "Where's Gary Hubbard?"

"I wish I knew," Carrie snapped without thinking. Oops. She corrected hastily, "He can't join us today. I'm here to shoot background shots and set shots we can use during voice-over sequences."

"But I thought Gary would come with you. It's his show, after all."

Carrie answered, "I'm so sorry. We've had some unexpected complications to our shooting schedule. Can you show me around, so I can pick out some spots to film for background? I'd love to do a preliminary on-camera interview with you. That will help Gary prepare questions to ask you when he's filming the actual episode."

Amalie preened at that and ran a nervous hand through her bottle-blond hair.

Carrie stepped inside and wrinkled her nose at the

scent of unchanged kitty litter. The front hallway was attractive in a faded-wallpaper-and-old-roses sort of way, and the front stairwell, made of beautifully-joined old cypress, really was gorgeous.

"Gary's going to love shooting on this staircase," Carrie commented appreciatively.

"This is one of the places Mignonette shows herself," Amelie announced. "She's the ghost. In fact, I've made a dress that's an exact replica of the one she wears. If you'd like me to, I can put it on and re-enact the appearance of the ghost."

Oy. This woman was obviously a fan of the show and knew the format. Gary often liked to use actors to portray the original historical figures who had later "become ghosted."

"Umm, great. Gary will decide whether or not to use you in the show." And no way was she touching that decision with a ten-foot pole. Gary could deal with his own crazy fans, thank you very much.

Was a crazy fan behind his kidnapping? Her gut said no. Those men in black who'd taken Gary had moved as if they knew what they were doing.

"Parlor's in there," her hostess said, pointing through an open pair of pocket doors. "That's where Mignonette appears most often."

Carrie listened to her hostess prattle on at length about sightings of the pre–Civil War belle who had pined away in this house for her true love and eventually died, herself.

Carrie wondered if the lover had died in the Civil War or from some other horrible nineteenth-century scourge. She tried to interrupt Amelie to ask, but the woman plowed ahead with the tour of the house, undeterred.

The original house had been joined to those on either side of it, and the resulting layout was a warren of narrow hallways that didn't line up with one another and odd, dark corners. No wonder Gary had chosen this place to shoot. It screamed of poltergeists and apparitions.

It took a while, but eventually, she captured every last mazelike nook and cranny of the home and wrapped up shooting for the day. As night fell, she climbed into the van and stared at the steering wheel. Where was she supposed to go now?

Her mind drew a complete blank. Idly, she looked around the interior of the beat-up van. "What's your name, old girl?"

She tried to imagine what a twenty-year-old van that had seen a lot of miles and better days would want to be called.

"I've got it," she announced to the vehicle. "You're Roxanne." Smiling a little, she coaxed Roxanne to start.

She drove randomly around the downtown area, which was magical at night. Bright neon signs and crowds of happy tourists juxtaposed against shadowed alleys and dawdling natives, all set against the lovely historic architecture created a seductive and moody ambience.

She couldn't go back to her apartment and the media sharks who would no doubt be waiting for her. She was tempted to go to Bass's place and seek shelter with him. But she had no idea what was up with him. He'd seemed so interested but then pulled back so quickly.

If only she could tell whether he had seriously been flirting with her or just doing his job, attempting to use pillow talk to get her to confess to kidnapping Gary.

As full night fell over the city, and the French Quarter became more than a little spooky, she pulled into a parking spot on a street at the edge of the historic district. In the peach glow of a streetlamp down the block, she ducked into the back of the van and retrieved Gary's duffel bag. Maybe there was some clue in it that might help the police find him.

She set aside the goofy artist's smocks and dug deeper. A spare razor and toothbrush spoke of Gary's eternal optimism when it came to picking up women. A cheap spiral notebook yielded plenty of Gary's chicken-scratchings. She glanced through it, and for the most part, his notes seemed to deal with upcoming episodes of the show.

Until she reached the last half-dozen pages.

Words leaped off the page at her. "…one of the greatest undiscovered treasures of our time…priceless… lost since 1795…best lead in decades, possibly ever…"

Whaaat?

She thumbed back a few pages to where the notes about this supposed treasure began. A string of bizarre sentences were painstakingly written down, with at least half the words crossed out and replaced by other words. And they seemed to be…a love letter?

Carrie frowned. The recipient was someone named Pierre. She knew for a fact that Gary wasn't gay. He was a hound dog after the ladies and had never wavered in that. So who was this Pierre guy? Honestly, the language sounded feminine and old-fashioned. *My beggared eyes weep for the beauteous wealth of your soul and my paupered heart yearns to beat in your presence.*

Nope. Definitely not Gary's style. She thumbed forward in the notes. Something about the return of Louisiana to France from Spain. Clearly, this had to do with the treasure hunt.

Which was unlike him, truth be told. Granted, Gary's work often involved historical tales and events, but the guy was no deep professor of history. He learned just enough to shoot the show and not one fact more.

The last annotation in the notebook was, "Stopped p 16, 6-1802. Arrived in New Orleans."

Confused, she laid the notebook down. The duffel bag appeared empty and she pulled it close to repack it. It thunked down onto the metal floor of the van and she frowned.

The bag was made entirely of canvas. The metal buckles hadn't made that sound. She turned the bag over to look at the bottom and it was plain canvas, too.

She turned the bag inside out and stared at a seam that appeared to have a clever fold built into it. She pulled the fold of cloth back. A hidden zipper. A secret compartment?

What did Gary have to hide? Given that his apartment had been ransacked twice, he obviously had something of value that someone else wanted.

She unzipped the secret pouch sewn into the bottom of the bag and slipped her fingers into the crack. Something smooth and cool was in there. It had a sharp edge. Paper. Another, smoother edge. That felt like leather. A book?

Working carefully, she eased out a very old-looking leather-bound book with rough-edged parchment pages. She opened it gently and spied brown handwriting. A journal. A very old one, written in a cramped hand. The tiny writing wasn't in English, either. She didn't speak French, but she could guess based on the accents over letters.

Was *this* what got Gary kidnapped?

* * *

Bass glared at his cell phone and jammed it back in his pocket. Again.

Carrie still wasn't answering his calls, and he had no idea where she was. He'd spent all afternoon cooped up in Gary Hubbard's apartment with the crime scene guys trying to figure out why on earth some goons felt obliged to destroy the place. So far, no answer had emerged.

On a personal level, he was worried as hell about Carrie. She'd looked like a firing squad was waiting outside for her instead of a bunch of reporters. Yes, she was an adult, and no, he wasn't responsible for her. But damned if it didn't feel as if he ought to be. She'd had a hell of a rough few days, and she was all alone in this town.

On a purely professional level, she was still a suspect in a kidnapping investigation. She couldn't just take off and not tell anyone where she was going. If she skipped town, she would be in even more trouble than she already was, and she'd looked fully panicked enough to bolt and leave New Orleans when she'd spotted all those cameras.

He hated to admit it to himself, but she was a definite flight risk.

Which chapped his butt, frankly. Hadn't she found the incendiary attraction between them interesting enough to stick around and see where it went? God knew, he rarely felt something like that with any woman. He knew how unusual, how precious, it was.

What did she have to be afraid of from reporters with cameras? He knew full well why he couldn't afford to be photographed. Not only did he work undercover as a cop from time to time, but as a SEAL, he seriously had to avoid his face being on public display. The police had spokespeople for a reason. It gave men and women like him a means of staying away from the press while someone else briefed journalists on high-profile cases.

"Hey, Bass," one of the crime scene investigators called to him.

He moved over to the dresser the guy was kneeling down in front of. "What's up?"

"There's a false bottom in this drawer. Looks hastily made and recently installed, like someone was hiding something. See these scratch marks on the interior side of the drawer? They're not deep and there aren't many marks, so this fake bottom hasn't been opened and closed more than a few times." The guy lifted a thin piece of balsa wood out of the bottom of the drawer, revealing a maybe one-inch deep space. Empty, dammit.

"Maybe the ransackers found whatever was in there," Bass suggested.

The crime scene guy shrugged. "I don't think so. The fake bottom isn't broken and was still in place when I found it. There's no deep scratching in the interior of the drawer to indicate a violent removal. In my professional opinion, the intruders didn't get whatever was supposed to be hidden in here."

"Was the vic into drugs?" Bass asked no one in particular.

A young woman, a rookie to the Missing Persons Unit, piped up. "No evidence of any drug residue in here. Appears Mr. Hubbard drank a fair bit, though."

Bass turned on the young woman. "Why do you say that?"

"He's got misdemeanor drunk and disorderlies in a half-dozen cities."

"What else did you find on him?" Bass asked.

"A bankruptcy a while back. Not long before he got the *America's Ghosts* gig. Doesn't do social media. Never married. Friends are mostly in the entertainment business. I found an article that described him as lacking any discernable talent, but hardworking."

Bass grinned. "Ouch." Then, "What about his email?"

"The lab still has his laptop."

Bass pulled the rookie aside and murmured to her, "Can you do me a favor?"

"Sure, B. Whatchya need?"

"Can you run a full background check on Carrie Price? She's Gary Hubbard's camerawoman and producer."

"Already tried. It's an alias."

Bass stared at her. "Come again?"

"She's got no history prior to three years ago when she started working on *America's Ghosts*."

"Nothing?"

"Nothing. Nada. Zip. She doesn't exist before she showed up on this show."

"Then who the hell is she?" he burst out.

"You're the one who's all cozy with her. Why don't you charm it out of her?" The rookie waggled her eyebrows suggestively.

Jesus, Mary and Joseph. Carrie was a fraud? Who the hell was she and how in the *hell* had she conned him so convincingly?

"Keep digging. I need a name. Something concrete on her."

"Will do, Bass."

"Let me know the second you figure out who she really is."

The rookie nodded, studying him a little too intently

for comfort. Bass turned away cursing in a steady, silent, well and truly pissed-off stream.

Evening turned into night, and still there was no sign of, nor word from, Carrie.

He finally broke down and got on the police band radio in one of the squad cars parked out front. He tuned to one of the unofficial frequencies and said, "LeBlanc here. Has anyone seen a white van with New York plates in the French Quarter in the past few hours?"

Someone answered quickly, "I saw a van like that parked on a side street near Dauphine and Urseline about a half hour ago."

"Thanks, man," Bass replied. He jumped in his Aston Martin and headed for the northeast French Quarter. With every block that passed, his irritation grew more intense. Although whether it was directed at Carrie—or whatever her name was—or at himself, he wasn't sure.

She'd *lied* to him…and he'd fallen for it. She'd potentially impeded an investigation by not telling the truth, and now she was hiding from him. He ought to arrest her and let her spend a night in jail thinking about it—

There. He spied a pale shape down a dark side street. Her van. Cripes. This was one of the uglier parts of town. Gang activity and drug deals were frequent in this area, particularly after dark. He pulled a U-turn that would have been illegal were he not a cop and turned into the narrow street. He parked behind the van and got out of his car, stalking up to the driver's side window with every intent of reading Carrie her rights and placing her under arrest—

She was crying.

The sight of her tears was a punch in the gut. It stopped him dead in his tracks. Then a burst of adrenaline shot through him, flinging him into full combat alert. What was wrong? Who'd hurt her? A need to commit violence, to protect her from harm, surged through him.

Sitting in the driver's seat of the van with tears streaming down her face, she looked like a lost child. He knocked on the window and she jumped about a foot straight up in the air, reaching frantically for the van's ignition before she recognized him and rolled down the window.

Good grief. She looked up at him with those huge, sad, brown eyes of hers, and his gut twisted like a rope of toffee folded over on itself. If he arrested her, he might as well kick a puppy while he was at it.

He exhaled hard, and that single breath whisked away his fury and frustration. "What's wrong?" he heard himself asking in a much gentler tone than he'd planned.

"I tried to go home, but I couldn't. Reporters were waiting for me and I have nowhere to go and Gary's gone and I don't know anyone except you and you're a cop and you think I'm guilty and I don't know what to do—"

He cut off her babbling, asking quietly, "Why do you say I think you're guilty?"

"The way you look at me. Like you're trying to see inside my head. And…" She hesitated, and then rushed forward, "…and the way you kissed me. I felt you holding back."

"Maybe I was holding back because I'm a decent guy, and I don't just fall into bed on a whim."

"And maybe you don't trust me."

She had him there. He changed subjects. "Are you planning to camp in the van all night? I can recommend much safer streets to do that on. Frankly, I'm surprised you haven't already been mugged sitting here."

"Really?" She looked out the windshield as if she hadn't noticed where she was before now.

"Any street in New Orleans that's this deserted this early in the evening is a sure bet to be dangerous as hell."

"Oh." Dammit, her eyes went all wide and innocent and sexy as hell again.

Business, man. Do not think about what she feels like in your arms, kissing you like you're some sort of conquering hero. "When I left Hubbard's apartment about fifteen minutes ago, there weren't any reporters camped out front. It's probably safe for you to go home."

She shook her head. "They'll be back first thing in the morning."

"Well, you can't sit here all night."

She nodded miserably and reached for the ignition again.

"Where will you go?" he asked quickly. "You can't leave town."

"I won't leave town. Not until Gary comes back, safe and sound. I wouldn't dream of abandoning the search for him."

He had to give her full marks for loyalty.

"As for where I'll go, I'll find a motel or something."

He winced. If her taste in motels was as bad as her taste in streets to park on after dark, he didn't want to think about how much trouble she could land in. Reluctantly, he said, "You can stay at my place. You'll be safe, and I won't have to sit up all night worrying about you."

"I don't want to impose. I'll just get a room—"

He cut her off. "I would end up sitting outside your

hotel keeping watch anyway. This way, at least I'll get some sleep. I insist."

She blinked up at him owlishly. Damn, she was cute when she did that. Irresistibly so.

"I'll lead the way out of here. You follow me in the van." He strode away from her before she could object and jumped in his car. He moved ahead of her and waited while she pulled into the street behind him. He led her back to his place.

As he waited for the iron security gate to slide open, he caught a motion down the block that had him reaching under his seat and pulling a pistol into his lap. He chambered a round by feel. The figure melted into the shadows and didn't move again, which only made his suspicions ratchet up even higher.

Was someone following him or following her? Could be either. He'd made plenty of enemies both as a cop and a SEAL. More likely, it was someone tailing her, though. Although reporters usually didn't move like Special Forces operators. Maybe paparazzi were that stealthy. But still. The hackles on the back of his neck never lied. And they were standing up right now.

He waited for Carrie's van to clear the gate before he hit the remote control and the gate started to close. He watched like a hawk to make sure no one slipped in at the last moment.

When the gate clanged shut, he proceeded to the garage and waved out his window for Carrie to follow him inside. While she parked the van, he slipped outside quickly and made a circuit around his property. He knew every possible hiding spot, where every concealing shadow fell, and he checked them all.

Who had that person down the block been? A very

sharp reporter? Or someone more ominous? Could whoever kidnapped Hubbard now be after Carrie?

He even let himself out of the compound and took a quick spin around the block in search of the mysterious lurker. Whoever it was, he or she was gone.

His gut was screaming a warning that something was not right. He hustled back to the compound and Carrie. Time to put her and the whole place on lockdown.

He closed the iron security gate and flipped on the electrification. Not only the gate, but all of the decorative iron spikes atop the steel perimeter fence would now deliver a cool fifty thousand volts of get-the-hell-out-of-here to anyone who touched them.

When he stepped into the garage, Carrie was standing by his front door, with something bulky slung over one shoulder. A backpack maybe?

"Stay where you are," he called to her.

She nodded, and he locked down the garage, turning on motion, pressure and heat sensors that covered both the immediate exterior of the building and the entire interior. He hustled over to her in the thirty-second gap before the system went live.

He unlocked the front door, ushered her inside, and then moved over to the panel in the corner, activating cameras and the house's security alarm. No one was getting close to Carrie tonight without him damned well knowing about it.

"What's up?" she asked nervously as he finally turned to face her.

"Just buttoning up for the night."

"It looks like you put Fort Knox on lockdown."

He grinned reluctantly. "Call me paranoid."

"You don't strike me as the paranoid type."

He had no intention of telling her about the shadowed figure down the street. The last thing he needed was a panicked houseguest on his hands. "Hungry?"

She frowned. "I am actually. But I'm more interested in knowing why you're changing the subject."

"Ever had a po' boy sandwich?"

She huffed in what sounded like exasperation, but caught the hint that he wasn't going to answer her question. "No. What's in it?"

"Po' boys can have anything from roast beef to hot sausage to hamburger in them, but the classic po' boy is fried seafood. One of my guys picked up a couple pounds of shrimp from the docks for me this afternoon. Wanna learn how to shell shrimp?"

She made a disgusted face as he showed her how to strip the shell and devein shrimp, but she caught on fast, and in a few minutes, they had a pile of shrimp ready to fry. He set her to work shredding lettuce and slicing tomatoes while he breaded and fried the shrimp in his own mix of spicy batter.

They worked well together in the kitchen. Which was to say, he gave clear instructions and she followed them to the letter.

The act of battering and frying shrimp, and then slicing thin and frying French fries, calmed him, and he felt more in control of his emotions by the time they sat down to eat the crusty French loaves filled with hot fried shrimp, cold, crisp lettuce, fresh tomatoes, and his secret sauce.

Carrie bit into her sandwich and groaned in delight. The sound vibrated right through him, terminating somewhere in the region of his groin. She took a second bite and groaned again. His zipper felt tight all of a sudden as a fast, hard erection filled his pants.

Dammit, he wasn't going to be able to stand up and do the dishes for a while at this rate.

He was tempted to distract himself by getting good and drunk. But, if that mysterious person down the street decided to get froggy and come mess with him, he needed to be on top of his game. Besides, he wasn't sure it was possible for him to get drunk enough to not be horny for the woman seated across from him.

"What did you do today after you fled the scene of the crime?" he asked in an attempt to distract himself.

"Hey, I may have fled, but you vanished."

He shrugged. "I can't afford for my face to be seen in public."

"How long have you been a SEAL?"

"I was active duty Navy for twelve years. Nine of which was on the teams. Then I shifted over to the reserves and have been there for two years."

"How does being a reserve SEAL work?"

"I mostly train active duty guys. I help out with the paperwork and coordinate mission briefings and intel reports. A few times a year, I take vacation or my annual reserve leave and go out on missions." He added ruefully, "And then I pray I get back home in time not to lose my job with the NOPD."

"I can't imagine they'd fire someone with your training and experience."

He replied, "That may be true, but I wouldn't want to strain my welcome with the police force. I like the investigative work. It's relaxing after a SEAL mission."

She looked amused. And he supposed she was right. Not too many people would find police work relaxing.

She asked, "Have you always worked in missing persons?"

"So far. I hope to move up to homicide in the next year or two."

"Why?" she exclaimed.

"More variety of cases. More stuff to learn."

She shuddered. "Better you than me."

He smiled, relieved that the conversation had, indeed, mellowed out his crotchular discomfort to the point that he could take a chance on standing up. Carrie helped him carry the dishes to the kitchen, and he finished cleaning up while she turned on the television to surf the news.

"I'm going to tune up your van," he told her. "I'll be out in the shop if you need me."

He went out to the workshop to give her van a quick tune-up and re-gap its spark plugs. He had the engine running half-decently again and was just about ready to button up the van and call it a night when a thought occurred to him. It wasn't exactly ethical to do it. But it wasn't illegal. And Carrie had shown herself to be a runner.

He went over to his shelves of spare parts and pulled out a GPS tracker.

This was a bad idea.

She would never know about it.

It was just a precaution. So he could keep her safe.

Keep telling yourself that, buddy.

He argued with himself the entire time he was wiring the unit into the van's electrical system. Good Lord willing, he would never need to use the damned thing. But if he ever did need it, he was going to be exceedingly grateful he'd installed it.

He finished, washed up in the big sink in the garage, and headed back to the house, toweling himself off as he went. He reset the alarm system and went inside.

He'd just stepped into the living room when a gasp of dismay from Carrie had him throwing down the towel and racing to her side. "What's wrong?" he demanded.

She pointed wordlessly at the television.

The house she and Gary were living in loomed large on his big, high-definition television. A mob of reporters jostled for position, shouting questions at the NOPD spokesman. Behind the guy, a door opened.

Bass winced as Carrie appeared onscreen and the camera zoomed in on her face. He watched carefully over her shoulder and spotted a big dark shape moving backward fast out of camera range. That would be him. Thank God. His face was never visible on the television. He was in the clear.

He glanced over at Carrie in time to catch her dashing tears off her cheeks. Oh, God. Not more tears. They were kryptonite coming from her.

"Who are you afraid of seeing you?" he asked her directly.

She shook her head.

"Look. I'm a cop. A good one. I'm going to find out eventually, so you might as well tell me."

Silence.

Dammit, why wouldn't she trust him?

He opened his mouth to ask her real name. To inform her he had the power to get access to sealed court records and that he fully intended to do so. But the house went black as the power suddenly went out.

He counted to five. That was weird. His backup generator usually kicked in so fast he hardly knew there was a power outage. The room was still pitch dark.

Why hadn't the emergency generator kicked in?

God dammit.

"Carrie, take my hand." He pulled her up off the sofa and raced to his bedroom, dragging her along with him. "We've got a problem."

Chapter 7

"Can you shoot a gun?" Bass asked tersely as he opened his gun safe by the glow of the tiny flashlight he kept on his key chain.

"No," Carrie answered in a quavering voice.

Damn. He jammed a clip in a small pistol by feel and handed it to her anyway. "Safety's on. It won't shoot until I show you how to take the safety off."

He grabbed a pair of NODs—night optical devices— and yanked them over his eyes. His bedroom jumped into green relief. Too bad he had only one set of them. Carrie was going to be operating blind. But there was no help for it.

He announced, "I'm wearing night vision gear and can see perfectly well, so there's nothing to worry about. I'll see anybody coming long before they can see me."

"Someone's coming?" Her voice broke on the second word.

"Put these in your pockets." He shoved two spare clips of ammunition for her weapon at her as he buckled on his SEAL utility belt, already fully loaded with spare clips for the pistol and short-range urban assault weapon he pulled out of storage slots. He shoved a KA-BAR knife in his hip holster and another in his boot holster, and he was ready to rock and roll.

"What's happening?" she whispered, sounding utterly terrified.

"Intruder."

He closed the safe, spun the combination lock, and took Carrie's hand again. Heading for the front door, he talked low and fast. "I'm taking you to the parking garage and putting you in a Hummer. It's fully armored. Do what I say when I say and don't ask any questions. Don't speak unless I ask you a direct question. Try to make as little noise as you can. Got it?"

"Yes," she gasped.

Crap. She sounded like she was trying to hyperventilate. No time to stop and wait for her to catch her breath, though. They had to go. He slapped his palm on the alarm pad inside the front door and disabled the system quickly. He planted Carrie's right hand on the left side of his belt and muttered, "Don't let go. Stay with me."

He didn't bother telling her to keep her head down. She was already short enough that it wasn't necessary.

He eased open the front door and scanned the workshop carefully using the heat sensing function of his optical devices. No human heat signatures in here. Moving fast, he raced across the open space of his shop and headed for the second garage where his car collection was housed.

Carrie stumbled once beside him as he ran, but she righted herself with only a slight yank on his belt and kept up with him. He stopped in front of the door to the parking area. It was *open*. He never left it open.

He hooked his left arm around Carrie's body, pushing her behind him.

He eased into the doorway and scanned the large space. The cars would block him from seeing heat signatures, so he bent down, scanning beneath the rows of vehicles—

Four feet clustered close together. Crouched in the back right corner behind his '63 Impala convertible. Not moving. Looked like they were hiding.

He could back out and flee with her in the Aston Martin behind him or on foot. But the Asty wasn't armored, and Carrie wasn't wearing Kevlar. If the bastards shot at her, she would be in mortal danger. He decided to stick with the plan and take Carrie to the Hummer. It was the second car on the left.

Placing one foot carefully in front of the next, he moved with glacial slowness toward the Hummer, giving Carrie plenty of time to keep up with him and remain quiet. Please God, let her follow instructions and not say anything or make any noises.

They made it to the driver's door of the Hummer and he bent down to peer under the vehicle's high carriage at the back corner of the garage. Bastards were still crouching there. Must not have heard them, then. Perfect.

Opting for speed over stealth, he opened the door, picked up Carrie, and swung her inside. She scrambled out of his way as he jumped in the driver's seat after her. He reached for the keys in their hiding spot under the hinged stereo speaker cover.

He heard running footsteps as he slammed his door shut, hit the garage door opener, and started the big engine. He backed it up fast, squealing the run-flat tires as he did a combat one-eighty, spinning the large vehicle aggressively. He stomped on the accelerator, and the Hummer leaped forward, barely clearing the still rising garage door as a burst of metallic pings sounded against the rear of the vehicle.

"They're shooting at us!" Carrie cried.

Grimly, he drove on, flying down the drive to the security gate, which was already open. A black SUV blocked the entrance enough that there wasn't room for the Hummer to go around it.

"Hang on!" he shouted as he gunned the Hummer, aiming for the rear corner of the SUV. Quickly, he flipped off the power to the airbags.

They smashed into the SUV hard enough to spin it out of the way with a crash of breaking glass and crunching metal. The Hummer swerved, but he righted it forcefully, careening into the street. He slowed at the next corner just enough not to squeal rubber and leave tracks for the assholes behind him to follow. He flew down the next street for a few blocks and then slowed to turn again. The next turn put him on a broad avenue with great rearview visibility, and he sped south for a few more minutes until he was positive they hadn't been followed.

He dug out his cell phone and dialed 9-1-1. "This is Detective LeBlanc of NOPD. I have hostile intruders at my home. I have vacated the premises, so anyone remaining at the residence should be considered armed and dangerous." He rattled off the address and then disconnected the call.

Not that he expected the intruders to stick around long enough to get themselves arrested. They'd been expert enough to get around most of his security measures. They would be smart enough to get the hell out of Dodge once he and Carrie bugged out in the Hummer.

He slowed to something more closely resembling the speed limit. His adrenaline was still sky-high, though. Weird. He never got adrenaline hits in the middle of an op. Why this time?

Was he that worried about Carrie's safety? Had all his years of training gone right out the window when danger threatened a woman he—

He what? Had the hots for? Was developing actual feelings for? Liked...a lot?

Swearing under his breath, he forced himself to do his own breathing exercises until his pulse came down out of the stratosphere. He finally was able to slow it to a normal speed.

He glanced over at Carrie, who was hugging her knees to her chest and looked nearly catatonic with terror. "We're good," he bit out. "You're safe."

"What the *hell* was that?" she demanded.

"The more pertinent question would be, who the hell was that?" he replied dryly.

"The power went out. How could you be so sure that meant there was an intruder?"

"I have an emergency generator that kicks in so fast we shouldn't have seen more than a flicker of the lights. The fact that it was disconnected or sabotaged clued me in."

"How do you know the generator didn't just fail?"

"Because through my night vision gear I saw two men hiding in the back corner of the garage."

She did hyperventilate then. When trying to talk her through controlling her breathing utterly failed, he finally suggested, "Lean over and put your head between your knees. At least you won't faint that way."

He probably ought to pull over and stop so he could help her, but he urgently wanted to get her to safety. There would be time later to talk her down off the bridge of panic.

She surprised him a few minutes later by asking, "Why do you have so much security installed on your property? Are you that big a target?"

"Not me. My cars and my guns."

"What?"

"In addition to the girls, I own a substantial collection of weapons. Don't want any of them stolen. So, I make it hard to get to them."

"Wouldn't thieves leave your place alone because you're a cop?"

He snorted. "They leave it alone because I'm a SEAL. I've got the local gangbangers convinced I'm a tiny bit crazier than they want to tangle with."

"Are you?"

He glanced over at her. "Am I what?"

"Crazy?"

"Hell if I know. Sometimes I think so."

She asked thoughtfully, "So if the intruders weren't local thieves, who are they?"

"That's an outstanding question." He added grimly, "One I need to answer."

Carrie was so rattled she could barely string thoughts together. First Gary and now her? Surely, she was who those men back at Bass's place had come for. A person would have to be completely suicidal to go after Bastien LeBlanc given his training and skills. What on earth was this all about?

Even if Lonnie Grange had seen her impromptu television appearance this morning, surely he hadn't been able to send a pair of his thugs all the way to New Orleans to come after her this fast. Right?

This had to be Gary's mess spilling over onto her. She was sure of it. The diary she'd snatched up as they ran past her backpack on the way out of Bass's house practically burned a hole in her shirt. She'd stuffed it down her sports bra as they'd run across the garage. It stuck up under her neck and was awkward as heck now that she thought about it.

She pulled it out and caught Bastien's shocked expression as the book emerged from the neck of her shirt.

"Do I want to know?" he asked.

"I found it today. I'm not sure what it is, but I called a professor at Tulane University not long before you found me in the van. He's going to translate it for me."

"Translate it?"

She responded, "It's a diary of some kind. It's really old—dated 1802. I think it's written in French. It was in Gary's duffel bag."

"Why didn't you tell me about it before now?" he demanded.

"Because I didn't find it until this afternoon. It was hidden in a secret compartment sewn into the bottom of his bag."

"I speak some French. I'd like to look at it when we get where we're going."

"Where *are* we going?" she asked.

"Safest place in Louisiana." He didn't elaborate, and she was too freaked out to ask.

They drove in silence for perhaps ten more minutes, and then approached a brightly lit gate with a brick guardhouse beside it. A big sign proclaimed it to be Naval Air Station New Orleans.

She'd never been on a military base before and

looked around curiously at the manicured lawns, boring but painfully neat buildings, and general air of order and discipline. Well, didn't this explain a lot about Bass? No wonder he was Mr. Hard-core Law-and-Order.

He parked beside an unmarked building, then came around and opened the passenger door for her, took her by the waist, and lifted her down from the high vehicle. She glared up at him and he shot her a crooked grin. "It seemed faster to just pick you up rather than teach you how to climb down out of Bessie."

"Bessie?" She looked over her shoulder at the big, beefy Hummer. "I'd have called that beast Godzilla."

"Godzilla was a boy. My cars are all girls."

"You seriously need to get a life," she retorted.

"Yeah, I get told that a lot."

Her gaze shot to him. He sounded more serious than joking. Her tummy fluttered at the idea of being the woman who finally lured Bastien LeBlanc away from his monastic soldier's life.

Aww, who was she kidding? It would never happen.

He stepped in front of her to use a biometric scanner for the building's entrance. The security system buzzed and he held an inner door open for her. He led her to a large room with perhaps twenty desks clustered in the space. A half-dozen men looked up, and then, to the last man, did a hard double take at her.

"Hey, Bass," one of them said cautiously.

"How's the world tonight, Skip? Safe for democracy?" Bass replied to the guy.

"Working on it."

"Any major ops running?"

"There's always something going," one of the other men replied cryptically, throwing her a cautious look.

"This is Carrie Price," Bass announced. "Someone

just broke into my place and tried to abduct or harm her."

Everyone's eyebrows shot up at that, and now they all were staring at her unapologetically. Obviously, none of them had missed the implication that she'd been spending the night with Bastien.

Skip commented, "What idiots thought they could get past you?"

Bass frowned. "They made it all the way into my car collection. I had to throw Carrie into my Hummer and bug out."

That caused exclamations all around. Finally, Skip asked, "What's up with the girl that she's got hostiles coming for her?"

Bass threw her a look she didn't know how to read. Was that apology in his eyes? Regret? Or maybe disappointment? He said, "I was hoping you guys could apply your superior research skills and help me answer that question."

Oh no. He was going to sic a bunch of SEALs on cracking her past? Not good. Hastily, she spoke up. "I can tell you why I'm of interest to your intruders. It's because I found Gary Hubbard's diary. Well, not *his* diary. A diary he had in his possession. I think it was written by a woman two hundred years ago. My guess is that Gary believes it can lead him to a hidden treasure."

"Isn't he that ghost hunter guy on TV? I thought he got kidnapped or something? Some stunt for his show."

Carrie replied indignantly, "It wasn't a stunt. He really was kidnapped, and he's still missing."

Bass interjected, "I got tagged by the NOPD to investigate Hubbard's disappearance, and Miss Price is correct. He was legitimately kidnapped."

"How's she connected to him?" someone else asked

shrewdly. This SEAL was fair in coloring and had light, light blue eyes. He looked way too smart for her good. His gaze had that same predatory alertness Bass's did when he was asking her questions she didn't want to answer.

Crud. These SEALs were as sharp as Bastien. How was she ever going to keep them from tearing apart her secrets? She pulled out the diary. "I was going to send this over to a professor at Tulane to translate, but maybe you guys know someone who can get it done faster? This was written around the year 1800, in French."

Bass took it from her and thumbed through it carefully, pausing and seeming to actually read portions of it. But then, he was a Cajun. The dialect must be fairly close to the early nineteenth-century French it derived from.

"Who wrote it?" one of the men asked.

Carrie answered, "According to Gary's notes, a woman named M. de Parais. She spends quite a bit of time swooning over someone she refers to as P.C. In his notes, Gary named the last French governor of Louisiana as Pierre-Clément Laussat. Gary thought this M. de Parais was Laussat's mistress."

"Gary's notes?" Bass asked ominously.

"I found a notebook in the same bag the diary was hidden in. Mostly Gary wrote down show ideas. But there are several pages about some treasure he thinks the diary will lead to." She added reluctantly, "Or, more accurately, it will with the help of a ghost."

Bass looked up sharply from the diary. "He really believes in ghosts?"

"Absolutely."

"And yet he's never found one on his show."

"He believes that the lighting anomalies and power glitches we film are created by ghosts."

"Do you?" Bass demanded.

Why was he doing this in front of a room full of avid listeners? It was embarrassing to talk about this under the best of circumstances. But Bass seemed determined to air the show's—and her—dirty little secrets in front of all his buddies.

She answered reluctantly, "No. I don't believe in ghosts."

"So you admit you Photoshop in fake stuff that looks like ghosts after the fact? Your show is a fake?"

"First of all, it's not my show. And second, I don't add in fake anything. It's my job in post-production to crop and enhance the footage in such a way as to hold open the possibility of the existence of ghosts."

"Don't play coy. Do you or don't you fake ghosts on the show?"

He was really starting to get on her nerves. "I told you. I enhance anomalies that are already there. I might highlight a light flickering or add contrast to a shadow that's already present, but I don't make up anything."

"And that's how you know your boss didn't fabricate his own kidnapping?" Bass asked.

Cripes, he was being a bastard. For the first time, he sounded like a cop who suspected her of being involved in the kidnapping. Was it being in the presence of his fellow SEALs that brought out his nasty side like this?

"Do you always have this much trouble remembering what someone's already told you more than once?" she snapped.

The men laughed, and it seemed to break Bass's train of thought. He closed the journal gently. "I speak a fair bit of French, but I can't read the whole thing. It uses archaic words and spellings I don't recognize."

One of the guys across the room spoke up. "We can fire it off to the Defense Intelligence Agency. They ought to be able to roust out some historian who can translate it for us."

"It's a police matter, not a national security matter," Bass objected.

"Your home was invaded. It's a SEAL matter, now," the guy with the light eyes declared.

"Thank you, sir," Bass said formally.

Sir? That scary man outranked Bass? She would never have guessed. All the men in here looked pretty much the same—hard, smart and way too observant for her own good.

"You need a place to crash tonight?" asked the one he'd addressed as sir.

"Now that you mention it, yeah," Bass replied.

"Grab a couple of racks upstairs. A few of the ladies are in town. Miss Price can bunk in with them, and she'll be that much safer."

"Thanks, Frosty," Bass murmured.

Carrie followed after Bass as he left the room. "Frosty?" she asked under her breath as they reached the hall.

"That's Commander Cole Perriman. He's the leader of all the SEALs in this unit. His field handle is Frosty. He got the nickname because of his pale blue eyes. That, and the guy has nerves of pure ice."

Bastien ducked into an office across the hall and dug in a filing cabinet for a piece of paper. He shoved it across a desk at her. "Read and sign, please."

"What is this?"

"A nondisclosure agreement."

"What on earth for?"

Ignoring her question, he explained implacably, "You will need to read the whole thing, but basically, it says that you agree not to speak about anything you hear or anyone you meet in this building—ever—or else you'll face serious criminal charges."

Whoa. She carefully read the document, which spelled out dire consequences for breaking the agreement she was about to sign. Apparently these military people, they took their privacy extremely seriously. Yet another disheartening insight into the heart and mind of Bastien LeBlanc. She signed the paper and shoved it back across the desk at him. He filed it without comment and then led her back out into the hall.

He jogged up a flight of stairs fast enough to leave her a little out of breath at the top. He, of course, seemed to not even notice the exertion. "There are quarters up here for SEALs passing through town or getting ready to go out on missions. You're going to stay in the women's bay tonight, and you're going to meet a few of the people you can't talk about outside this building."

"Women?"

"Yup."

Lord, she hated it when he went all cryptic and silent on her like this. "Who are these women?" she prodded.

"They're Tier Two support staff to the SEALs."

"What does that mean?"

He shrugged. "They have specialized skills that SEAL teams use. Sometimes they deploy with us, and sometimes they help us from some forward operating base. They speak oddball languages, do photo intelligence analysis, fly drones, that sort of thing."

How cool was that? And she got to meet some of

them! Eagerly, she stepped into a big room with rows of single beds down each wall.

"Hey, Catfish!" one of the four women at the far end of the room called out. "You got a new recruit for us?"

Carrie looked up at him in alarm.

"Nah. This is Carrie Price. Civilian. Never fear. She already signed an NDA about you. Take it easy on her tonight, will ya? She's had a rough couple of days."

"She's in good hands," one of the other women replied. "Scram, Bass, so we can grill her about you."

He rolled his eyes and looked down at her. "Come get me if they bug you too much. I'll be directly across the hall. I'm not averse to kicking some butts in here."

"You think you could take us, big guy?" one of the other women declared. "Go ahead. I dare you."

Bastien's gaze narrowed. "Who trained all of you in hand-to-hand combat? You think I give up all my secrets to recruits?" He shot one last general scowl around the group before retreating.

A pretty brunette said pleasantly, "Hey, I'm Kalli. Pull up a chair."

Carrie sat in one of the chairs at a round table.

Kalli asked, "So, Carrie Price. How do you know the most eligible SEAL in Louisiana?"

"Who, Bass?"

"Who else? You gotta admit, he's some serious man candy."

Carrie grinned. "He is not hard on the eyes, no."

"So what's the deal with you two? You dating?"

Carrie jolted. "Good grief, no!"

"Then why was he hovering all protective-like over you? His body language screamed relationship in progress."

That made her snort. "Not hardly. He's highly ticked

off with me at the moment. I've been keeping secrets from him, and it's driving him crazy."

One of the other women leaned forward. "I'm Freda. Nice to meet you. We may pick on Bass, but he's got a good heart. A really good heart. He's the kind of guy you can trust with your life."

The other women all nodded, and the last two introduced themselves as Logan and Suzanne.

"Bass was one of the guys who trained us," Kalli explained. "He was a giant pain in the ass most of the time, but he pushed us because he cares about us. He wants us to survive anything we encounter in the field."

"You really work with SEALs?" Carrie asked.

The women laughed. Freda answered for all of them, "In the flesh, babe."

"That is so freaking cool," Carrie replied.

"You have no idea," Kalli replied, grinning. "So what brings you to these luxurious accommodations in the company of Bastien LeBlanc?"

"Some guys broke into his property, possibly to kidnap me."

The women's eyebrows all shot up. "They still alive?" Freda asked skeptically.

"Well, yeah. Bass threw me in a Hummer and drove away like a bat out of hell."

Kalli frowned. "He didn't take out the intruders?"

"No."

"That's weird," Suzanne replied.

Freda leaned forward, also frowning. "He must really have it bad for you if he was so concerned for your safety that he ran rather than confronting a couple of thugs."

"Me?" Carrie laughed. "He hardly knows I exist."

All four women guffawed. Kalli spoke for all of

them. "Are you kidding? We saw the way he hovered over you, and the way he looked at you. We know him like we know our own brothers, and I'm here to tell you, that man is *seriously* into you."

Carrie was speechless. Bastien into her? For real? How had she missed it if these women were correct? Eventually, she managed to sputter, "But he's mad at me all the time."

That sent the women off into gales of laughter. Freda finally retorted, "Sure sign he's got a huge crush on you."

"Is this some perverse SEAL thing? They show affection by yelling at people and being angry at them?"

The humor evaporated from Kalli's face and she leaned forward to speak. "Seriously, Carrie. Bass is one of the calmest men I know. Nothing flaps him. He's nearly as chill as Frosty Perriman, and nothing *ever* rattles that guy. The fact that you're getting flashes of any kind of strong emotion from Bass LeBlanc speaks volumes about how far under his skin you've gotten."

Freda added earnestly, "Don't hose him over, Carrie. He's one of the good ones."

The women didn't exactly threaten her, but Carrie got the distinct impression these women would take deep exception with her breaking Bastien's heart.

Thing was, he would have to give her his heart before she could break it. And she wasn't sure he would ever get around to doing that. Not unless she revealed secrets she'd never revealed to another living soul. Not even to the police back home who'd driven her away from everything and everyone she'd known and loved.

She couldn't do it. She'd locked away that part of her life forever, and she had no intention of dredging it up again. Not for love. Not even for Bastien.

Chapter 8

Carrie slept terribly that night. The combination of an unfamiliar bed, the shocking revelations from the women about Bass's possible feelings for her, and worry for Gary made for a mix of toxic dreams.

When she woke in the morning, the four women were gone. Wow. They'd been really quiet not to have awakened her. But then, she supposed they were trained in the art of stealth. She went looking for Bass and found him in the ready room talking and joking with a bunch of guys there.

When she appeared in the doorway, he looked up instantly, and his face lit with a smile for her. *Oh. Was that what the women SEALs had been talking about?*

Warm little squiggles erupted in her stomach.

Bass held an arm out to her and she stepped up beside him, startled as he wrapped his arm around her shoulders and said, "This is the woman I was telling you about."

She recognized Commander Perriman from last night, and in the light of day, his eyes were silver. And they were frankly alarming when he turned that icy gaze on her as if he could look right into her soul. Even his voice was cool as he spoke to her. "Bastien's been telling us about your recent problems. We're expecting the translation of your journal back today, and maybe it can tell us more about who's so interested in you. Then we can form a plan to take out whoever's threatening you."

She blinked, shocked. "The SEALs aren't responsible for me."

That got a round of laughter, but she didn't see what was so funny.

Perriman said gently, "We take care of our own, Miss Price."

She got that. But she didn't belong to—

Oh. She looked up at Bass in quick surprise. Had he claimed her as someone he cared about to all these other SEALs? His deep blue gaze gave away nothing as she searched his eyes for an answer. The guy definitely held his emotional cards close to his chest.

Of course, he might have told his buddies he was interested in her purely so they would help him capture whoever'd broken into his garage.

That made more sense. Sure, he'd kissed her once. But that didn't make for an actual relationship. For all she knew, he'd kissed her because he felt sorry for her and not because he was actually attracted to her. Who could blame a healthy, red-blooded male for kissing a woman he woke up to find draped all over him in his bed? Surely, it hadn't meant anything to him.

She'd been needy and naïve to think it had signaled actual interest in her. Just like she'd been silly to believe the patter of a bunch of women who'd trained with Bass. For all she knew, they were playing some kind of joke on Bass by setting her up to throw herself at him.

The men around her were talking animatedly, and she tuned back in. They were debating the merits of her and Bass returning to his place with a contingent of SEALs hiding in the bushes, and using her as bait to draw out whoever was interested in her.

Bass was adamantly opposed to the plan, but pretty much everyone else seemed to think it was a great idea. Personally, she had no desire to dangle on a hook like a helpless little worm.

She eventually caught Bass's eye and looked over at the door significantly.

Immediately, he broke into the conversation. "Back in a minute." He guided her out into the hall without ever removing his arm from around her shoulders. It was almost as if he liked the contact.

"What's up?" he asked.

"I can't sit around being bait for you guys. I've got a show to film. I can do all the background shots and can even do a bunch of the night filming without Gary present. Once he shows back up, we can do a bunch of quick clips of him, and then he can do voice-overs for the stuff I shoot now. Frankly, it works out well for the show to do it this way, because, God bless him, Gary can't act his way out of a paper bag."

"Where are you supposed to film over the next few days?" Bass asked.

"I'm scheduled to start the night shoot at the bed-and-breakfast I was at yesterday."

"Is the night shoot when you film your ghosts?"

She smiled up at him ruefully. "Congratulations for asking that with a straight face. And yes, it is. I try to capture shadows and flashes of light and filming anomalies that can be enhanced into alleged ghost sightings."

"Congratulations for saying that without putting air quotes around the phrase, ghost sightings," he replied dryly.

She laughed. "Hey, it's a job."

"I'm not letting you do any filming without me. Not until we catch whoever kidnapped Gary and is coming after you now."

"You think it's the same people?" she asked in alarm.

"It has to be. What are the odds that two members of the same television crew would be attacked within days of each other by entirely separate people?"

She had to agree with him. Even if her past did come looking for her, it would take more than a single day to get to her.

"Where's this bed-and-breakfast?" Bass asked. "I want to let the guys know where we'll be."

She gave him the address and watched, perplexed, as he poked his head back in the door of the ready room and called out the address. "Carrie has to film at this place tonight. Anyone wanna go ghost hunting with her?"

She rolled her eyes as the jokes flew thick and fast at that. She'd heard them all before, and she stood by her standard response. Filming the show paid her bills.

They might have joked about it; but as she stepped out of the Hummer with her big bag of camera equipment that Bastien had fetched from her van, still parked in his garage, no less than six SEALs were waiting on the front steps of the bed-and-breakfast. And one of them was holding her overnight bag. Oh, Lord. Had one of them gone to her place to paw through her underwear and toiletries?

But as the guy held it out to her, he said, "One of the female cops who works with Bass got this stuff for you."

Thank goodness. "What are all of you guys doing here?" she asked the group at large.

Bass answered, "The guys will be spending the night with us. No one's getting close to you on the SEALs' watch."

Oh my. The owner was going to swoon over all these hot guys moving in with her.

Carrie's prediction turned out to be entirely accurate. Amelie, indeed, was so flustered she had trouble fetching eight room keys and passing them out, let alone instructing everybody on how to get to their rooms in the warren of winding hallways.

After she set her little bag down in the middle of her bed, Carrie stepped out into the hall in time to see SEALs heading off in both directions. Bass stepped out of his room directly across the hall from hers, and she asked, "Where are they going?"

"Reconnoitering the hotel layout. We couldn't find any floor plans on this place before we came over here. In a little while, we'll be able to move around this place blindfolded."

"It's an old house, not a military installation," she responded.

"It's the site of potential operations." He shrugged. "Even if this weren't a security assignment, SEALs would roam around and get the lay of the land in a place like this out of force of habit."

"Because it's important to be prepared?"

"Exactly."

"Has anyone told you you're a little bit crazy?" she queried.

"I'm a SEAL. I'm a lot crazy."

The way he said that, with pride and affection, made her understand why the idea of giving up being a SEAL to be a full-time cop was so hard for him.

She asked him, "What made you choose to be a SEAL?"

"The challenge of doing the impossible, I suppose."

"Are you that big an overachiever, or are you simply an adrenaline junkie?"

He stared down at her. "Why do you care?"

"Just trying to understand what makes you tick."

"You're overthinking it, Carrie. The mountain was there. I climbed it."

He wasn't being honest with her. People didn't put themselves through the rigors of SEAL training just because it was there. What wasn't he telling her about himself or about his background? Obviously, the truth was something private and personal to him. And just as obviously, he didn't trust her enough to share it with her.

She sighed, belly-punched yet again with the fact that she wasn't good enough for a man like him. "I'm going to shoot a fill of nighttime background shots and then turn in. You have fun traipsing around the house."

"We'll try to stay out of your shots."

She grinned. "Go ahead. Let me catch you guys on film. You'd be the hottest ghosts ever recorded."

"No thanks. We're better off if there's no public record of our faces." He added, "If you get scared or can't sleep or just get lonely, my door will be unlocked," Bastien replied.

Okay, she hadn't seen that coming. An open offer to join him in his bed, huh? Taken aback, she blurted,

"Aren't you worried that the ghost will come in your room and haunt you if you leave it unlocked?"

Bass laughed at that. "The day I'm worried about a ghost is the day I check myself into the loony bin."

"Oooh, you shouldn't have said that. Now you're gonna get haunted for sure," she teased.

Grinning, Bass shook his head. "Go take your pictures. I'm gonna stroll around a bit and get my bearings. This place is a maze."

With Amelia not hanging around bugging her, she got the footage she needed in under an hour and packed it in for the night.

She tried to sleep, but the stress of everything was catching up with her. She stared at a crack running across the ceiling plaster over her bed for hours, but no answers came to her. She had no idea what had happened to Gary or why, and she had no idea what the deal was with her and Bastien.

She was definitely interested in him. He was at least mildly interested in her. But enough to do something about it? Enough to break his stated rule about not dating suspects and his unspoken rule about not having serious relationships at all? Should she take him up on his invitation and crawl into bed with him? Maybe strip off her pajamas and go for the gusto? Of course, with her luck, Bass would think it was a joke and laugh his head off at her. Or worse, he would kick her out of his bed.

A cheap alarm clock on the nightstand said it was just after 1:00 a.m. when the first hard splats of rain hit her window. A gust of wind sent tree branches rattling against the side of the house, and something banged not far away, making her jump.

A faint moaning sound caught her attention, and she shook her head ruefully. Good thing Gary wasn't here.

He would be knocking frantically on her door, demanding she get up and go ghost hunting with him right away. She would tell him it was the wind, but he would insist it was spirits calling to him from the nether world.

Maybe that was why, when she finally drifted off to the pounding of the rain, she dreamed of Gary. He was calling out to her to help him, moaning rather like a ghost himself. Then he exhorted her to finish the work he'd started. To finish the quest.

She tried to ask him if he meant his treasure hunt, but the ghostly image of him either didn't hear her or didn't want to answer. A pair of faceless men came up behind him then and carried him away, down into a dark abyss she knew to be death. In her dream, she cried out to him. But he never looked back at her.

She sat bolt upright, mumbling, "Don't leave me…"

Carrie flopped back against the flattened feather pillows. God, she was so lonely. Gary might have been a pain in the butt, but he'd been her constant companion and had staved off the ugly truth that she was all alone in the world except for him.

Meeting Bastien had been a stark reminder of what she was missing by cutting herself off from other people, by traveling all the time and never staying in one place long enough to develop friendships, let alone actual relationships. She could totally relate to Bastien's choice not to date seriously. But the price of it—these moments in the dark, late at night, when the scary world was banging at her window…

Had she done the right thing by running away all those years ago? By not facing her attacker? By taking the coward's way out?

Oooooooh. A sigh of breath, as if someone moaned in great pain, disturbed the patter of rain.

What was that?

She was no rookie to creepy sounds associated with ghost hunting, but that strange moaning noise was unnerving. No wind she'd ever heard had made that noise.

Her curtains stirred, and she jolted away from them, staring. The window was definitely closed and locked. She'd checked it before she went to bed. There must be an air vent somewhere in the room, making the curtains flutter like that.

The moaning sound came again, so close it sounded as if it was practically in bed with her. What the hell?

She sat up, clutching the covers close to her chest. Of all people, she knew for sure that ghosts were not real. Which meant a human was making those noises. If someone was trying to freak her out, they were doing a darned good job of it, though.

A flash of lightning outside was followed by an almost immediate crack of deafeningly loud thunder that made her jump. She thought she caught a glimpse of a shadow outside her window, a human-sized shape in the tree, as if someone had climbed it and was peering inside.

Ohmigod.

She bolted out of bed and flew out of her room, shooting across the hall to leap into Bastien's room in about one second flat. She plastered her back against the door, breathing hard.

Bass was out of bed and standing in front of her in about the same amount of time. Crud, that man could move fast. "What's wrong?" he bit out.

"I thought I saw someone outside my window. It was nothing, I'm sure, but it spooked me."

He touched his throat with a finger and ordered tersely, "I need someone to check out Carrie's room, inside and out, ASAP. She thought she might have seen someone outside her window."

"Who are you talking to?" she asked.

"My men. We're all wearing earbuds and microphones."

"You went full commando in a bed-and-breakfast? Isn't that a tiny bit of overkill?"

"What if there really is a guy outside your room?" Bass responded.

Oh, God. There went her pulse again.

Bass gathered her into his arms as if he sensed her panic. "I've got you. You're safe. No one's going to hurt you."

She mumbled against his chest, "I feel so stupid."

"No need. You have every reason to be jumpy." A pause, then he added, "You're freezing. Come get under the covers and warm up."

He deposited her in his bed, which was still warm from his body. Heat wrapped round her like the hug he'd just given her, comforting and secure. She was disappointed when he didn't join her. Instead, he continued to stand over by the door, listening at the panel.

Without warning, he slipped outside, leaving her alone in his room. Great. Now she could freak herself out in here.

She stared fixedly at the alarm clock on his nightstand, her tension climbing with every passing minute. What was going out there? Why had he bolted out of the room like that?

The door flew open and she froze in terror, her gaze darting around frantically in search of a weapon. That alarm clock was her best bet. She started to dive for it when Bass murmured, "It's me."

She collapsed across the pillows. "Good thing you

identified yourself. I was about to bean you with the alarm clock."

Bass lifted the covers and slipped in beside her. "Come here."

She rolled toward him, and he drew her into his arms. He smelled of rain and fresh cut grass and his shirt was damp. "You're wet," she announced. "You should take off that shirt before you catch a chill."

"Our body heat will dry off my clothes soon enough."

"Why did you go outside?"

"The guys spotted someone moving around out there."

"Did you catch him?"

"Nope. Whoever it was took off when we closed in on him."

"I thought you guys were super stealthy."

"We are. Which makes it interesting that the person noticed us and managed to slip away."

"Interesting how?"

"Whoever's after you is no amateur."

Her heart sank. She couldn't hide behind Bastien and his buddies forever, and Lonnie Grange was a patient man. If he'd found her and decided to take revenge upon her, he wouldn't ever give up. She said heavily, "I've got to leave New Orleans. Go somewhere far away from here where no one can find me."

Was she going to have to change her name again? It had been a royal pain to jump through all the legal hoops to make that happen the first time. If it was a matter of life and death, though, she supposed she had no choice. But the prospect of starting over again, from scratch, of starting a new career in a new place, of living like a mouse, catching no one's attention, speaking to no one, making friends with no one—

Bass interrupted her grim thoughts. "Have a little faith. We'll catch this guy and make him talk. We'll figure out what he wants. Between the SEALs and the NOPD, we'll solve this puzzle."

"If you catch this guy, a new one will replace him. They'll just keep coming," she mumbled.

Bass went still against her. "What makes you think that?" he asked alertly.

Because Lonnie Grange was rich and powerful and had an endless supply of thugs eager to do his dirty work. Yup, she could really pick bad guys to tangle with.

She blinked, realizing too late what she'd let slip. "Nothing. It's just that if these guys are after Gary's treasure, there will always be another treasure-hunter greedy for whatever he thinks Gary can lead him to."

It was a lame excuse and sounded ridiculous even to her ears. Bastien made no comment, but she could literally feel his brain working overtime.

Crud. Desperation to distract him rushed through her. She did the only thing she could think of. She snaked her arms around his neck and tugged his head down to hers.

"Kiss me, Bass."

He resisted her for a moment, and she felt his stare upon her in the dark. But then his mouth closed on hers, and she sighed in relief. His lips were warm and restless, gentle and demanding, all the things she remembered from their first kiss and more.

His arms tightened around her and her stomach pressed against the hard ridges of his abdomen, her legs tangling with his. Her toes barely came to the top of his feet, and for once she enjoyed feeling small and fragile in someone's embrace.

As big and overpowering as he was, though, he handled her with a gentleness that said he knew the extent of his strength.

His mouth slanted across hers, his lips warm and firm. She kissed him back eagerly, inhaling the taste of him, lingering toothpaste and that hint of the outdoors that always clung to him.

Using the tip of her tongue, she tested his lips, and his mouth opened immediately. With a groan in the back of his throat, he deepened the kiss, drawing her even closer to him. His left hand plunged into her hair, cupping the back of her head, angling her to fit him more perfectly, and holding her as if she was made of precious crystal.

But then he tensed and lifted his mouth away from her.

"What's wrong?" she asked anxiously.

"I don't want to mess this up."

"You have a lot more experience at this romance stuff than I do. I wouldn't know if you got it all wrong or not."

"Still."

"You won't mess anything up," Carrie declared. "You can do anything you set your mind to."

He kissed his way across her cheekbone to the sensitive spot behind her ear. "Thanks for the vote of confidence."

"You're a SEAL, for crying out loud."

He kissed his way down her neck and across her collarbone before lifting his head. "That only means I know how to be a warrior. It doesn't mean I know a damned thing about how to do relationships."

"You say that like I have some idea what I'm doing," she replied, raising her chin to give him better access to her throat.

"Then I guess we'll have to figure this out together."

Figure out what, exactly? She stared at him as he loomed over her, only able to make out the general lines of his face, the planes of his cheeks, the angles of his nose and brows. She reached up with her fingertips to trace the familiar outlines. "You're so pretty," she murmured.

"I thought that was supposed to be my line to describe you."

"I'm nothing to write home about. But you're kind of spectacular."

His lips curved against hers, inviting her to participate in the smile. As if she could refuse that. She smiled and kissed him back until he muttered against her mouth, "I'm glad we've established that you're kind of blind, then."

"I'm a camerawoman! I'm not blind, and you're hot!"

He laughed then. "I'm glad you think so. You are rather delectable, yourself, Miss Price."

"Now who's blind?"

He kissed his way down her throat to the V-neck of her T-shirt, pulling the soft cotton down out of his way as he explored the gentle valley between her breasts. His breath was warm and his mouth warmer against her skin. "Everything about you is just right."

"I'm a midget."

"Sweetheart, I wouldn't have you any other way."

His hands slipped under the hem of her T-shirt and up her ribs, lifting her to his mouth. One hand slipped around her side to cup her breast, and his thumb rubbed lightly across her nipple, making her cry out a little and arch up into the contact.

"So sensitive," Bass murmured. "So damned soft."

His big, calloused palms swept up her body, shoving her shirt over her head. Cool air wafted across her skin, making her shiver a little. But then he was there with his mouth and hands and furnace-like heat to chase away the cold, the gentleness of his touch belying the hardness of his hands.

For a moment, she froze up, panic consuming reason. But then she told herself firmly, *This is Bass. He would never hurt you.* She repeated that to herself over and over until the moment of anxiety subsided, leaving only his heated hands and soft mouth on her skin, and her pulse racing frantically in response.

She plunged her fingers into his silky hair as his lips roamed across her stomach, seeking and finding all her ticklish spots. She cradled his head in her arms as he laid his cheek against her stomach, pausing there as if making a memory of the moment.

It was exactly what she needed—a reminder that Bass was a good man who appreciated her as a person, respected her as a woman, and genuinely found her attractive. Not to mention he was both honorable and honest. He was precisely the kind of man she'd wished for all these years and never expected to find.

"You smell like a woman," he murmured against her belly button.

"Is that good or bad?"

"All good. You smell sweet. Edible. Like home. Like…fresh-baked cookies."

"That must be the vanilla shampoo I use."

"You're everything I'm not," he said as he dipped his fingers into the waistband of her flannel pajama bottoms. "You fascinate me."

His hand cupped her rear end, his fingertips skimming the base of her spine and the incredibly sensitive spot there. Her nether regions melted a little, and suddenly her limbs felt boneless.

Her own hands roamed across his chest, frustrated by his damp T-shirt, and she tugged it up impatiently. Better. Skin.

She kissed his chest, loving how his pectorals jumped under her mouth and how his stomach tightened into a sexy washboard as her hands stroked his waist. She found the deep, muscular indent at his hips and traced it downward to where it disappeared into the top of his jeans. Hungry for more, she reached for his zipper.

One of his big hands closed over hers. "Before we go any further, are you sure about this?"

Everything inside her went deeply still.

Was she sure? She'd had sex now and then in college, and she'd gotten through it okay. Trauma from the past hadn't intruded too much. But then, she also hadn't been very emotionally involved during those encounters. Unlike now.

This was Bass. Kind, stern, uncompromisingly decent Bass.

"Yes," she said firmly.

"Yes what?"

"Yes, I'm sure about this. About you."

He smiled against her mouth, "All right then. Last one naked's a rotten egg."

She laughed as he rolled away from her fast. She reached for her pajama bottoms, but he was there before she could hardly touch them.

"Slowpoke," he declared. "Let me do that for you."

She squeaked as he disappeared under the covers, grabbed the waistband in his teeth, and dragged them down her body. When he got to her ankles he quickly stripped away the flannel and kissed his way slowly back up her leg. He paused at the back of her knee and licked her until she giggled, then he continued up her thigh until she gasped.

How could the act of kissing her leg make her feel so wanted like this? Or maybe it was that he was willing to take his time with her, make sure she was enjoying herself first. Either way, something warm and fragile unfolded inside her heart.

"Open for me, baby. I want to taste you."

The intimacy of what he was suggesting staggered her. She might have protested, except he commenced murmuring words of praise about how beautiful she was and how much he wanted to give her pleasure, his mouth all the while teasing the incredibly sensitive flesh of her inner thigh. He nuzzled the juncture of her thighs with such undisguised enjoyment that her reservations melted away. Her leg muscles relaxed, and he kissed his way toward her core, taking his sweet time about it.

She'd never been with a man who savored the experience and felt no rush to get to the finish line. But then, Bass was a lot more confident and sure of his masculinity than the few college boys she'd had sex with.

Gradually, she relaxed as he cupped her hips in his hands and kissed everything but the throbbing center of her nervous desire. The longer he delayed, the more a strange tension built in her lower belly, straining toward...something.

"Bastien," she finally mumbled in complaint.

"Hmm?"

"What are you doing to me?"

"I don't know. You tell me. How does this feel?" He kissed the softness where her thighs ended and then drew his tongue along the sensitive crease.

"Umm, it feels nice. But…" She trailed off, unsure of what was missing.

"But it's not this?" he murmured.

She lurched as his tongue licked slowly and deeply between her labia, finding the core of her desire and exploding it to life in a single hot, wet stroke. Lights exploded behind her eyes, and her entire being jolted at the crazy pleasure ripping through her. *Oh. So that was what all the fuss was about.* Well, then. No wonder people liked sex.

"Again?" he asked.

"Uh-huh," she panted.

He obliged, sucking and licking and tugging at her throbbing flesh until she cried out, fisting her hands in the sheets and writhing beneath his mouth. She vaguely realized that her legs were thrown wide, granting him full access to her most private places, that her nipples were hard and hungry for attention, and that her entire consciousness had narrowed down to where his mouth was slowly but surely driving her out of her mind.

A wild buzzing sensation started to build in her extremities, racing inward toward her core, growing stronger and stronger until it crested all at once, crashing through her in a rush of pleasure that made her cry out as her entire body spasmed, arching off the mattress and into his mouth. Shock tore through her. She'd never expected to enjoy sex at all, let alone thought it could feel like this!

"That's it. Sing for me, Carrie." Barely giving her a moment to draw breath, his mouth closed on her again, and her hypersensitized flesh throbbed again. His lips closed around the bud at her core. One graze of his teeth as he sucked on the swollen nub, and she came again, even more sharply and powerfully than the first time.

Tears of gratitude leaked out of the corners of her eyes, so overcome was she at realizing a normal, healthy sex life was possible for her.

Bass surged up over her, covering her body with his. He started to kiss her, then stopped abruptly. "What's wrong?"

"Nothing's wrong. In fact, everything's unbelievably right."

"So those are happy tears, not sad tears?" he asked cautiously.

"Those are ecstatic tears."

"Ahh. I can live with those." He confessed, "I'm a bit terrified when it comes to dealing with tears. They kind of freak me out."

"You?" she exclaimed. "I didn't think anything rattled you!"

"Honey, you rattle me so hard I don't know which end is up, sometimes."

"Me?" she asked in a small voice. That warm, fragile feeling in her chest expanded a little bit more, taking root a little more deeply in her soul.

"Yes. You." He kissed her deeply then, the taste of her still on his lips. It was foreign and erotic, and she surrendered to it—to him—too overcome with pleasure to do anything but ride the wave he'd created in her.

She vaguely heard a plastic tearing noise, and then something hot and smooth, hard as steel touched the core of her pleasure. Impatient for more of this brand new world he'd opened up to her, she wrapped her legs around his hips, urging him to hurry.

"Easy, darlin'. I'm trying not to hurt you, here."

"You won't," she panted. "I want you. Now."

Bass groaned in the back of his throat. "You're killing me, woman. Let me be a gentleman, here."

The burning heat of him slowly pressed a tiny ways into her.

"Bass! Stop teasing me!"

"As the lady commands," he muttered. And then he kissed her and stroked all the way home, filling her to bursting and absorbing her cry of pleasure into him at the same time.

Her internal muscles contracted and released spasmodically, and her hips rocked forward hungrily. "More," she gasped.

Bass withdrew a little ways, and she tightened her legs around him in alarm.

"Never fear," he murmured against her lips. "I'm not going anywhere. Not after I waited so long to get here."

He plunged into her then, filling her once more. Drugging pleasure speared through her and she groaned her approval. "Again."

"Demanding little thing, aren't you?" he teased. But he didn't keep her waiting and plunged into her again, wringing a keening cry of joy from her this time.

She hung on for dear life as he established an unhurried rhythm that her body picked up on and mimicked immediately. But he was definitely in the driver's seat as she clung to him and he cradled her, carrying her higher and higher toward she didn't know what. This was all uncharted territory for her, and she was happy to let him steer this ship wherever he wanted to take it.

A deeper pleasure built inside her this time, rising steadily to fill not only her body but also her mind, an emotional connection to Bastien that was a hundred times more seductive than the explosive pleasure of before. She looked up at him, losing herself in his shadowed gaze, amazed and overwhelmed to share her-

self with him like this and to have him share himself
with her.

And a sharing it surely was. This was not a colli-
sion of self-absorbed bodies seeking momentary grat-
ification that sex had been for her in the past. This
was something entirely different. For the first time, she
truly understood why people called it making love. She
used her body to express everything she couldn't say in
words, opening herself to him, using her legs and arms
to draw him closer, kissing him with unbridled hunger,
touching his face with her fingers in the same wonder
she felt throughout her body.

Bastien never took his gaze off her, watching her
with hawklike intensity. God only knew what he was
reading in her face. But it was okay. She was willing to
share everything she was with him in this magical space
they'd created, separate from the real world.

Emotions built up inside her until they refused to be
contained any more, and as Bass increased the speed
and intensity of his movements, her own body matched
him. She strained with him toward wherever their final
destination might be, eager to get there. With him.

An urge to laugh and cry and shout out her pleasure
came over her and she stared up at Bass, her only life-
line to anything at the moment. Bass's jaw tightened
and his eyes glazed over as she looked on. She'd done
that to him. She'd sent him to a place of pleasure so intense he was totally lost in it.

As her own orgasm clawed its way toward release,
she, too, gave in to the primal demands of her body,
losing herself in the slide of sweaty flesh, the piston
strokes of Bass's body against her swollen, pulsing
flesh, the flex of his back muscles beneath her hands,

the woodsy smell of him, the salty taste of his neck as she kissed him.

Bass surged into her one last time, his entire body arching against hers, and she met him halfway, crying out her own magnificent release. They shuddered violently against each other, clinging convulsively as their bodies and souls emptied into each other.

Everything she'd ever dammed up inside her heart broke loose, and she cried out as too many emotions to name—both good and bad—tore through her, laying her utterly bare to Bastien.

He stared down at her, and she stared up at him, too stunned to hide everything she was feeling from him. She regained feeling slowly in her fingers and toes. Gradually, awareness of his weight registered, but it was a delicious sensation she relished. He was breathing hard. Hah! She'd winded a SEAL! Of course, she was panting just as hard.

They lay like that for a long time, recovering from the intensity of their lovemaking. Her thoughts were disjointed, jumping from one observation to the next in random fashion. *That was amazing. Shockingly, she felt safe. Sex done right really wasn't related to violence. She trusted Bass.*

Eventually, Bastien murmured, "You okay?"

Always the perceptive one, wasn't he? "Okay wouldn't be the word I'd choose to describe myself."

Quick alarm flashed in his eyes. "What word would you choose?"

"Flabbergasted."

"Umm, as in good?" he asked.

"Not good—great. Fantastic. Spectacular."

He chuckled and kissed the tip of her nose. "Glad to hear it. And yeah. You're all of that."

She let out a long, slow breath. He thought that of her? Really? She had to let that sink in for a minute. Eventually, she murmured, "Thank you for enlightening me."

Bass leaned to one elbow and used his free hand to push her hair back from her face. "It's not usually like that for you?"

"Umm, no," she replied vehemently.

He frowned. "Why not?"

"Lousy taste in guys. Rotten past. Low self-esteem. Too shy to let go and enjoy. Trust issues. Take your pick."

"Wow. Good thing I'm a brave man or that list might send me running for the hills."

Yikes! The last thing she wanted to do was to spook him now. "Good point. Never mind," she said quickly.

"No. Not never mind. I want to know you. All of you." He gazed down at her searchingly, as if he would, indeed, peel back her emotional armor and discover all her most closely held secrets.

She waited for the panic to come, the need to run from him and keep running until he couldn't possibly find her. Except it didn't come, tonight. At all.

Flummoxed, she stared up at him. What was so different about this man that she might actually contemplate revealing everything about herself? Heck, she barely did that inside her own mind. Surely it was more than the amazing sex that made her want to tell all to Bass.

The answer was obvious, but she wasn't sure she was ready to admit to herself how far and how hard she was falling for him.

In a bid to shift the subject to safer territory, she said, "What are you thinking, right now?"

"I'm thinking that I've never met a woman like you."

"Is that good or bad?"

"Definitely good."

That earned him a smile from her. She wriggled a little beneath him and his eyes widened as she felt him stirring where their bodies were still joined.

The humor faded from his eyes as he stared down at her and he spoke quietly. "I think it's time you told me your real name."

Chapter 9

He'd had some great sex in his life, but nothing—*nothing*—compared to what he and Carrie had just shared. The deep vulnerability she brought to his bed, her genuine surprise, and then that shattering explosion of joy from her had brought a level of emotion to the lovemaking that he'd never experienced before. It was a revelation. And here he thought he knew a lot about sex. Hah! Turned out he knew zilch about making love. Until now.

"I beg your pardon?" Carrie stammered up at him.

"Your name. Your real name. If you're willing to share your body with me, willing to let me see inside your soul, and willing to make love with me like that, the least you can do is let me know your name."

"My name is Carrie Price. Carrie Ann Price."

"So you legally changed it, then? From what? What name were you born with?"

She shook her head, looking panicked that he would force her to tell him.

He spoke more aggressively. "You're a suspect in a criminal investigation. You need to answer my question."

"So this is an official conversation, then?"

He nodded grimly, once, just the tiniest dip of his chin.

"Then you should probably not be in bed with me. Unless of course, it's standard police interrogation procedure to have sex with the people you're questioning."

Dammit. Her tart words stung with barbed truth.

She frowned and pushed at his shoulders. He propped himself up on his elbows to stare down at her earnestly, but he didn't release her lower body from beneath his. She didn't get to evade the question or run away from him this time like she had every time he'd brought up her past so far. He was being an ass, but he couldn't help it. He was so damned frustrated that she wouldn't tell him something as simple as her real name.

"Look, Bass. I have a past, and I want to keep it in the past. I swear I'm not a criminal and I've broken no laws. If you want to be with me, the deal is you have to accept me for who I am now and move forward."

She didn't trust him. The realization was a cold bucket of water on his libido and he rolled away from her and sat up. An urge to swear and throw something came over him. What the hell was it going to take to get through to her? If she wouldn't tell him herself, he was going to find out some other way.

He muttered, "I'm going to go check in with the guys." He got out of bed and went hunting for his clothes. "I want to see if they found any tracks for the guy in the tree outside your room." He jerked on his jeans and bent down to tie his shoes. "Stay here. My room faces the courtyard, and I've got two guys sitting down there on watch. No one's coming in through my window to get you."

He yanked on a T-shirt and left without a backward glance, grabbing his laptop off the desk by the door on his way out.

It took him about ten minutes to visit the six men lurking in various corners of the bed-and-breakfast. After the excitement with the person outside Carrie's window, all had been quiet. Perhaps whoever was sniffing around her had finally figured out Bass was serious about keeping her safe. Or maybe the bastard had merely retreated to call in reinforcements.

Time was not only running against Gary Hubbard, but the longer it took to figure out why Carrie was in danger too, the more time the bad guys had to organize themselves and become combat effective. He had to figure out what the hell was going on with Carrie and her boss, and fast.

To that end, Bass found a desk in the library on the ground floor, turned on a small lamp, and sat down at his computer. It took him only a few minutes to find the court case where Jane Doe changed her legal name to Carrie Price. It had been filed in the State of Idaho three years previously. Idaho? That was a long damned ways from upstate New York. What was she running from?

He wrote up an official request for the file to be unsealed and sent it to the court in Idaho. Then he went hunting for a girl matching Carrie's description in the news in New York State. Without her real name, it was hopeless, though. Hell. She might not have been telling him the truth about being from upstate New York, anyway. Whatever had happened to send her across the country and ultimately to change her identity could have taken place any time in the past decade or so, more or less anywhere in America except the deep South. She bore no hint whatsoever of a Southern accent in her voice. For all he knew, whatever had happened to her hadn't made the newspapers anyway.

Frustrated, he went looking into Gary Hubbard's past and found nothing to indicate why anyone would find the guy kidnapping-worthy.

Of interest was the fact that Gary had lived in Albany, New York, for some years before moving to New York City and launching his television career. Maybe that New York connection explained why Gary had hired Carrie to be his camerawoman.

Too wired to sleep, he checked in with the SEAL unit and was surprised to hear that the translation of the old French diary had just come back. One of the night watch guys emailed it to him.

Bass spied a printer across the room and went over to check it out. While dated, the thing looked operational, and a stack of blank paper filled the feeder tray. He downloaded the proper drivers for it to his laptop, and then hit print for the file of the diary translation. Fifty-plus pages later, he sat down with the results.

He was maybe a dozen pages into it, when the library door opened, causing him to look up sharply. Carrie stood in the doorway. Memory slammed into him of her body beneath his, her internal muscles clenching him sweetly, her arms holding him close—

He swore under his breath and his brows came together in a frown. "I told you to stay in the room. It's not safe for you to wander around this place alone."

"Why? Worried the ghost is going to get me? I've been filming spookier places than this for years and have never been attacked by a ghost. Heck, the young woman who haunts this house isn't even supposed to be hostile."

He huffed. "This place is a maze. If an intruder got in, they'd have no trouble hiding. You shouldn't be strolling around unaccompanied, especially at night. I want one of my men with you at all times when you're out of your room."

She looked crestfallen. Had she been hoping he would personally play bodyguard to her going forward? That would've been a great idea had she bothered to trust him enough to tell him the truth about herself.

As it was, his emotional detachment was ruined, and he was angry enough with her to make a fatal mistake. Better that his men babysit her for now. His expression hardened and he looked away from her, staring down at the pages in his lap without seeing the words.

"What's that?" she asked.

"The translation of the diary came through. I just printed it out."

"Can I see it?"

His first inclination was to refuse her, but he knew that for the knee-jerk reaction it was. She'd been working with Gary on this supposed treasure hunt for months. Maybe she would recognize something in the diary that he wouldn't. He sighed. "Yes, you can see it. It'll go faster if we split it up." He held out a wad of pages to her. "Look for anything that could explain what the hell Gary's been up to that got him kidnapped."

She sat down in the chair beside his and dug into the pages. Her mere presence within arm's reach of him was distracting as hell. He could barely focus on the pages before him, let alone make out words and absorb meaning. The curve of her cheek in the lamplight, the way strands of her hair caught the light and shone gold—

Focus, for crying out loud.

Whoever had translated the diary had written directly onto an enlarged photocopy of the original, mostly translating word for word with notes in the margins about possible alternate translations and the occasional grammar notation.

He found it tedious going and wasn't particularly interested in the passionate romance between the female author, who referred to herself only as M., and her wealthy patron, P.C.

Carrie, however, seemed fascinated. He even caught her dashing away a tear from her cheek at one point.

"What's so tragic?" he broke down and asked.

"She loved him so much, and he couldn't be with her because his job was too important to walk away from. It's sad. Such a loss of what they might have had."

The words resonated deep in his belly. Was Carrie talking about him, or about the dead guy in the journal? He shook off the sensation. Of course she was talking about Pierre. But a niggling feeling remained.

A voice spoke quietly in his earbud. "I've got movement in the upper hallway heading toward the main staircase." Bass leaped to his feet, scattering papers on the floor, and turned off the lamp quickly.

"What's happening?" Carrie asked, her voice quavering in the sudden dark.

"Intruder." He thought fast. "You and I are going to stay put and take cover behind the desk while my guys check it out."

He heard Carrie fumbling around and moving toward him. He reached out and his hands brushed her skin. She gasped, which helped him locate her in the dark. Throwing an arm around her shoulders, he drew her down beside him behind the desk.

Chagrin roared through him that he wasn't armed and equipped with night vision gear. The only saving grace to being caught out like this was that he trusted his teammates completely. They would deal with the intruder as efficiently as he could.

No sooner had the thought crossed his mind than a blood-curdling scream ripped through the house.

Carrie lurched against his side. She whispered, "I've never heard a ghost make a sound like that."

Neither had he. That was a human, and a female if he wasn't mistaken. He tightened his arm protectively around her.

One of the other SEALs' voices spoke in his ear, dripping with disgust. "We caught the intruder. You gotta come see this. We're on the front stairwell."

"C'mon," he muttered to Carrie, standing up.

"Are we running away?" she asked nervously.

Oh, right. She didn't have an earbud to hear his guys. Must get her one. "Nope. Intruder's been apprehended, and you and I have been asked to join my teammates to see who it is."

He turned on the desk lamp, and he and Carrie made their way to the door. It was a quick walk down the main hallway to the foyer, where three of his guys clustered around one of the craziest sights he'd ever seen.

Amelie Reigneaux was wearing a tattered, once-white ball gown with a giant hoop skirt. It was an off-the-shoulder affair she was far too old to pull off decently. But more bizarre was the pale blue-white pancake makeup covering all of her exposed skin. Her eye sockets had been darkened with charcoal makeup, too. The overall effect was of an elaborate Halloween costume gone terribly wrong.

"Oh, dear," Carrie muttered.

As soon as Amelie spotted Carrie she squawked. "Why did these men scare me to death? Why aren't all of you in your rooms? I thought you would enjoy me making an appearance as the ghost! Shouldn't you go get your camera and shoot me?" The woman shook her left arm free from the SEAL gripping her elbow, declaring in a ridiculous Southern accent, "Take your hands off me, you rude young man!"

"We won't shoot the actual show until Gary gets here," Carrie explained.

"Then why is your crew traipsing all over my house in the middle of the night?" Amelie demanded.

Bass dived in, throwing as much charm at their irate hostess as he could manage. "We thought we saw an intruder earlier. When we heard you moving upstairs, of course, we immediately jumped to rescue you."

"Well, I never." Amelie fanned herself with a ratty lace fan that all but fell apart under her vigorous swishing of it.

"Can I make you a cup of tea, Miss Amelie?" Bass asked solicitously. "Your nerves must be rattled."

More fanning. "They're shattered!"

"Why don't you gentlemen take Miss Amelie into the parlor and sit with her while I go to the kitchen and make her a nice cup of tea?"

His men looked at him like he'd completely lost his mind. None of them were Southerners, let alone native New Orleanians. They didn't get how encounters like this worked. There were rules for moments like these.

Carrie made as if to follow him to the kitchen, but he muttered to her, "You need to go sit with her. Calm her nerves and let her rant. See if you can get her to talk about something she's interested in and get her mind off my guys scaring her half to death. And for God's sake, don't comment on her crazy appearance."

Carrie flashed a quick grin at him. "You forget. I spend my life filming people who sincerely believe in ghosts. I'm good with crazy."

Thank God for small favors. He rushed off to the kitchen to make Amelie's tea. He knew without even having to ask the woman to load it up with enough sugar that a teaspoon would practically stand up in it.

Carrie headed thoughtfully for the parlor and their hostess in her ridiculous ghost outfit. Honestly, Carrie had seen worse. This outfit was elaborately decorated with festoons of ruffles, lace and ribbons. It actually would look good on the show if...no, *when*...Gary returned and they resumed filming.

She stepped into the parlor, where Amelie was currently suffering an attack of the vapors. Probably had as much to do with her overtight corset as it did with the three good-looking men hovering around her. Poor guys looked completely flummoxed by their red-faced, panting hostess.

Taking pity on them, Carrie picked up Amelie's fan. "Lie back and let me fan you, Miss Amelie."

It took a minute or two, but she began to breathe more normally.

"If you're feeling better, perhaps you could tell us about the history of this house? When was it built?"

"Oh, it was built before 1800. It's one of the oldest standing homes in the city. That's because it never burned down in any of the great fires."

Carrie followed up. "Do you know who the original owner was?" She'd just been reading the diary of a woman who'd lived in New Orleans in 1800 and who might have known the person who built this home. It was pretty cool to think about, actually.

"Oh yes. Louis de Parais built it."

Carrie jolted. The woman who'd written the diary Gary'd hidden was named *de Parais*. "Was Mignonette his wife or his daughter?"

"His daughter."

"And she's the ghost?" Carrie confirmed.

"Correct. This is a replica of the dress she's seen wearing when she appears."

The SEALs all frowned. "There's an actual ghost?" one of them asked skeptically.

Carrie murmured to him, "Just go with it."

The SEAL clammed up but continued to look incredulous.

Carrie turned back to their hostess. "Tell me more about Monsieur de Parais."

"He was a merchant and owned a ship. He sailed it up the Mississippi River to buy furs from traders, and then sailed to the Caribbean to trade the furs for spices and silk from France."

"Why didn't French traders bring silk directly to New Orleans?" Carrie asked.

Amelie waved a vague hand. "Oh, well, there was all that trouble between the English and the French. English privateers laid in wait for French ships that were trying to make the port of New Orleans. It was far too dangerous for the French to sail here directly. But we New Orleanians—we had to have our little luxuries— like French wine and fashion."

And French mistresses, if the diary was accurate and Mignonette had really been the girlfriend of the governor of Louisiana.

"What do you know of Mignonette?" Carrie asked.

"You've seen her diary, yes? I lent it to Gary Hubbard a few months back, and I'm a bit vexed that he hasn't returned it to me, yet. Nothing's happened to it, has it?"

"Oh, no. I saw the diary just yesterday. It's perfectly safe." In fact, it was locked in Bass's desk back in the SEAL operations center.

"It's a priceless artifact. Legend in my family is that it holds the clue to finding a great treasure."

"The same treasure Gary's hunting on this season of his show?" Carrie asked.

"Exactly! He said he's basing his entire show around dear Mignonette's secret. I don't understand why Gary hasn't come to see me, yet. He was very excited to return here and film Mignonette's story."

Carrie sighed. "Gary is missing. We don't know when he will return, and that's why there's a delay in shooting the show."

"Is that why all these big, strong men are here? They're protecting me?" Amelie exclaimed.

In point of fact, they were protecting Carrie, but she wasn't sure it was worth splitting hairs with their dotty hostess. She said carefully, "We're concerned that treasure-hunters may try to come after Mignonette's secret, and it made sense to up security until we figure out who's interested in the treasure besides Gary."

"Oh, dear. Oh dear, oh dear!"

Carrie fanned Miss Amelie some more and was greatly relieved when Bass turned the corner carrying a tray with several cups of tea on it.

He fussed over the older woman, unfolding a linen napkin over her lap and handing her a teacup and saucer. Amelie simpered, enjoying the attention.

Carrie took one sip of the syrupy sweet tea and set

her cup down, suppressing a grimace. "You were telling me more about Mignonette."

"She didn't write about treasure exactly. She more hinted at it than wrote about it," Amelie replied.

"Do you have any other writings from Mignonette? More diaries, maybe?"

"No, but we have a whole pile of letters she got from relatives in France. They were royalists, you know. Had to go into hiding and flee with their most valuable possessions."

"Is the treasure something of theirs, then?" Bass asked.

Amelie laughed. "Oh, no. It belonged to the royal family of France."

Carrie dived in. "Any idea what it was?"

"Well," Amelie said conspiratorially, "the story in our family goes that it was part of the French royal regalia. A crown or scepter or something like that. It belonged to King Louis himself."

"Which one?" Bass asked.

Amelie threw him an exasperated look. "Does it matter? All the French kings were named Louis."

Carrie threw a warning look at Bass for him to behave and interjected soothingly, "Did Mignonette keep the treasure? Maybe hide it somewhere in this house?"

"Oh, no. My relatives have torn into every wall and ripped up every floorboard in search of the treasure. It's definitely not in this house. Besides, Mignonette never possessed the treasure. Her lover had it."

"Pierre-Clément de Laussat?" Carrie asked. "The last French governor of Louisiana?"

Amelie sighed. "That's him. So romantic and tragic, their love."

Carrie got the distinct impression from Mignonette's

diary that the guy had been married and refused to leave his wife for her. Which wasn't exactly the stuff of romantic love stories. She glanced up and caught Bass's wry gaze. They shared mutual mental rolled eyes.

"Did Mignonette have any idea what happened to this supposed treasure?"

"The family legend is that her lover gave it to her father to hide where only he could ever find it again."

"Her father the merchant. With ships?" Bass asked.

"Correct," their hostess answered. Amelie finished her tea and declared herself exhausted. She put up a rather theatric act of being too weak to make it all the way back to her room under her own power, and Bass volunteered one of his men to walk her back to her bedroom. Carrie bit back a grin at the guy's long-suffering look over his shoulder as he walked Amelie and her ridiculous ghost costume out of the parlor.

Bass burst out, "How are we supposed to find something—and we have no idea what it is or if it really exists—that was last seen over two hundred years ago and could be hidden anywhere along the entire length of the Mississippi River or the whole of the Caribbean?"

Carrie swiveled to stare at him. "Why do you care about finding this supposed treasure at all?"

"If I knew what people were looking for, I'd stand a much better chance of identifying who took Gary."

Carrie tilted her head thoughtfully. "What if you made everyone believe you knew what and where the treasure is? Wouldn't that have the same effect of drawing the kidnappers out?"

"How would we get the word out?" Bass asked curiously.

She replied, "What if we give a press release that

there's treasure, say, in this house? Wouldn't that force the kidnappers to come to us?"

Bass commented, "We could make a big fuss over security. Not let anyone into the building."

Carrie nodded. "We could say that because of the time-sensitive nature of the treasure hunt, the show is going to resume filming in Gary's absence. That would put huge pressure on the treasure-hunters to come here for the treasure."

Bass nodded. "My guys already know the layout here. We'd have the tactical advantage. But we'd need other people around to disguise our presence here."

"What can I do to help?" Carrie asked promptly.

"Make as big a production as possible of your filming. Close down the entire street outside. Make a movie set of the place."

She laughed. "Well, that would be a stretch for a television show of this type, but I'll do my best. I can call in a few favors. I ought to be able to get light booms, power generators, maybe even a makeup trailer. A bunch of films get shot in New Orleans, and there should be plenty of movie supply companies. As long as no big production is filming in town right now, there should be plenty of equipment sitting around, ready to be rented. Best case: I can have them here sometime tomorrow."

"Perfect." Bass turned to his guys, and they began walking through various scenarios for how and where to trap whatever treasure-hunters showed up. Carrie got lost quickly in sight lines and fields of fire and dozed on the couch while they planned. She sure wouldn't want to be whoever got caught in their web.

She was deeply asleep when Bass woke her sometime later, murmuring that she needed to go to bed. Stumbling up the stairs and down the long hall to her room, she turned right when Bass told her to and fell into bed, asleep within seconds of her head hitting the pillow.

It ended up taking two days to arrange for all the snazzy filming equipment to show up in front of Amelie's house. But when it arrived, it was a zoo.

The commotion drew local photographers and news crews, all of whom were dying to know what the fuss was about. Bass called in the NOPD spokesperson to read a prepared statement to the crowd. As expected, a buzz went up at the mention of a priceless, long-lost treasure being hidden in the house.

As the press conference dispersed, Carrie, watching from inside with Bass, muttered to him, "You do realize every nutball in New Orleans is about to show up here, right?"

He grinned ruefully. "Oh, yeah. But I figure the serious players will wait until late at night to make a run at the treasure."

The New Orleans police had their hands full through the afternoon maintaining a security perimeter around the bed-and-breakfast. Amelie got a new case of the vapors every hour or so, but the woman was obviously thrilled at all the publicity her place was getting.

Meanwhile, Carrie decided to take advantage of all the cool movie equipment and set up a number of elaborate shots she wouldn't normally be able to pull off with her single, shoulder-held camera. If these New Orleans episodes of the show ever did make it to television, they were going to be spectacular.

She was exhausted when the last crewmembers finally left the house a little before midnight. She had a ton of great footage to rough cut and send to New York, but that could wait until tomorrow.

It had been a disappointment to wake up alone in bed this morning. But then, she and Bass hadn't exactly parted on good terms the last time they'd been in a bed together. No way was she going to tell him her real name. From that, it would be only a hop, skip and a jump to the whole sordid story of her past. Well, the whole story that the police in New York were aware of. Nobody knew the whole story except her. And Lonnie Grange.

The mere thought of him gave her chills. She wasn't a violent person, but if anyone had ever been in need of killing, he was that guy. He'd stripped away her innocence. Taught her fear. And he'd taken away any chance of a normal life from her. That was probably what she resented the most. She'd grown up wanting to have a family some day. A home. Kids. Roots.

But all of that was gone.

Tired after a long day of shooting, she headed for her room, pausing to stare at her door, then at Bass's door. With a sigh of defeat, she turned left and went into her room.

She pulled up short at the sight of Bass just stepping out of her bathroom with a towel wrapped round his hips. *Yowza*. Talk about a rack of abs that wouldn't quit. She struggled to lift her eyes away from his godlike torso to speak to him.

"What are you doing in here?" she stammered.

"I thought I told you I was trading rooms with you. My old room faces the courtyard, which is patrolled by one of my guys at all times. It's a lot safer than this room with a window facing the street."

Her stomach dropped in disappointment. He really didn't want anything to do with her. Not since she'd refused to tell him her name. Now that he knew the full extent of her inability to trust him.

"Sorry. I forgot in all the chaos. Where's my stuff?" she asked in resignation.

"Across the hall. I moved it for you."

"Thanks." She backed toward the door. "Sorry to have disturbed you."

He didn't want her any more. They'd had sex, he'd scratched that itch, she'd screwed up, and he'd obviously moved on. She was just another notch in his bedpost. Fine. If that was how he wanted things to be, so be it.

She marched across the hall and closed the door behind herself.

If only she didn't have an uncontrollable urge to fling herself across the bed and sob into a pillow. She tried telling herself sternly that he wasn't worth crying over. That sleeping with him had been a giant mistake. That he hadn't earned her tears.

But it didn't help. The tears still came.

It was a long, lonely night.

Chapter 10

Bass sat under Carrie's window, pulling a shift in the courtyard, watching the light in her room go off. Then on for a half hour or so. Then off again. She couldn't sleep either, huh?

What the hell was he doing? He knew better than to get involved with her. Even if it had become clear she wasn't part of the kidnapping plot, it still was a lousy idea to get involved with any woman, given his line of work.

As the night aged and cooled, he occupied himself with trying to imagine a hypothetically normal life with Carrie. Being a cop might even become just a job. Something he left at the office at the end of the workday. If he had a family to go home to, maybe he could finally learn to set aside the cases, even if just for a few hours every day.

The Navy's psychologists told him he was too invested in his work. That he should get a hobby and have a real social life. Hell, he spent hours and hours restoring cars, didn't he? That counted, didn't it? Although it was a pursuit he did alone. It didn't exactly check the having a social life box. Carrie was what the shrinks were talking about. A living, breathing, walking, talking human being to spend time with.

He did enjoy being with her. She was witty and sweet, and they fit together in bed—both physically and emotionally.

Even if she were to agree to give up her nomadic lifestyle and settle down in New Orleans, could he give up his obsession with his work? Could he walk away from being a superhero out to save the world?

The very thought gave him the heebie-jeebies. His entire adult life had been spent doing one thing—chasing bad guys. Was he even capable of sustaining a longterm relationship of the romantic variety?

More to the point, did he want to find out?

He knew as well as any shrink that the only way to answer the question would be to try. Carrie was exactly the kind of woman he would want to try with if he ever did go for it and dive into a deep, meaningful relationship…with one glaring exception, of course.

He would never, ever, be able to trust a woman who couldn't—who *wouldn't*—tell him her real name.

An ugly sensation nibbled at his gut, and it took him a while sitting in the shadowed corner of the garden to identify it. Fear. Not the pulse-pounding, adrenalineinduced, about-to-die terror that happened in the field if a guy wasn't properly trained or if a hostile got the jump on him.

No, this fear was a great deal more insidious. It crept

through his skin and wormed its way into his gut, coiling like a snake waiting to strike.

Surely he wasn't this terrified of a little thing like Carrie Price.

Which was, of course, an evasion from the truth. He wasn't scared of Carrie. He was scared to death of how she made him feel.

Feelings got in the way of doing the job, of catching the bad guy and solving the crime. Hell, they got in the way of pretty much everything. Life was so much simpler without a bunch of messy feelings cluttering up the works.

Dawn was just starting to lighten the sky in the east to dull gray when his cell phone buzzed. Who was calling him at this time of night? It was a police number. "Detective LeBlanc."

"Sorry to bug you, sir, but Homicide has a body that roughly matches the description of your missing TV show guy."

"Where's the body now?"

"Washed up on the north shore of the Mississippi. We can wait for the medical examiner to compare dental records and run DNA, but I thought it might be faster if you came down and took a look. Corpse still has a face. Fish didn't get it, yet."

That was a small silver lining on some potentially very bad news. He radioed the SEAL due to come on watch in an hour and asked him to come downstairs early. As soon as the guy arrived, Bass bugged out and headed for his Hummer. It was a short drive with no traffic to where the body had been found.

He jumped out at the edge of a cordon of crime scene tape, ducking under it to join a cluster of cops and crime scene investigators standing around a blue tarp draped over a bulging shape.

"Hey, Bass. Thanks for coming down to peek at our dead guy."

"No problem. Thanks for the call." He knelt down and lifted the corner of the tarp to peer at the body.

Homicide detectives vowed that they eventually became immune to looking at dead and disfigured bodies, but he had yet to develop that tough hide. Sure, he'd seen corpses in his military work. But those were casualties of conflict for the most part.

Setting aside the twisting tightness in his gut, he studied the bloated, waterlogged features. He even pulled out the folded picture of Gary Hubbard that he kept tucked in his jacket pocket to compare it to the corpse.

"Not my guy," he announced. "You've got a John Doe on your hands."

"Damn. I was hoping this would be an easy one," the detective in charge muttered. To the medical examiner standing by patiently, the detective said, "Bag him and tag him, boys. John Doe."

Bass chatted with the homicide guys for a few minutes, making nice. He'd made no secret of wanting a transfer into the elite division, and the homicide guys seemed interested in him, too. He'd finished his master's degree in criminology a few months back and now had all the prerequisites to transfer over.

"Sorry to drag you out of bed so early, LeBlanc," the chief inspector told him cheerfully.

"No worries. I was on a stakeout anyway. Sorry I couldn't help you."

The cop slapped Bass on the shoulder and strolled back to the crime scene.

Bass pointed his vehicle toward the B&B, arriving in the middle of an uproar. "What the hell's going on?" he demanded.

The guy he'd left on the watch explained, "Carrie snuck of the house on us. She's gone."

"How the hell did that happen?" Bass exclaimed. "We're supposed to have eyes on her twenty-four seven!"

One of the other SEALs stood his ground. "Our perimeter was set up with an eye to keeping bad guys out, not to keeping good guys in."

Bass cursed, furious with his men and furious with himself that he hadn't seen this coming. He *knew* she was a runner.

"When did she leave?" he asked tersely.

"Best guess is she slipped out right behind you. It would explain why we didn't think anything of the motion detectors alerting. We thought they were you. The sound of your Hummer must've masked the sound of her van."

She had about an hour's head start on him, then. Where would she go in the early hours of the morning? Knowing her, she would go back to her place to get her stuff before she left town. She didn't carry much, but it was all she had in the world. It would be important to her.

"I'm heading over to her place. Call me if you hear anything at all."

"Maybe call the police and have them search the traffic cameras for her van?" one of the SEALs asked.

"I could, but the department may not have the resources to do it if they're tracking someone else already." Besides, it wasn't the NOPD's job to pick up the slack because his SEALs had gotten tricked by a lone civilian female with no covert training whatsoever.

He raced outside and jumped in his Hummer, pointing it at her place. It was about a fifteen-minute drive, and he chewed on his irritation at her for bolting the whole time. She had to quit running away on him like this!

He pulled up in front of her residence, relieved to see that the media wasn't camping out there anymore. They'd moved their stalking operation over to the B&B.

He jogged up the stairs to the third floor and banged on her door. No answer. Not that silence meant anything. She could just as easily be hiding in there, waiting for him to go away. Ticked off now, he ran downstairs and had a look in the garage. Empty. She wasn't here.

Swearing, he strode back to his Hummer. Where in the hell was she? Surely, she knew better than to leave town and risk being jailed for impeding a police investigation. He slammed himself into the seat and revved the engine angrily. Did she hate him so much that she'd felt a need to sneak away from him?

A kernel of betrayal poked at his heart, hurting like a pebble under his bare foot. What the hell made her run? What had changed since last night? She had seemed perfectly willing to continue down this path of investigation, helping him draw out the treasure-hunters after Gary's secret.

He pulled up in front of his place, dismayed to see the security gate still hanging from one hinge where he'd left it when he blasted through the gate three nights ago. He'd selfishly hoped his SEAL buddies might have been able to get it repaired by now. Of course, none of them were trained welders, and it could take a few days to get a skilled wrought-iron worker to make a house call.

He pulled up to his garage and spied a taillight sticking out from behind the metal building. Reaching beneath his seat, he pulled out a pistol and chambered a round. Easing the door open, he moved fast and silently toward the corner of the building. Slowly, he peered past the corner.

Sonofa—

Carrie's van. What the hell was she doing here? He moved up beside the driver's window and threw open the door. She lurched inside, screaming a little.

"Jeez, Bass. Are you determined to scare me to *death*?"

"You're the one parked suspiciously behind my house. What are you doing here?"

"I left Mr. Paddles here."

He frowned. "Mr. Who?"

"Paddles. Mr. Paddles. My turtle. He and I have been through a lot together over the years. No way could I leave him behind."

"Leave him? You planning on going somewhere?"

"Oh. Uhh. Yeah."

"You do remember that I told you not to leave town, right?"

"Well, umm, of course I remember." A pause, then she said in a rush, "But I thought that was more of a suggestion than an order."

"You thought wrong. If you leave New Orleans, I'll arrest you and drag you back here. You're a material witness in an ongoing investigation. You may not leave the city."

"Oh." She frowned, obviously thinking hard. "But I still need Mr. Paddles back."

"Why?"

"Because he's mine! I've had him as long as I can remember."

It was more than a little tragic that her only friend in the world was a stuffed turtle. His initial impulse was to feel sorry for her. She was a genuinely likable person who, if she would just stand still for a little while, would have plenty of friends.

In the meantime she sounded jittery, and she was acting jumpy. "What's wrong, Carrie? What happened? Why did you leave Amelie's house so secretively?"

"Well, obviously I didn't want to be stopped."

He rolled his eyes as he unlocked the big door and waved her into the garage. She parked the van and climbed out reluctantly.

As he methodically searched the garage, he picked up their conversation where they'd left off. "Why exactly did you run this time?"

"I had to get away."

"Thanks for that answer, Miss Obvious."

He entered the code for his home's front door and activated the biometric scanner. She slid past him into his living room, and he flipped on the lights. Only when she'd returned from his bedroom carrying the ratty stuffed sea turtle did he plant his feet wide, cross his arms, and ask evenly, "Why did you have to get away, Carrie?"

"Personal reasons."

"What personal reasons?"

"Sheesh, give it a break. I don't want to talk about it."

"I do."

"Tough," she declared stoutly.

He had to give her credit. None of his men would dare to cross him when he was scowling at them like he was scowling at her right now. "Carrie, don't push me," he warned her.

"Then don't push me."

"Look. I'm done with your secrets and evasions. You can tell me right now what the hell's going on with you, or I'm going to find out for myself. I've requested the file of your court case to change your name in Idaho three years ago. Within the next day or so, I'm going to have your real name."

She gasped in dismay, but he pressed ahead, well and truly ticked off. "And then, so help me God, I'm digging up every last bit of information there is on you. I'll know the name of your kindergarten teacher, and every person you ever knew. Hell, I'll know who gave you your first kiss."

She stared at him in undisguised horror. "You can't do that," she whispered.

He took two long strides to bring himself chest to chest with her. He loomed menacingly over her, taking advantage of every single inch of height he had on her. "I can, and I will."

She wilted all at once, her face crumpling and the tears coming freely. He was so angry that her crying didn't move him in the slightest. He was sick and tired of this cat-and-mouse crap with Carrie. It stopped now.

Carrie paced Bass's living room, too agitated to stand still. This was *exactly* why she'd run away from the bed-and-breakfast. She knew he would react like this if she told him she had to leave New Orleans. That she had to flee before her past caught up with her. He would demand to know everything. Everything she'd never told anyone else. Everything she barely acknowledged to herself about who she was and where she'd come from.

"Don't make me ask again, Carrie."

"What will you do to me if I refuse to answer you?"

"I'll place you under arrest and put you in jail until that case file comes through and I can investigate every aspect of your life."

"You can't do that!" she exclaimed.

"If I deem you a flight risk, which I bloody well do, I most certainly can."

She subsided, stymied. She didn't doubt for a second that he would throw her in jail. He wasn't a cop for nothing. And he looked about ready to throttle her. What had she been *thinking* getting involved with a man like him? Of course, the answer to that was she hadn't been thinking. At all.

Ominously, Bass walked over to his alarm system and deliberately activated it. She was locked in with him. Crud.

"What's your real name, Carrie?"

"We've already been over this. My real name is Carrie Ann Price."

"What name were you born with?"

He had her in an impossible situation. She was damned if she did and damned if she didn't. Had he really requested her sealed court records, or was that a bluff? He was a police officer, after all. He probably had the power to get the stupid thing unsealed. As much as she hated to admit it, he had her cornered and outmaneuvered.

She collapsed onto the sofa, clutching Mr. Paddles. Defeat rolled through her, oppressive and inevitable. "You're a bully, you know."

"Yup."

"This isn't fair."

"Nope."

She sighed. Closed her eyes. And mumbled, "Katherine Hubbard."

"That's your name?"

"No! My *name* is Carrie Ann Price."

She thought she heard him mutter, "Stubborn woman."

"Tell me about Katherine Hubbard."

"You wanted my birth name. You have it. Can't you let it go?"

"Carrie—Katherine—"

"Carrie," she insisted.

"Fine. Carrie. I do not have time for compassion or sensitivity. A man's life is on the line, here. I'm trying to save your boss—"

He broke off as if something had just dawned on him. And she knew what it was. Carrie winced, waiting for the explosion.

"Katherine Hubbard? As in Gary Hubbard? You two are related?" Bass's voice rose in volume with each word, ending in a near shout.

"He's my uncle."

"Why on God's green earth didn't you see fit to tell me that before now?" he bellowed.

"Because of how you're reacting."

"I'm reacting like this because you withheld a vital piece of information from me in a police investigation."

"It's not vital that he's my uncle. He's still missing. I'm still worried sick about him, and we still need to find him."

"Wanna bet? You're a relative. Your possible motives for wanting him to disappear just multiplied a hundred times."

"I had no motive and I had nothing to do with his disappearance!"

"How am I supposed to believe you now after you've been lying to me all this time?"

"I haven't lied to you. Granted, I've withheld the truth. But I've never lied to you." Not that she expected him to accept that she was telling the truth. He saw the worst in everyone. Including her.

He strode down the hall to his office and came back bearing a sleek laptop. He set it down on the coffee table, sat down angrily on the couch beside her, and asked grimly, "What am I going to find when I type Katherine Hubbard into my police database?"

"I have no idea. I'm not a criminal."

"Where's your hometown?"

"Apple Grove, New York. It's north of Albany."

He typed rapidly, alternately scowling at her and frowning at the computer.

Lord knew what was going to pop up on her. She hadn't searched her old name for years. That life was water under the bridge, and she had no intention of going back to it. Ever.

"Captain of the JV cheerleading squad at Apple Grove High School. One brother. Parents married, father works at a public utility company."

"He's an electrical engineer. Manages power usage for our county," she supplied.

"No police reports associated with your home address on Orchard Lane," Bass declared.

Please God, let his search yield only more of the same innocuous information.

"Who's Shelly Baker?" Bass asked abruptly.

Carrie felt the color drain from her face. Her whole body felt hot, then cold, then hot again. If she knew how to swear like a sailor, she would do it right now. "My best friend in school," she answered reluctantly.

Images of Shelly flashed through her mind's eye. Shelly laughing at her, running across the football field, blond hair flying, calling back over her shoulder, daring Kathy to keep up with her as they raced to flirt with the boys on the football squad. Lord, they'd been naïve back then. Life had been a summer dream, warm and hazy and innocent.

"What happened to her?" Bass asked, interrupting the reverie.

Carrie stared down at her hands, her twined fingers wringing at one another. She whispered, "I don't know. Nobody knows."

"And her mother?"

"She disappeared, too."

Carrie was startled to see a tear drop onto her knuckle. She dashed at her cheeks, wiping away the evidence of how painful these memories were.

"I'm pulling up the Apple Grove police database, now. Wanna tell me what I'm going to find in here before I find it myself?"

She squeezed her eyes shut. Better that the information come from her than some dry police report. At least she had a chance to explain herself this way. Try to make Bass understand. To do some badly needed damage control.

"Shelly's mom remarried when Shel and I were in the eighth grade. He was from New York City. Some kind of construction manager. Lonnie Grange was his name. After he married Mrs. Baker, Shelly and her mom changed."

"How?"

"They became nervous. Tense. Secretive."

"Was he abusive?"

"I guessed that he was," she blurted.

"Did Shelly or her mom turn him in?"

"No." A long pause. "I did."

Bass jumped all over that. "What did he do to you?"

She took a deep breath and lied. Again. Like she'd lied to everyone since that awful night all those years ago. She'd heard that if a person told the same lie enough times he or she would start to believe it. Not so in her case.

"He didn't do anything to me. I just started to get suspicious. I hung out with Shelly all the time and I… heard things. Snippets of phone calls. Comments Lonnie made to Mrs. B. And they made me believe he was some kind of mobster."

"Construction in New York City? It's a distinct possibility," Bass commented.

"I told the police I suspected he was up to something criminal."

Please God, let Bass drop it there. He'd heard enough. And the truth didn't lie far below the surface of her words, now.

"And?"

Dammit. Bass's cop instinct was too sharp for his own good.

"And what?" she echoed.

"I don't know. You tell me. Or, I can always read what the police had to say."

Grudgingly she gave up a little more ground. "Lonnie was supposedly gone on a business trip, and the police went out to their house and had a conversation with Shelly and her mom about my accusations."

Bass didn't speak, but his waiting silence was crystal clear. He sensed there was more to the story.

"Shortly after that, Shelly and her mom disappeared."

"Disappeared how? Did they leave town?"

The horror of those first days after Shelly dropped off the face of the earth flooded her as if it had all happened yesterday. A huge weight pressed down on Carrie's chest until she could hardly breathe. "If they did leave town, they didn't take a single thing they owned with them. Not even their purses or identification. Their cars were in the driveway, and they disappeared with nothing more than the clothes on their backs."

"Did Grange kill them?"

"He was never charged with murder."

"What happened to him?"

"He went to jail on other charges. I guess the police found something when they dug into his finances."

"Where is he now?"

How did Bass do that? How did he ask exactly the right question to get to the heart of the matter? Was it talent or luck? Either way, it was a pain in the butt.

"You're almost there, Carrie. Keep going with your story," Bass said quietly.

Huh. As if he had any right to encourage her, when he was the one ripping the scab off the wound and rubbing salt in it.

"Where's Grange?" he repeated.

"That's the thing. My mom called me bright and early this morning to tell me I was on the morning news in Apple Grove. They were doing a story about Uncle Gary's disappearance. He grew up in Apple Grove. Anyway, she was all excited to see me on TV."

Bass waited, but his body looked tensed. Ready to pounce on some poor prey animal—like her.

"Anyway, my mom happened to mention that Lonnie's out of jail. Came back to Apple Grove a couple of months ago. He actually showed up at my parents' house to ask about me. The gall of the man!"

Bass leaned back, his thinking face firmly in place. Carrie swore some more to herself. He was far too clever for his own good, and she seriously didn't need him filling in the blanks.

As if on cue, Bass said, "So Grange is out of jail and free to come after you. And you were just seen on national television and placed in New Orleans hunting for your missing uncle. You're afraid Grange is going to do what? Come after you to kill you? Or maybe question you about the whereabouts of his missing family?"

"They're not his family," she snapped.

"I stand corrected," Bass replied mildly. "Is that why you felt a need to flee the city with Mr. Paddles?"

"Don't make fun of my turtle. He's been the only constant in my life since I was five years old."

Bass actually looked sympathetic.

"I don't want your pity!" she exclaimed.

"And you don't have it. But you do have my understanding. Losing a friend under mysterious circumstances sucks. Believe me, I see it often enough in my police work, chasing down missing persons."

"Satisfied now?" she demanded.

"I don't know. Is there more?"

Heck yes, there was more. But she would never tell. She shook her head stubbornly in the negative.

He shoved a hand through his hair. "I wish you had told me this before. We may have wasted all this time in the search for your uncle. I hope it hasn't cost him his life."

A sob rattled its way out of her chest whether she wanted it to or not. If she'd killed Gary, too—how would she go on living? The guilt of having killed Shelly and Mrs. Baker was almost more than she could stand already. She couldn't bear the weight of another life on her conscience.

She asked Bass cautiously, "Have you ever killed people in combat?"

One of his eyebrows lifted sardonically. "I'm a SEAL. What do you think?"

"How do you live with it?" she blurted.

"Live with what?"

"Knowing you've killed someone."

"Ahh. That. When the choice is the other guy or me, I choose me. The people I've killed chose to put themselves in harm's way. They chose violence and knew the risks of their actions. I'm just the guy who caught up with them first."

Well, that was of no help. Shelly and Mrs. B hadn't signed up for anything at all. Carrie had been the one to lead the police to their doorstep and sic law enforcement on Lonnie Grange. But the two of them had paid the price for her foolish belief that the police would get the bad guy and protect the good guys. Silly her. What *had* she been thinking?

Bass typed on his laptop for a while, and she lost herself in contemplating the woulda, shoulda, couldas. First on that list would be never, ever going to the police to accuse Lonnie Grange of anything, no matter how terrible a monster he was.

Bass spoke abruptly, startling her. "Says here Lonnie went to jail on racketeering and money laundering charges."

"That makes sense. Shelly and Mrs. B weren't around to accuse him of abuse or assault."

"So, he was physical with them, then?" Bass asked evenly. His voice betrayed nothing, but Carrie sensed tension in him.

"Of course he was. Not that Shelly or her mom ever complained to the police—or anyone—about it for that matter. They were too scared of him."

"Sounds like an asshole."

"A gigantic sucking one with an oozing rash," she added vehemently.

Bass grinned. "Why don't you tell me how you really feel about him?"

She answered soberly, "Scared enough to run for the past seven years."

Bass tilted his head, studying her. "It all makes sense now. The nomadic life as a camerawoman. Very little contact with your family. The lack of friends. The name change." He nodded. "You're hiding."

"Darned straight I am. Lonnie Grange is the scariest person I've ever met."

Bass's shoulders lifted in a shrug. "Then you haven't seen me in full combat mode."

That made her blink. Bass scarier than Grange? The thought was laughable. Bass was a certified, card-carrying good guy.

"You can't run forever, you know," he commented.

"Sure I can. I've been doing it for a long time. No reason I can't keep on doing it."

"What about you? Are you happy?"

"I'm alive," she retorted.

"What if you want to have a family someday?"

"Not in the cards for me," she replied bitterly.

"Do you like being alone? Without friends? Estranged from your family?"

She scowled at him, but paused to give the questions actual thought. She rarely paused to question her path since it was the only path that kept her alive.

Bass pushed, "If you had a choice, if you could live

some other way, would you? What life would you build for yourself if Grange was out of the picture?"

She stared at Bass, shocked. Was it possible? Was there a way to be free of the ever-present pall of fear that hung over every breath she took? Did she dare hope? "How?" she breathed.

Bass shrugged. "There's always a bigger, badder fish in the pond. If Grange understands that he'll be eaten if he comes after you, he'll back off."

She wilted. "I'm no shark."

Bass smiled coldly. "I am."

She stared at him. "I can't ask you to get involved in my personal life."

"Fine. Then involve me in a police investigation of the guy."

"How?"

"Does Grange know you're working for your uncle?"

She considered. "I doubt it. I'm never on camera, and I work under my new name."

"So, it's entirely possible that his guys went after your uncle as a means of finding you, without realizing you were already right under his nose."

Horror erupted in her chest. Was she responsible for Gary's kidnapping after all? Oh, God. Her chest squeezed tight and drawing breath became nearly impossible. Without waiting for Bass to prompt her, she started holding her breath, counting and exhaling slowly, the way he'd taught her.

Eventually, she was able to answer him, "I guess it's possible Lonnie's guys went after Gary to find me."

Bass nodded briskly. "It's a valid line of inquiry. I'll send the fingerprints we lifted from Gary's apartment up to New York and see if they get any hits on the assailants. I'll also send out a request for a list of known associates of Lonnie Grange. We'll run financials on them and see if any of his boys have headed down this way recently." He typed in his computer in a rapid burst and then leaned back with a satisfied expression on his face.

"And in the meantime, you're with me. This jackass gets no chance to hurt you until you've faced him down and won."

"I can't face him!" she exclaimed in horror.

"You can, and you will."

"No way—"

He cut her off. "You won't be alone, Carrie. I'll be with you. I'll help you be strong."

She shook her head stubbornly. "I can't do it. The last time I tangled with him, Shelly and her mom disappeared. Because of me, Bass. *Their blood is on my hands.*"

Bass stared deeply into her eyes and spoke seriously. "Their blood is on the hands of whoever killed them. Not you. If nobody has the courage to stand up to evil, then evil wins. Yes, there can be a tragic cost to confronting evil, but it has to be confronted, nonetheless. You did the right thing."

"My friend is *dead.*"

"How many more people would be dead if you hadn't blown the whistle on him?"

And therein lay the heart of her guilt. She hadn't told the police everything about Lonnie Grange. How many more women would he attack because she'd been too afraid to speak up?

"He needs to be stopped," she declared.

"He needs to be taken out behind the woodshed and shot," Bass snorted.

She couldn't kill the guy! She must have looked

alarmed because Bass added, "We'll do this by the book. There won't be violence unless Grange starts something. And if he does, I'll finish it. I'll finish *him*."

Bass said the words quietly, but the cold conviction underlying them warmed Carrie's heart like nothing she'd heard in a very long time.

Hope flickered to life in her heart, and she hugged Mr. Paddles tight. It was scary as heck to think about taking on Lonnie Grange, but oh, the possibilities if she won. A home. Friends. A dog. Heck, maybe even a family. Longing flared in her gut for everything she'd ever dreamed of having as a kid that Lonnie Grange had stolen from her. Could Bass truly give her dreams back to her?

She looked up at him, her heart in her throat. "What do we do first?"

Chapter 11

Bass studied Carrie carefully, intrigued by the light in her eyes. He'd never seen it there before. It looked like... hope. He wanted to put a lot more of it in her eyes and make it permanent. She deserved to live a normal life.

And he might just have a vested interest in getting her to a place where she could settle down. Stay in one place. Consider long-term relationships.

"Do you have all your personal possessions with you?" he asked her.

"Everything's in the van. I was on my way out of town when I came here to get Mr. Paddles."

"Perfect. You're staying with me until Grange is dealt with."

"You make it sound so easy."

He snorted. "Honey, I've taken out entire international terrorist networks. Some two-bit thug who picks on women *is* easy."

Carrie launched herself from her end of the couch and threw her arms around his neck. He caught her lithe body in his arms, relishing the sweet feel of her pressed up against him. She was like a wild thing only he could tame, a fey creature he'd miraculously managed to lure close.

"Thank you," she whispered.

"No thanks required. It's what I do."

"Still. I'm grateful."

He stared down at her, and she stared up at him. An entire, unspoken conversation happened between them. Her desperate need to be free of the specter of her past, his compulsion to protect her from harm, both of their confusion at why they felt so irrevocably drawn to each other.

"What is this thing between us?" she asked, low.

"Whatever it is, it's meant to be." He added ruefully, "I've tried my damnedest to fight it, and I failed."

She smiled up at him. "I know the feeling." She continued slowly, "When I thought I was leaving town, my one regret was never seeing you again. I almost didn't go."

"Promise me you won't ever leave again without saying goodbye." He had to have a chance to talk her out of going if she tried to run again. To fight for her.

She stared up at him for a long time. Then, "I promise."

He leaned down and kissed her then, and her arms tightened around his neck. "I need to know you're not a flight risk," he murmured against her lips.

"I don't want to go anywhere," she murmured back, kissing him with sweet passion. "This is exactly where I want to be."

He stood up, sweeping her up with him, her weight

nothing in his arms. He strode back to his bedroom, carrying her in his arms, kissing her all the while so she would know he didn't think of her as a child.

And besides, he couldn't stop himself. He'd almost lost her, tonight, and the residual panic of that rode him hard, poking like a knife into his ribs. She could be exasperating, but now that he'd gotten to the bottom of her frustrating refusal to stand her ground and fight, he understood her much better.

If anything, his need to protect her had only grown with her admissions.

He laid her down on his bed, relishing the sight of her sleek body, her eyes warm as she looked up at him, a come-hither smile on her lips. He murmured, "God, you're beautiful."

Her gaze went bashful. Did she really not know how desirable she was? He stretched out beside her, shucking her clothes efficiently as he spoke. "Good thing you never stayed in one place long enough to have a steady boyfriend. Otherwise, he'd have convinced you of just how attractive you are, and you wouldn't ever have given me the time of day."

Her hands plucked at the buttons on his shirt and then at his belt buckle. "I still don't understand what a guy like you sees in someone like me. You're about as close to perfect as anyone I've ever met."

He grinned and leaned down to kiss her neck, inhaling the soft scent of her skin. "Then you haven't met many people, have you? I have tons of flaws."

She arched up into him, her bare hands skimming across his chest muscles and making them jump beneath her palms. "Name me your flaws," she challenged.

He rolled her onto her back and kissed his way down to the gentle valley between her breasts. He could lay his head there forever and die a happy man. The quick, light beat of her heart was music to his ears. "Well," he drawled, "I've been told I'm stubborn."

"More like pigheaded." She laughed as she wrapped her legs around his hips, rubbed her core against his erection, and made him groan with pleasure.

"And I'm overbearing."

"I have no idea what you're talking about," she teased as her body undulated invitingly against his.

"I won't take no for an answer," he muttered. Damn. He was actually a little out of breath at the mere idea of making love to her.

"Well now, that's not necessarily a flaw in the right situation."

He was having trouble following the conversation. The silken slide of her stomach beneath his lips and her fingers spearing hungrily into his hair were distracting as hell.

She tugged on his head and he rose up her body, kissing a path across her golden skin. And then her mouth captured his, open and warm and inviting, like her body and soul. "Make love to me, Bass."

He positioned himself above her, and then, looking deep, deep, into her dark, sultry eyes, eased into the tight sheath of her body. His eyes all but rolled back in his head at the glorious sensation of her slick heat clutching at his arousal, pulling him deeper and clenching him close when he would retreat.

"More," she gasped.

He groaned, fighting to restrain himself, hanging onto reason by a slim thread. But then she grabbed his glutes and pulled him all the way to the hilt within her. "Mmm. Better," she purred.

"You're an evil temptress," he growled.

"Then give in to the temptation," she replied breathlessly. Her hips moved impatiently against his, and he was lost. He surged into her, shuddering with pleasure. He withdrew partway and surged again. She arched up to meet him thrust for thrust, and his mind was blown by the passionate abandon with which she made love to him. He thought she'd been amazing before—but their previous lovemaking was nothing compared to tonight.

He stared down into her eyes, amazed at how generously and joyfully she met him, sharing her body and heart without reservation. Lord, the courage of this woman. She'd been living in her own private hell for years, but even the suggestion of breaking free was enough to transform her from a frightened mouse into a soaring falcon.

His body enforced a rhythm of its own upon the moment, and their lovemaking picked up in speed and intensity. But Carrie matched him every step of the way, her cries of ecstasy rising to mingle with his own shout of staggering joy as they took each other to the moon and back.

He sagged above her, supporting his spent body on his elbows, his forehead resting against hers. She clung to him with everything she had, arms and legs and internal muscles, and he felt more wanted, more loved, in that moment than he could ever recall.

"Am I crushing you?" he managed to mumble.

"Don't you dare move," she panted back.

His heart was pounding like a jackhammer, and not entirely from exertion. This woman did things to him that no other woman did. She made him feel things. Emotions. Possessiveness. Protectiveness. Joy. Hell, *awe.*

"You're magnificent," he murmured. He kissed her

brow, her temple, burying his nose in her hair and relishing the silky slide of it against his skin.

"Gee, I was about to say the same thing to you," she replied.

"We're agreed, then. You're perfect for me."

"Am I?" she asked in a small voice. "You're sure about that?"

He laughed. "Honey, I've been around the block a time or two, and I'm here to tell you that you're one-of-a-kind."

"Thank you, I think?"

He kissed her nose playfully. "I'm besotted. You've done me in."

She smiled up at him, and he could swear those were tears glistening in her eyes.

"Hey. What's wrong?" he asked quickly.

"Nothing. I'm just happy. I never dreamed I might have a chance at finding a man like you, let alone a chance at escaping Lonnie."

"Consider yourself already escaped. Now all we have to do is make sure he knows he's lost his hold over you."

Her eyes went dark and fearful, and Bass kissed her again quickly. "Don't think about him now. Focus on me. On us. On how incredible you make me feel…"

Carrie rolled over lazily, stretching residual stiffness from her muscles. After the third time they made love, Bass told her to take a nap, and she'd been happy to crash in the cool and dark of his windowless bedroom. Who knew it was possible to feel this happy? Overflowingly so. Not that she had any illusions that Lonnie Grange would go down without a fight. But she wasn't alone now. Having a man like Bass in her corner made all the difference.

She strolled out into the living room wearing one of Bass's T-shirts, which was a minidress on her. She pulled up short. Bass was sitting on the sofa, shirtless, laptop on his jeans-clad thighs, typing away. She demanded, "What are you still doing here? I thought you'd be out saving the world by now!"

He looked up at her and smiled. "I told you I'm with you until this Grange character is no longer a threat. I do need to go into the office this afternoon, though. You up for a field trip to a police department?"

"I've already been to your office," she reminded him.

He grinned. "Yeah, but I got you out of there as fast as I could. You didn't catch the full broadside of interrogation about you and me from my fellow cops."

"Sounds intimidating."

He shook his head. "It's a pain in the ass working with such nosy people. But I have no choice. You're not leaving my side until this situation is resolved."

"You gonna arrest me?" she teased. "Handcuff me to you?"

He looked up at her, eyes glinting in amusement. "Don't tempt me." He surged to his feet and she squealed, dodging him and running for the kitchen. He snagged her waist on the way past and spun her around easily, catching her against his big, delicious body.

"I hope you're not too hungry," he murmured, kissing her until her knees went weak.

"If you promise to make me one of your world-famous omelets, I could be convinced to delay eating for a little while," she teased, nipping at his lower lip until he growled and slid his hand behind her head, deepening the kiss until she forgot to breathe.

His sofa turned out to accommodate a large man and a small woman with no problem whatsoever. Of course it helped that their bodies twined together, and that both of them were feeling a little lazy after last night. They made slow, sensual love, smiling and trading murmured words of praise and pleasure until she was practically delirious with joy. Bass LeBlanc liked her. Enough to fight for her.

No one had ever put himself on the line for her before.

It was kind of spectacular to think about.

Bass made taking down Grange sound so easy. But in the hard light of day, she knew it wouldn't be a walk in the park. Lonnie Grange was a dangerous man, and he wouldn't take kindly to being crossed. The old fear crept into her mind insidiously. Was this a crazy idea? Supremely stupid? Was she endangering not only herself but Bass? It would be so much easier just to run away.

"Don't psych yourself out," Bass murmured, sitting up and pulling her into his lap.

"How do you do that?"

"Do what?"

"Read my mind like that?"

He grinned down at her. "I don't read your mind. I read your face. You wear every thought and feeling right out in the open."

She sighed. "Yeah, that gets me in trouble a lot."

"I like it. I always know where I stand with you."

"What about when I'm spitting mad at you? Will you like it then?"

He took her face in his hands, cupping her cheeks gently. "Even then."

She shook her head. "Who knew a SEAL could be such a sappy romantic? Next thing I know you're going to start writing love sonnets."

He put on a thick drawl. "I dunno. Low-country

Cajun like me? I kin barely read, ma'am. I don't take to no fancy rhyming, y'all."

She rolled her eyes and stood up. "I do believe you owe me an omelet, Detective LeBlanc. Can I help you make it?"

"You can set the table and entertain the chef."

Which turned out to include kissing the chef any time she walked past him and throwing the chef saucy looks every time he looked up from the stove.

In a few minutes, Bass put down two plates on the table, piled high with hash browns, sausage and omelets that were two inches tall.

"I've never seen such a fluffy egg in my life!" she exclaimed.

He swept an arm out to the side and took a bow. He said in a cheesy French accent, "I am zee tremendous chef, mademoiselle."

She laughed gaily. "You're tremendous at something. I'm just not sure it's cooking."

Laughing, he held her chair for her. "Don't mess with the chef or he'll poison the porridge."

"Note to self: don't eat porridge," she retorted.

They continued bantering throughout the meal. He had fully as quick a wit as she, and he kept her on her toes throughout their conversation. They cleaned up quickly after brunch and climbed into a vintage Dodge Charger to drive to the office.

"And who's this car?" Carrie asked.

"Who else? Daisy Mae. Fastest car I own. They don't make 'em like this any more."

She shook her head, enjoying the rumble of the powerful engine and Bass's smooth driving. They parked in a garage attached to the police station, and Bass came around to get her door for her. He murmured low, "We need to play it cool in the precinct. These guys are barracudas and will leap all over any hint of a personal relationship between us. I can take the heat, but I'd like to spare you the brunt of it if I can."

"Sounds ominous."

"They're not that bad. But they all can sniff out secrets at twenty paces. They're not cops for nothing."

"Ugh. They sound like you. But not quite as bad," she groaned.

"I'm not that bad!"

"Wanna bet, Mr. Truth, Justice and the American Way?"

He held open the door to what he called a squad room, and she registered the noticeable dip in volume as she stepped into the space. She followed him over to one of the neatest desks in the space, while Bass's desk was still populated by several tall piles of folders and papers.

"Carrie, this is Jarred Strickland, my boss."

She nodded pleasantly at the gray-haired cop while Bass added, "Miss Price is the closest friend we have for Gary Hubbard."

"How's the case going?" Strickland asked.

"Caught some new information last night. May give us a new direction to pursue."

"Good. Because that case is going cold fast. Still no ransom demand?"

"Nope. Nothing."

Strickland shook his head direly, and his grim expression spoke volumes about what that meant for Gary. Carrie's heart tumbled to her toes. Here she'd been having a rollicking great old time with Bass while her uncle's life was in mortal danger. He had to be alive. He just *had* to be.

"Tell me everything you can remember about Lonnie Grange," Bass instructed her.

"I mostly remember not liking him…"

Over the next half hour, Bass teased all kinds of details out of her that she didn't realize she knew. Coupled with what he'd found online earlier, Bass declared himself prepared to take on the gangster. He finished by stating, "The plan will be to draw out Grange and provoke or tempt him into coming down here into my jurisdiction. Then I'll nail his sorry ass."

"How do you plan to lure him down here?" Carrie asked nervously. "New Orleans is a long way from Apple Grove."

"Easy," Bass said blithely. "I have what he wants. I dangle the bait under his nose."

"What bait?" she asked.

"You."

Oh.

Oh dear.

"Umm, I'm not sure I like the sound of that."

"I didn't expect you would. But if all you say about him is true, he'll come for you, aggressively."

"Oh, I'm telling the truth about him, all right. That's why this idea stinks!" She jumped to her feet in dismay.

Bass muttered under his breath so the other cops in the big room couldn't hear, "I promise I'll take good care of the bait."

"The bait still thinks fishing is a lousy idea." She planted her fists on her hips.

She was on the verge of launching a full-blown tirade at him when one of the other cops, a pretty young woman, called out, "Bass! Evidence guys got two hits on the fingerprints from the Hubbard home!"

Carrie whipped around and said in unison with Bass, "Who are they?"

"Guy named Tony Sicarrio, and a guy named Stevie Desilva."

"Sounds mob," Carrie observed.

Bass grinned. "People are innocent until proven guilty, my bloodthirsty minnow. Lots of perfectly law-abiding Italians live in New York."

"These two broke into Gary's place and left behind fingerprints!" she exclaimed.

"True." To the woman cop, he asked, "Where are these guys from?"

"New York City. The Bronx."

"They're mob, I tell you," Carrie insisted.

"They staying in the local area?" Bass asked.

"Got a credit card hit a few days back on a motel in Lakeview for Sicarrio."

"Text me the address," Bass called over his shoulder, already heading for the exit.

Carrie trailed along, alarmed. Bass wasn't going to drag her into the middle of a shoot-out, was he?

His last words before they left the squad room chilled her to her toes. "Call for a couple of black-and-whites to meet me there. Tell 'em to move in within a couple of blocks with no sirens, and then await my call. Don't want to spook our guys before I take them down."

Bass slouched behind the wheel of his vintage pickup truck, while Carrie fidgeted in the seat beside him. He'd gone home to switch out flashy Daisy Mae for this much more anonymous truck before heading for Lakeview.

He'd never been on a stakeout with a woman he was sleeping with, and it felt weird in the extreme. This wasn't supposed to be an intimate, sexually charged event. But damned if he could keep his mind from drifting to thoughts of pulling Carrie on top of him, unzipping his fly, and sliding into her tight heat—

Stop that.

"How long do you suppose it'll be before they get back?" she asked.

"Could be a few minutes, could be hours."

"Why aren't we busting into their room now to make sure Gary isn't there?"

"Because they've been having the motel's maid clean the room every day. They would hang up a Do Not Disturb sign and keep everyone out if your uncle was tied up in there."

"What if he's drugged or hurt?"

"All the more reason to keep strangers out of the room. The maids cleaned the room as recently as this morning. I guarantee you he's not there."

She deflated, disappointed.

"We'll find him, darlin'."

"You can't be sure about that. You've said yourself that the more time passes, the less chance we have of finding him."

"We've got solid leads now. Have a little faith."

She chewed on the end of her finger nervously. Taking pity on her manicure, he reached over and snagged her hand, pulling it to his lap and twining their fingers together.

Just holding hands like this was nice. The physical contact did something strangely soothing to his heart. She gave him hope that everything would work out in his life, and that he wouldn't end up alone.

Since when was he worrying about being alone? He'd been fine for all these years. He had his buddies and his cars, and a steady stream of women. And yet, having met Carrie, all of that wasn't enough any more. He apparently craved an emotional connection, a real relationship, more than he'd realized. Although how he was going to make time for a relationship on top of his day job and his weekend job, he had no idea.

Of course, he was assuming that Carrie would want to stay with him, to put down roots in New Orleans, if he asked her to. She'd been a nomad for a long time. She might have lost interest in any permanence in her life.

His gut tightened in alarm at the notion, and he realized he was crushing her hand. He loosened his grip apologetically.

A car turned into the parking lot of the motel, and he went onto high alert. Were these his guys? They parked in front of room 114, where the manager said Sicarrio was staying. Bass picked up a pair of small binoculars and peered at the man getting out of the car.

He grabbed the microphone from the radio unit mounted under the dashboard and broadcast tersely, "I've got visual on our suspects. Get ready to move."

He watched Sicarrio and a second man who matched the description of Desilva open the trunk, carry grocery bags to the door of room 114, and disappear inside.

Bass transmitted, "Suspects are in their room. Unit 51, move in behind the motel and radio when you're in place."

Carrie asked, "Why are you putting cops behind the motel?"

"In case our guys jump out the bathroom window and try to make a run for it. We could give chase on foot or get a helicopter to give us air support, but it's a lot less hassle to just cut off all escape routes before we make the collar."

"Collar?"

"Arrest," he clarified.

"Unit 51 in place," a voice announced over the radio.

"Stay here," he ordered Carrie. "If you hear gunshots, lie down as best you can and cover your head with your arms."

"Where are you going?" she asked as he reached for the door handle.

"To arrest these bastards and find out what they know."

He climbed out of the car and tugged his bullet-resistant vest down into place as he jogged across the street. He headed for the other end of the motel from the room in case one of the suspects was looking out the window and saw him coming. No sense warning the dudes they were about to get busted. He reached the covered walkway in front of the rooms, out of sight of room 114. He raced down the breezeway until he stood beside the door. He drew his pistol.

The second cop car pulled around the corner and started to turn into the parking lot, and Bass knocked on the door.

A voice called from inside, "Who's there?"

"Hey man, you driving the blue Taurus out here? You left your trunk open."

Bass heard from inside, "What the hell?" Bass moved off to one side slightly so he couldn't be seen from the room's window. He heard fumbling at the lock and exhaled slowly, dropping into the combat calm that made SEALs so deadly.

The door opened about a foot before the guy inside spied him standing there in body armor with his weapon drawn. The suspect tried to slam the door shut, but Bass was faster. He jammed his steel-toed boot in the door, blocking it open, and then slammed his shoulder against the door. Hard.

The man trying to jam the door shut staggered back, but the second man jumped at Bass, trying to shove him aside, presumably to flee. Bass lowered his shoulder and took the charge, bracing himself against the impact. The runner grunted, and Bass whipped up his elbow, cracking the guy hard across the bridge of the nose. The suspect fell back, crying out and clutching his broken, bloody nose.

Bass spun away from the first guy and brought his pistol to bear on the second, who was just pulling a gun from a holster at his hip.

"Don't do it, man," Bass said coldly.

The second suspect's hand froze, his weapon half-drawn. Undoubtedly the guy heard Bass's promise of a lethal double-tap of lead to the center of his forehead. To reinforce the perp's decision, Bass said calmly, "I'm a cop. If you finish drawing that weapon, I'll kill you. Put the gun back in the holster and clasp your hands behind your head."

The suspect did as ordered.

Bass said, "On your knees, my friend. Let's keep this all nice and calm and everyone walks out of here alive. Okay?"

The first guy was not so sensible, however, and charged forward, taking a wild swing with his fist at Bass. For his part, Bass sidestepped neatly, leaning back out of the path of the fist and swinging fast with his pistol, clocking the guy on the side of the head. Suspect number one dropped like a rock.

"You've killed him!" the second suspect shouted.

"Nah," Bass replied casually, kneeling and planting a knee in the middle of the downed man's shoulders. "He's just taking a little nap. He'll wake up with a killer headache in about sixty seconds."

To the conscious guy, he asked, "So where's Gary Hubbard?"

"Gary who?"

Dammit. Either the guy didn't know where Carrie's uncle was, or he wasn't going to give up the information easily.

Just then, a voice called from outside, "Clear?"

"Clear," Bass called back. "Come on in."

A pair of uniformed cops stepped into the room, crowding it. Any sense of hope the second suspect had left whooshed out of him, and he slumped, sitting on his heels, hands still behind his head.

"Restrain the suspects, if you would," Bass directed the uniforms.

One cop quickly handcuffed the guy on the ground's wrists behind his back, while the other cop relieved the kneeling suspect of his weapon and handcuffed him.

Suspect number one started groaning on cue about sixty seconds after Bass struck him. Which made Bass smile. He still hadn't lost his touch. The blow had been delivered perfectly. Hard enough to take out a hostile, but not so hard as to cause the guy any serious damage.

"Where do you want 'em?" one of the uniformed cops asked.

"Downtown. I'll meet you there. Me and my guys are looking forward to having some conversation with these two."

"You got it, Detective."

Bass stuck around while the uniforms searched the room. They confiscated another handgun and some ammo, and Bass took both men's cell phones. There was nothing else in the room to point at where Gary Hubbard might be hidden.

As the uniforms stuffed each of the suspects into

a different squad car, he strode across the parking lot and crossed the street. He opened the truck's door and slid into the driver's seat…and was assaulted by Carrie, launching herself across the truck's bench seat to nearly strangle him.

"Easy, darlin'. I'm right as rain. Nothing to cry over."

For crying she was, tears wet against his neck.

"That was a routine arrest. Couldn't have gone much more smoothly," he tried. But Carrie's tears didn't stop.

He finally pulled her into his lap, wrapping his arms around her, and kissing her until she mumbled, "I was so scared for you."

"Honey, trust me. That was not a scary arrest." He refrained from telling her he was routinely in situations a hell of a lot more dangerous than that one. No need to give her a full-blown panic attack.

He relished her weight in his lap, her sweet curves in his arms, the gentle smell of her hair. Everything about her was feminine, and he couldn't get enough of her. It would be so easy to push back the seat, to help her straddle his hips. To lean back and let her ride him to oblivion—

The suspects, dammit. He needed to follow the squad cars downtown and interrogate Tony and Stevie, ASAP. With a last, lingering kiss for her, he reluctantly set Carrie in the passenger's seat. But he couldn't resist. He leaned across the interior to kiss her again.

"I want you all the time," she muttered against his lips. "It's like I'm addicted to you."

He knew the feeling. "Hold that thought until we get home tonight," he murmured against her mouth.

"I'll hold you to it," she declared.

He laughed, "Honey, you'll be holding all sorts of things, tonight."

The drive to the station took nearly half an hour in traffic, which barely gave Bass enough time to stop thinking about all the ways he wanted to make love to Carrie and to get his head back in the game.

He quickly planned out the questions he wanted to ask the two men. He would separate them, of course. And then he would lie about what each one had confessed, to see if the second man would corroborate Bass's guesses as truth.

These guys didn't strike him as rocket scientists. One of them would crack. His money was on the guy who'd knelt out right away. He'd shown a stronger survival instinct than Broken Nose had. It was never smart to take a swing at a cop. Especially a cop with his gun already pulled.

Bass parked and took Carrie inside, putting her in a darkened observation space sandwiched between two interrogation rooms. One-way glass windows on each side of the observation room overlooked both interrogation setups. Speakers from each room piped sound into the dim space.

He told her, "Stay in here. I'll check in with you from time to time, and you let me know if you can think of anything I ought to ask one or both suspects."

She nodded, her eyes big and scared. He got why she was scared of cops, but she was going to have to get over her fear of all of this police procedure to be with him for any length of time—

Whoa. Wait. What? Since when had he decided to definitely go for a long-term relationship with her?

Stunned, he stumbled out of the observation room and leaned against the closed door to calm his racing heart. Things were happening so damned fast between him and Carrie. He needed to slow down. Catch his breath. Hell, think with his brain and not his crotch.

Right now he needed to get his mind on business and break these two jerks. Get them to admit they worked for Lonnie Grange and most importantly, get them to tell him what had happened to Gary Hubbard and where he could be found, alive or dead. For Carrie's sake, he sincerely hoped her uncle was still alive.

As it turned out, Broken Nose—who identified himself as Stevie Desilva—caved first. He wasn't the brightest bulb in the bin and fell for the ruse that his buddy had decided to save his own hide and confess.

Broken Nose was furious that Siccario was going to get immunity from prosecution for talking first and burst out, "Tony's the one who should go to jail! He's the one calling the shots. I just do what he tells me to!"

"Oh, dude," Bass replied sympathetically, "he's screwing you over hard in the other room. Totally threw you under the bus. He said you were the one in charge of kidnapping that ghost show guy."

"Not even close!" Stevie replied indignantly. "Tony got orders from his boss to do it! Tony only brought me onto the job to help out."

Bingo. Confession to kidnapping. "Who's his boss?" Bass asked casually.

"Some guy in Philly. Grunge. Grange. Something like that."

"Lonnie Grange?" Bass echoed. "I've heard of him. You work for him? I'm impressed. He's in Philly now? Last I heard he was running a crew in New York."

"Hell, yeah, we work for him. And he moved to Philly to get a new start after he got out of jail. You know. Less heat in a new town. And he's got the best lawyers in the business."

Confession number two. They worked for a known felon. Now that these yahoos had tied Grange to the kidnapping, he could investigate ole' Lonnie hard-core. In addition to finding Gary, maybe Bass could find out what the deal was between the bastard and teenaged Carrie. Unfortunately, his internal radar still wasn't satisfied he'd heard the whole story from her.

Now the trick was to keep these two thugs talking. The more they said before they clammed up and lawyered up, the better. Although Bass highly doubted any lawyer, no matter how good, was going to get these two out of the long and growing list of charges against them.

Bass nodded sagely at Stevie. "A good lawyer can get pretty much anybody out of any charges. I doubt we're going to be able to hold you more than a day or two before someone screws up some police procedure and we have to let you go. You've got nothing to worry about."

Stevie visibly relaxed.

"Soon as you and I are done talking, I'll call Grange for you and tell him to get his lawyers down here. That way you can save your phone call for someone else."

"That's decent of you, man," Stevie replied.

"No problem. You help me, I help you, right?"

"Sure thing."

Bass was equally comfortable playing bad cop or good cop, but given that Carrie was watching the interrogations, he was abjectly grateful he got to play good cop today. His version of bad cop would probably send her running, screaming, for the hills, never to return. It wasn't that he was actually that big a bastard. He was just very well trained to make hardened criminals think so.

"Okay. So after you guys picked up Gary out of that

alley and threw him in your vehicle, where did you take him?"

"First we took him back to the motel. Tony had some stuff he made the old guy breathe that knocked him out. Then I stayed at the motel and Tony took him somewhere. I don't know where."

"How long was Tony gone?"

"Couple hours. I dunno. I fell asleep."

"Is he going back to Gary and taking care of him?"

"Oh, yeah. Every other day or so, Tony takes a couple a' bags of groceries and drives off for three or four hours."

"That's square of him," Bass commented pleasantly. "Is the car muddy when he gets back to the motel?"

"It was a few nights ago. The night we had that big rainstorm come through."

"That was a big one, wasn't it? Woke me up from a dead sleep," Bass replied conversationally.

"Me, too. Tony was plenty pissed when he got back. Said that storm was a bitch to drive through."

"I can imagine." Bass stood up. "Well hey. Thanks for your help, and you sit tight. I'll be back in a little while and we'll get you out of here. You need anything to eat or drink?"

"Yeah. I could use a beer, but I'll take a soda. Something caffeinated."

Bass grinned affably. "I *wish* we could have beer around here. I'll send in a drink."

He stepped out into the hall and paused in front of Tony's door, collecting himself. Time to put the screws to this jerk. He stepped inside.

Chapter 12

Carrie moved across the small, dark room to the other window as Bass shifted from Stevie's room to Tony's. She was impressed by how good Bass was at questioning these guys. He'd put Stevie completely at ease and had the guy singing like a bird without even realizing he was confessing to a bunch of serious crimes.

The female cop Carrie'd seen before in the squad room ducked her head into the room, asking, "How's it going?"

"Great. Stevie just confessed to kidnapping Gary Hubbard and to working for Lonnie Grange."

"Wow. That was fast. Usually these types hold out for a few hours before they break." The woman came into the room all the way, closing the door behind her.

Carrie watched as Bass sat down in front of Tony, who looked a great deal more hostile than Stevie. She listened closely as Bass said gently, "Your friend, Stevie, is a talkative guy."

Tony swore long and hard, and Bass seemed content to let him rage. As the guy's tirade eventually ran down, Bass said calmly, "You know the score, Tony. He who talks first, walks first. Unless you can offer me some information that Stevie hasn't already spilled, he's walking out of here in a few minutes, and you're going to jail for the rest of your life."

"Life? I didn't kill no one!"

"What you would call first-degree kidnapping in New York, down here in Louisiana, we call aggravated kidnapping. Unlike in New York, where you can be sentenced to twenty years in prison for first-degree kidnapping, in this fair state it's a mandatory life sentence without probation or parole. Did you know that?"

Another storm of swearing erupted from Tony. Carrie was impressed at its breadth and creativity. That must be what swearing like a sailor referred to.

"Your boss, Lonnie Grange, had to know that. It's why he didn't kidnap Hubbard himself. He threw you to the sharks, man."

When the guy wound down from a third outburst of profanity, Bass leaned forward in his chair, staring hard at Tony. Carrie wasn't even the target of that lethal stare, but still, it made her squirm. Guilt did that to a girl.

Bass growled, "Your best bet is to tell me where to find Gary Hubbard. I can get you put in a lower security prison, get you privileges. Trust me, you don't want to go into general population in the federal penitentiary in this state. Gen pop in Angola is a very, *very* risky proposition."

"Maybe I'm the guy who'll make it risky."

Bass looked Tony up and down. "You're soft. Going to fat. Approaching middle age. The boys in Angola would chew you up and spit you out." Tony bristled as

Bass continued, "Lonnie G.'s got no pull down here. He and his boys can't protect you at all. You go into the pen without a hard-core gang affiliation, you're going to be for sale to the highest bidder. You can't even begin to imagine the stuff they'll do to you. Bending you over in the shower's gonna be a walk in the park before they're done with you. Guys *die* from the stuff they do to cream puffs like you."

There was notably less swearing from Tony this time. Bass's warnings appeared to have gotten inside the guy's head.

Carrie silently cringed as Bass stepped on the gas pedal a little harder. Lord, he was scary when he talked like this. "You wanna die in prison, Tony? You got any family back home? Kids? Grandkids someday? You wanna *ever* see them? Hug them? Only way you're seeing any of them is through Plexiglas, my friend."

Tony was silent this time.

Bass let the silence draw out until it was so uncomfortable that even Carrie was fidgeting. "Where's Gary Hubbard?"

"I can't tell you," Tony replied.

Carrie's hands fisted in frustration. He *knew*. She could feel it. Through the glass, Bass asked the guy, "You can't tell me, or you won't tell me?"

"Same diff. I'm a dead man either way."

"Lonnie G. tell you he'd kill you if you rolled over on him?" Bass threw out. "Guys like him always say stuff like that. They make big threats to get their guys to shut up and take the fall for them. Lonnie's just out of prison. He knows how bad it really is in there. He'd do anything not to go back, including giving you up."

"He would not!"

Carrie nodded. Bass was good at this interrogation

stuff, all right. Tony had just confessed to knowing Lonnie Grange.

"You're willing to go away for the rest of your life for Lonnie? Is he that good a guy? He must be some kind of special friend for you to die for him. Are you really willing to go to hell for him?"

Carrie was ready to confess everything to Bass, and she wasn't even in the same room with him. Who knew he'd been taking it as easy on her as he had been so far? Thing was, the day would come when he would demand to know what she wasn't telling him about her past. He would come at her *like this*.

And she wouldn't be able to hold out against him. She was deluded if she thought she was going to be able to keep her secret from Bass. He would tear her open like a cheap tin can and pry every last, humiliating detail out of her.

The thought made her physically ill.

"You okay?" the female cop asked her.

"No," she muttered. "Yes. Never mind."

"You look like you're about to faint."

Carrie waved off her concern. If the woman went next door and told Bass his girlfriend was sick, he would rush in here and demand to know what was going on. He would interrogate her like he was going after Tony Sicarrio, and it would be all over. She leaned against the wall, gasping like a dying fish.

On the other side of the glass, Tony was stubbornly silent.

Bass leaned even further forward and began describing in a quiet, terrible voice the graphic, violent detail of things he'd heard of happening to inmates in federal prisons. Bile rose in Carrie's throat at some of the abuses he described. They were nothing short of the sickest forms of torture. It appalled her to know that Bass was even aware of such things, let alone familiar with them.

Tony paled.

Carrie glanced over at the female cop, who seemed completely absorbed in the interrogation. She glanced up at Carrie. "Bass is the best, isn't he? I love watching him work over perps."

"If being gross constitutes being good at this stuff, then I guess Bass is pretty good at it," Carrie managed to reply.

The other woman nodded, seemingly oblivious to Carrie's reaction. "Being good means doing whatever it takes within the law to get the criminals to confess. Saves us a ton of time and resources if we can get them to confess instead of having to go out and gather physical evidence to prove they're guilty beyond a shadow of a doubt."

Bass's voice—unusually clipped for him—floated out of the speaker on the wall. "And then there's the torture…"

Oh, God. It could get worse than he'd already described?

Carrie tried to tune out his words, the cruel way he battered at Tony, the way he broke down a hardened criminal's defenses, waxing eloquent in describing the worst excesses of torture Tony could expect to experience in prison. It sounded to her like Bass had dipped into his military training for some truly gruesome forms of torture to describe.

She couldn't unhear any of it. How did Bass live with having seen, or possibly even experienced, horrors like that?

"Jeez, you've got a twisted mind!" Tony finally blurted.

"No kidding," she muttered.

The female cop shrugged. "Bass breaks everybody. They all spill their guts to him in the end."

He breaks everybody.

The words were daggers to Carrie's heart. She couldn't spill her guts to him. Ever. If he knew the truth, he wouldn't want anything to do with her. She would take her shame to the grave with her.

But she knew him too well. Bass would never stand for secrets between them. Telling him the truth would totally be a condition of their relationship. She would have to rip off the scabs she'd so carefully nurtured over her worst emotional wounds.

She couldn't do it.

Tony blurted, "You're sick, man."

Through the glass, Bass smiled so coldly that Carrie felt the chill in here. "Hey, I'm not even a criminal, and I'm not bored out of my mind, sitting around in my cell all day long, thinking up ways to entertain my psychotic self. I'm nothing compared to the boys in orange. They're gonna have a field day with you, Tony. You're gonna take that tough guy attitude inside with you, and they're gonna smash you like glass. You're gonna be left in so many pieces they have to sweep you into a body bag."

Carrie was appalled. Bass was showing a streak she was scared to death of. Surely it was all an act. But the cop beside her was staring at Bass in open appreciation, as if that was the real Bastien LeBlanc revealing himself in there.

An overwhelming urge to bolt from the room and run for her life tore through her, leaving her entire body shaking and her mind jumping from thought to thought like a manic rabbit standing on an electrified panel.

"Where's Gary, Tony?" Bass asked forcefully.

"Why in the hell should I tell you? I want a plea deal before I'll cough it up."

She gaped. The man had basically just admitted to knowing where Gary Hubbard was stashed.

Bass stood up, moved around the table and loomed behind Tony. Then Bass looked up, straight at the mirror, and said clear as day, "Get her out of there."

The woman cop reached for the door and said, "You heard him. Let's go."

"But I have to know where my uncle's being held!"

"Bass needs you gone. And he's the boss."

Carrie might have resisted further, but the woman officer actually reached out and took her by the elbow, politely, but firmly steering her out into the hall.

Even though she wanted nothing more than to run, she owed Gary. Carrie demanded, "Why can't I stay?"

"Think about it. Why would a cop not want a civilian witnessing an interrogation?"

"Is he going to beat up Tony?"

"Cops don't beat up prisoners," the woman replied scornfully. "But we sure as hell jog their memories when someone's life is on the line."

Bass was going to rough up Tony Sicarrio? If she'd been shocked before, she was stunned speechless, now. In an intellectual way, she understood that Bass was capable of violence. But somehow, she'd always pictured him shooting a gun at terrorists from a long way away—something bloodless and technical. But using his fists to pummel the truth out of Tony? It was so… real. So *violent*.

That was it. She was out of here.

Her thoughts must have shown on her face because the cop paused in the doorway of the squad room to ask her, "Do you want to know where Gary Hubbard is or not?"

"Of course!"

"Then let Bass do his job, and don't overthink it."

Carrie fell into the chair beside Bass's desk and absolutely overthought it. With every passing minute, her imagination spun more wildly out of control. The more she thought about it, the more she convinced herself that Bass was probably murdering Tony. Slowly.

The hell of it was that even if he hadn't murdered the guy, she knew without a shadow of a doubt that Bass was capable of it. Every fear she'd ever had of Lonnie Grange, of men in general, roared to the front of her mind, blinding her to anything else.

Must. Run.

Now.

She couldn't take the waiting any more, imagining Bass pounding another human being into pulp. She jumped up from the chair, mumbling something about needing to find a restroom, and all but ran out of the building. She had to get some fresh air!

She burst out of the precinct, hyperventilating so badly she felt as if she might faint. But she didn't stop. She headed down the street, stumbling along blindly, going nowhere in particular.

She had to get away. Away from Bass's aggressive curiosity. Away from his willingness to resort to violence to get the answers he wanted. She spied a park and veered into it, drawn by the green grass and inviting benches. She fell onto one, and wasn't surprised to realize tears were streaming down her cheeks.

She couldn't do it. She couldn't stand and fight like Bass wanted her to. She wasn't as strong as him and not anywhere near as tough as he was.

Yes, she was a coward. She owned that about herself, and she was okay with it. Running away had kept her alive for this long—there was no reason to believe continuing to run wouldn't continue to work for her.

Except for Bass himself.

She'd thought she knew him. Thought she could trust him. But who was the man back in that interrogation room? Was that all an act to get a criminal to talk, or was it a glimpse into the real monster lurking beneath the nice guy?

Or was she just overreacting? He hadn't done anything to Tony Sicarrio in her presence. He'd just talked to the guy. Sure, he'd painted some horrifying pictures with words, but it wasn't as if he'd actually tortured the guy. But then he'd ordered her out of the observation room.

What had happened *then*? No way would he ever tell her.

Run or stay.

Stay or run.

If she ran, she would be abandoning Gary. She might also be saving her own life.

If she stayed, she might die. Or she might be able to have Bass for herself. Assuming she could find a way to reconcile her feelings for him with what she'd seen of him today.

All of her stuff was at Bass's place. How was she supposed to get through the gate and past all that fancy security of his to reach her personal belongings and the van? He had her neatly trapped.

Was that his plan all along? Was he that calculating? Lord knew, she'd had no idea he had such a hard streak in him until she witnessed that interrogation.

She had to stick around. For now.

She had to play the game for a few more hours, get back inside his fortress-like compound, and wait for an opportunity to make a break for it.

Plan in place, she sat there until her breathing finally slowed and stabilized, and then she looked around. She had no idea where she was. She headed for the busiest looking street bordering the park and looked for a taxi. It took her a few minutes, but she finally spotted one and waved it down.

She asked the driver to take her back to the police precinct. Sitting in the backseat, she carefully schooled her face to calm. Bass was so perceptive that she dared not give away any hint of her plan to escape him.

The cab pulled up in front of the precinct, and sure enough, Bass was standing out front, looking up and down the street. The look on his face shocked her. He looked...ravaged. She looked more closely, not believing what she was seeing.

His entire body was taut, tense. He looked close to panic. And the expression in his eyes was one of total devastation.

Her plan to run away from him wavered in the face of his distress. Did he really care about her that much? Could she forgive him for what she'd seen earlier?

She climbed out of the taxi, and Bass spotted her instantly. He rushed forward and wrapped her in a bone-crushing hug. He mumbled into her hair, "Thank God you came back to me."

"I had to get some air," she wheezed from the iron grip of his arms. "Speaking of which, could I have a little now?"

His arms loosened slightly. Very slightly. "What happened?"

"I started feeling really claustrophobic in there. I

went for a quick jog but I got lost, so I grabbed a taxi and had it bring me back here."

Keeping an arm around her shoulders, he guided her into the precinct. "Let's get out of here," he murmured.

Completely thrown by the intensity of his reaction to seeing her return, she followed him to the parking garage and climbed into his pickup truck.

Was she wrong to run away from him? The mental whiplash of seeing him go from violent to solicitous was too much to process.

As he pulled out into traffic, she asked, "Why did you choose to drive this car today?"

"In the first place, this is a truck, not a car, and in the second place, what do you mean?" he asked, never taking his eyes off the road.

"I've observed that the vehicle you choose to drive on any given day reflects your mood at the time. So, why the beat-up old truck now?"

He glanced over to her, looking surprised. "Huh. I never thought about it before."

She stared at him expectantly.

He continued, "For the record, the exterior of this truck may be fifty years old, but the engine under the hood and the chassis is state of the art. She may not look like much on the outside, but Esther is fast and powerful."

"Esther?"

"My grandmother was named Esther. She had white hair and came to about my chin, but she was a swinging dame. Loved to dance and laugh and shop. I have a lot of good memories of her."

This was the first time Bass had spoken of his family to her. Carrie studied him thoughtfully. "Have you got a car named after your mother?"

His face closed, and his eyes went hard. "No."

"Wow. That's revealing."

"My mother wasn't a bad person. She just couldn't handle it when my father walked out on her. She crawled into a bottle and never made it back out."

Holy cow. "How old were you when your dad left?"

"Eight."

Yikes. He'd been old enough to remember it, then. If possible, his face closed even more tightly. Obviously not a subject he liked to talk about. At all. "I'm sorry," she murmured.

"Why? It's not your fault my parents' marriage sucked."

She sucked in a sharp breath. A bad marriage, huh? She'd lived through the end of Shelly's parents' marriage and the disaster of Mrs. B's second marriage. The toll on Shelly had been rough.

To Bass, she said, "I'm sorry you got caught in the middle of it and got hurt."

"Granny Esther was great to me. I spent a lot of time with her after the divorce. I'm not totally screwed up."

"You're in your thirties and showing no sign of interest in long-term relationships. I'd say you were screwed up at least a little by your parents' divorce."

Bass's spine went rigid at that.

"Don't get me wrong," she added hastily. "We're all screwed up in one way or another by family baggage."

"How are you screwed up—aside from, of course, having to change your name?"

"I got no support from my family. I learned early on to take care of myself and not trust anyone else."

"And how's that working out?" he asked dryly.

"I'm alive."

"But not much more," he observed.

She sat back, startled. Was he right? Had she sacrificed a normal life, normal relationships—heck, even friendships—in the name of protecting herself? Was she as messed up as him?

Truth be told, she'd never slowed down long enough to really think about it.

They arrived at his place, and she watched closely as he punched the left-hand garage-door opener and the iron security gates swung open. The right-hand garage-door opener raised the big steel door at the end of his parking garage. She memorized the numeric code that let them into his workshop, and despaired of how she was going to get past the palm print pad that let him into his house. Maybe, if she was lucky, she could get out of the house without the palm print thing.

Bass went immediately to the kitchen and started cooking. An act she now knew to be another coping mechanism of his. Cooking was how he de-stressed. In a little while, the smells of frying sausage, seafood and the pungent spices of jambalaya emanated from the stove.

She went into the bedroom and quickly organized her clothes and personal items so she could pop them into her bags and be ready to go in a matter of minutes. She returned to the main room, her heart heavy.

She set the table for dinner, and sat down with Bass to unquestionably the best jambalaya she would ever taste.

Bass let her eat in peace, but then at the end of the meal, he laid down his napkin and said seriously, "We need to talk."

Uh-oh. "About what?"

"About today."

She *knew* he was mad that she'd bolted from the police station! "What about today?" she asked cautiously.

"About my interrogation of Tony Sicarrio."

Oh. Whew. Not something she particularly wanted to revisit, but at least she wasn't the target of this conversation. "Umm. Okay. It was pretty graphic."

"Yeah. It was. He was a tough nut to crack."

She took a deep breath and forced herself to ask the question she'd been dying to ask ever since she bolted from the precinct. "Did you hurt him?"

"No."

Did she believe him? He'd never lied to her before. But he also wasn't elaborating. Doubt ate at her gut, and she chewed her lip, unsure of what she believed.

Silence fell between them. Bass seemed to expect her to say something, to react to his horrific descriptions of torture. But she had no idea what to say. His utter determination to get at the truth—at any cost—had appalled her. Made her distrust him. Sealed her decision to get away from here, away from him, as soon as possible.

She had to say something. The silence was getting downright uncomfortable. "Where did you learn about all those torture tactics? Is it something you were taught in the military?"

"Good Lord, no! The US uses enhanced questioning techniques, and some of them can be fairly…challenging…but we don't torture anyone."

"Not officially."

He shook his head. "The stuff I talked about isn't stuff I've ever done to anyone. It's all stuff that's been done to me or my fellow SEALs."

Oh. My. God. "That's horrible!"

"Yes. It is."

"How does somebody walk away from something like that and not be a complete head case?"

"Some guys don't. Some guys never recover physically or emotionally from what's done to them."

She stared at him in horror. "What was done to you?"

He shook his head, his eyes hard and cold. "It's in the past. I survived. I walked away from it. I got some counseling, and I let it go. I don't need or want to talk about it ever again."

Fair enough. She wasn't sure she could stand to hear the details anyway. If only he would offer her the same understanding. But it wasn't in his nature to let something important go. If she had a secret, he would insist on knowing it.

Aloud, she asked, "Is it common for SEALs to get tortured?"

"Not at all. We have to get caught to get tortured, and that's rare indeed."

"Can you talk about how you got captured?"

"Bad intel. Politicians back home interfering with important decisions. Everything that could go wrong did go wrong. It was just one of those things. The stars aligned to blow a mission to hell. At least everyone on my team lived. Most of the time when a mission goes sideways, guys die."

"Still. That's terrible," she responded.

"Life is a roll of the dice. We were lucky."

"Lucky that you were captured and tortured?"

"Lucky that we lived. SEALs are trained to put up with a lot of terrible stuff and not take it personally. The funny bit is we actually accomplished the mission. The bad guys revealed themselves by capturing us, and the team sent in to rescue us was able to take them out."

She had a hard time wrapping her brain around that

kind of thinking. "So your team was *bait*? You sacrificed yourselves and got tortured to lure out a bad guy?"

"More or less."

"That's insane!"

"That's the job."

"You SEALs really are crazy."

He shrugged. "Someone's got to do the job. Why not me? I'm stronger, tougher, and better trained than anyone else to pull off the tough missions."

She couldn't resist asking the question that bubbled to her lips. "Does that include being able to dish out the same kind of punishment that was done to you?"

He frowned. "That's not a simple question. Do I know how to do bad things to people? Of course. Do I think it's right to torture someone? No. Is there a circumstance under which I might actually torture someone? I know better than to say never."

That rocked her to her core. He was admitting that he could do terrible things to other people? He really was the monster she'd thought he was earlier!

"Don't look at me like that, Carrie. Everyone's capable of doing things they thought they could or would never do, given the right motivations. I'm trying to be honest with you, here. I wouldn't just randomly grab someone and do awful things to them."

"When might you torture someone?" she demanded, outrage growing in her chest. "Give me an example."

"All right." He thought for a second. "If someone kidnapped you, and I had one of the kidnappers in custody and they wouldn't tell me where you were—I wouldn't hesitate to do whatever I had to in order to get them to tell me where to find you."

She was only slightly mollified by that answer.

He must sense her reluctance to buy his explanation,

for he continued, "Everyone's got a hot button. Everyone's got someone or something they'll break all their personal rules and taboos for. If you were a mother and someone was harming your child, are you telling me you wouldn't hurt them, given the chance?"

"I suppose I see your point."

"Trust me. It's what becoming a SEAL is all about. We will die to defend our country and protect our brothers. Period. Someone's got to be willing to go that far, and we're those guys. We'll die to defend the people we love, as well."

"That's really intense."

"I suspect most people will get violent to protect the people they love. Thankfully, most people aren't ever put in that situation."

But SEALs were put in that situation. Routinely. How did that change a man? Did it unleash something terrible inside him, or did it refine his priorities into something heroic? She studied Bass intently. Maybe it did both to a man.

She just wasn't sure she was brave enough to love a man who could be both.

Bass stood up and picked up the dinner dishes. "SEALs are extremely carefully trained to control the violence. We're not psychopaths waiting to tear the head off anyone who crosses us."

This afternoon's interrogation notwithstanding, apparently. "Then why did you go after Tony Sicarrio like that?"

"I didn't lay a finger on him."

Truly? Then why did Bass order her out of that observation room? She declared, "You scared the hell out of him."

"Do you want your uncle back?" he shot back at her.

"Yes, of course!"

"At what cost? Is it worth me scaring some two-bit criminal into telling us where your uncle is and who has him? I threw some ugly words at a bad guy. Not a hair on his head was touched. He got off damned easy if you ask me."

Carrie had no response for that. Bass was right. Her reaction wasn't on Tony Sicarrio's behalf. This was about her fear of violence in men. She'd been the victim of it once, and she had no intention of being a victim of it again.

Silently, she carried the rest of the dishes into the kitchen.

Bass commented, "I need to run over to the Navy base and check in with my guys. Do you want to come with me or would you rather stay here? This place is buttoned up tight, and our bad guys have been striking strictly late at night. You should be okay here for an hour or two."

Hah! A chance to get out of Dodge! She answered, "I'd rather stay here if you don't mind. It has been a long day."

"Cool. Feel free to go for a swim in my bathtub. It's fully jetted."

"That sounds amazing."

She waited until the rumble of Bass's Charger faded into silence before racing to the bedroom and throwing her clothes into her duffel bag. She was just heading to the pegboard in the kitchen to get the keys to one of Bass's cars when her cell phone rang in her pocket. She jumped about a foot in the air. Ten to one it was Bass checking up on her. Lord, that man had great internal radar. He must sense that she was about to pull a runner.

She schooled her voice to cheerful unconcern. "Hello?"

"At long last, Kathy. You're a hard girl to find."

She staggered and dropped onto the sofa. She hadn't heard that voice since the night long ago that changed her life forever. That changed her forever.

"What do you want, Lonnie?" she snarled. She would be damned if she showed fear to this man, even if her legs were too weak to hold her weight right now and her entire body was shaking like a leaf.

"You know perfectly well what I want. Except this time I want you wide awake."

She mentally swore, calling him every name she could think of in her head. The only reason she'd been able to recover and move on at all from his attack was that she'd been drugged and had no memory of the actual rape.

God. She hated to even think the word.

"You're a pig, Lonnie."

"You're an uppity little bitch who needs the starch knocked out of her."

Her breath whooshed out of her. But then a strength she didn't know she had flowed through her. She answered scornfully, "Whatever. You need to leave me alone, Lonnie, unless you want to end up like your men."

"What men?"

"Tony and Stevie. They're in police custody and singing like little birdies."

That caused a long silence at the other end of the line. She was on the verge of hanging up when Lonnie burst out, "You want your uncle back alive or not?"

"What are you talking about?"

"You come to me and I'll let him go. You refuse to come to me, and I'll kill him. Your choice."

Her brief moment of bravado crumpled, leaving her bent and broken and so scared she could hardly breathe. "Where is he?" she asked hoarsely.

"With me."

She closed her eyes in agony. Every instinct she had was screaming at her to run, run, *run*! But she had to keep him talking. Get him to reveal everything she could before he hung up.

"Where are you?" she asked in resignation.

"Outside New Orleans."

"Give me an address."

"Head southwest out of New Orleans on Highway 90 and call me when you get to Morgan City. Be there in two hours, or your uncle's a dead man."

The connection went dead in her ear.

She quickly did a map check and found out the drive to Morgan City would take her a solid hour and a half. She dialed Bass's phone number, but he didn't pick up. She left a hasty message. "Lonnie called and he's going to kill Gary. I'm on my way to Morgan City." She rattled off the phone number Lonnie had called her from, too.

And then she raced out of the house. Sure enough, the alarm system allowed her to open the house door from the inside without any problem. She punched in the numeric code to get into the parking garage and tossed her things in the back of the van. Unlocking Esther, she took the two garage door openers off the visor, left the keys on the seat, and headed out.

This was not how she'd expected to leave Bass's house. But somehow, it felt inevitable. Bass had been right about one thing, at least. She hadn't been able to run away from Lonnie forever. He'd finally caught up with her. And it was time to pay the piper.

Chapter 13

Bass got out of the classified briefing a little after 9:00 p.m. They had a team in trouble in a nasty corner of the world, and they'd spent the past hour scrambling to arrange a safe house and build an exit strategy for a SEAL team trapped in hostile territory. Finally, all was well and the team was secure, but it had been tense there for a while. He stepped out of the metal, anti-surveillance cage around the briefing room, and his phone exploded with texts, vibrating madly in his pocket.

It rang just then—the police department phone number flashed on his screen—and he picked it up. "Detective LeBlanc."

"Hey. It's Jarred Strickland. We just got that file you requested unsealed."

Oh. That. "I already know her real name."

"No, Bass. The other file."

"What other file?"

"You requested all information about the death of Shelly Baker and Susan Baker Grange."

He'd forgotten about firing off that request. "Oh. Right. They're unsolved murders that might have something to do with the Hubbard kidnapping."

"Turns out they're not murders."

Bass stopped in the middle of the hallway. "Come again?"

"They're not dead. They're in the WitSec program."

"Who did they testify against? Lonnie Grange?"

"Give the boy a gold star," his boss replied.

Oh, man. Carrie was going to be ecstatic when she found out she hadn't killed her best friend and her friend's mother. "Thanks for letting me know. I gotta go talk to someone."

He disconnected the call, hurrying toward the exit. As he went, he checked the sender of all the messages. Strickland must have been frantic to get that information to him—

Except the person sending him message after message was Santiago Perez, one of the SEALs keeping an eye on his house. Quickly, he punched up the texts. The guy was losing his mind because Carrie had driven out of the property in her van a little before 8:00 p.m. and Santiago had no orders on whether or not to follow her.

And then Bass spotted the phone message from Carrie. Furious and panicked, he pulled it up and listened in horror as she told him hastily that she was going to meet Lonnie Grange by herself to save Gary.

He sprinted to the ready room and pulled the card out of his wallet that had the identification code for the tracking system he'd installed in her van. Thank God he'd done that!

A map popped up on the screen with a blinking dot

that was Carrie's van. She was headed out of New Orleans on Highway 90. Only major thing out that way besides swamp and alligators was Morgan City. Lonnie Grange had made a mistake hiding out in Bass's old stomping grounds. He knew every inch of that part of the state.

Bass called Carrie and listened in dismay as her phone sent him to voice mail. Why didn't she answer? Was she in Grange's custody already?

Stone cold terror roared through him, making him shiver with fear. He took off running for the building's armory, forming a mental inventory of weapons, ammo and gear he would need to operate in a swamp. He'd grown up in the low country and knew its many dangers all too well.

"What's up, Bass?" his boss, Commander Cole Perriman, asked from the doorway moments after he barged into the supply room.

"Carrie's gone to meet with her uncle's kidnapper in a misguided attempt to get him back."

Perriman groaned, then said briskly, "How many men do you need?"

Bass stopped stuffing ammo clips into a utility belt long enough to look up. "I beg your pardon?"

"She's your woman, right?"

"No. Yes. No. It's complicated."

Perriman grinned. "Always is when a woman's involved." He strode into the room and commenced picking up gear off the metal shelves. "I'm going with you. Let's grab a sniper and spotter—Trina Zarkos and Ford Alambeaux are in the building. She's a top-notch shooter, and he's been spotting for her for a while."

"We got a tracker in town?" Bass asked as he stripped off his civilian shirt and pulled on a high-tech sea-land shirt knit with metal microfibers that acted as armor against bug bites and minor snake bites. It was ideal for swamp ops.

"You're the best tracker I've got. But Mick McCarty's downstairs."

Bass nodded. "Let's grab him." The Aussie transplant was a desert tracking specialist, but the guy had eagle eyes and was a hell of a tracker in any environment, in addition to being tough as nails.

He hated having to wait for the other SEALs to gather, and he occupied himself pulling gear for all of them while he fidgeted. But within about ten minutes, the five of them had piled into a big SUV with all their gear and headed out. Perriman drove, and he put a siren on the roof of the SUV, flying down Highway 90 after Carrie.

Bass tried Carrie's phone again. Still no answer. He was going to *kill* her when he caught up with her.

And then his fear got the best of him and he just wanted to wrap her up in his arms and never let her go.

Cripes. His emotions were all over the damned place. Thank God Perriman had chosen to drive.

Bass briefed the team with everything he knew about Lonnie Grange and Gary Hubbard's kidnapping. Tony Sicarrio had confessed that Hubbard was being held in a swamp shack somewhere, but he had no idea the exact location. Apparently, Tony met Lonnie Grange at a gas station every few days to deliver food and supplies to his boss.

But no matter how hard he'd pushed Tony, the guy swore he had no idea exactly where Gary was being held. He did confirm, though, that Lonnie was trying to get Gary to tell him where his niece, Kathy, could be found.

Apparently, Gary hadn't confessed that Carrie was actually his niece. Bass had to give the old guy credit for holding out this long. It was noble of Gary to protect her life with his own. Not everyone had the grit to suffer for someone else.

Sicarrio had mentioned there was "creepy as crap" swamp all around the spot where he met Lonnie. Which suited Bass just fine. He'd grown up in those creepy swamps.

Bass turned to Trina Zarkos in the backseat. She was tracking Carrie's GPS signal on a computer tablet. For the hundredth time, he asked her, "Where's Carrie now? Tell me you haven't lost her."

"I haven't lost her. She stopped at a gas station in Morgan City long enough to fill up her vehicle. Maybe to make a phone call or two. She's heading west from there as we speak. Looks like she's heading into your neck of the woods, Bass."

Trina leaned forward from the backseat to hand him the tablet. "I've got topographical maps pulled up and overlaid on the road map along with the blip from your girl's tracking device. You're the local boy. Any guess as to where she's headed?"

Bass studied the computer screen, translating roads and waterways into the familiar territory of his youth in his mind's eye. "I know a shortcut that'll get us into the area she's driving toward in ten or fifteen minutes less than going all the way into Morgan City."

To Perriman, he said, "Continue straight for about ten more minutes. I'll call the turn."

Gary Hubbard's life might hang in the balance tonight, but more importantly, so did Carrie's. If something happened to her, Bass wasn't sure he would ever be the same again.

They drove a bit further, and then Bass started watching the road carefully. "Slow down, Frosty," he muttered.

Perriman eased off the accelerator.

"About a tenth of a mile more," Bass told him.

The commander turned off the highway where Bass indicated. They weren't able to careen along at godawful speeds, but this road cut the corner and pointed them directly at Carrie's current position.

Perriman turned on the high beam lights, illuminating a narrow asphalt road pitted with potholes and crumbling in the harsh climate. They banged along, punishing the SUV's suspension and their bodies. Bass and the others braced a hand against the ceiling as Perriman pressed on grimly.

Trina grunted, "Looks like she has stopped moving."

Bass glanced at the tablet Trina held up for him and swore. "She's transferring into a boat." He thought fast about who lived nearby. "I have a cousin who lives about three miles ahead of us. He'll lend me his boat, no questions asked. We'll turn right, and it's not gonna look like any kind of road at all. There may be some water over the road before we get to Lou's house."

Perriman replied, "This vehicle will handle about three feet of water if it comes to it. Engine's sealed for rough terrain."

God bless his boss for thinking ahead. Personally, he'd been so panicked when he'd gotten Carrie's message that he was lucky he'd remembered to bring ammo for his weapons.

They bumped along for another couple of minutes, and then Bass said, "Look for a mailbox mounted on a tree stump. That marks Lou's driveway."

Perriman turned on the searchlight mounted by his

rearview mirror, and Bass leaned forward from the backseat to point at the right side of the narrow road while Perriman drove.

"There!" Bass called out.

Perriman hit the brakes and turned carefully onto what looked like a patch of shorter weeds among the taller weeds and brush. "You're sure this is a road, Bass?"

"Positive. Lou is my mother's cousin. We used to come here all the time."

Ford commented dryly from the backseat, "No wonder I hear banjos in my head any time I hear you talk in that Cajun drawl of yours."

Bass didn't take his eyes off the nearly nonexistent driveway as he muttered in his thickest Cajun accent, "Don' make me fillet yo' face, boudreaux."

Everybody chuckled as the road curved and a cabin on stilts came into view.

No lights burned in the windows of Louis's house as Perriman stopped the SUV.

"Anybody home?" Perriman asked as Bass threw open his door.

"We'll find out," Bass replied as he jumped out of the SUV and ran up the stairs to the porch. He banged on the door and shouted, "'Ey, Louis. It's me, Bastien. You home?"

Nothing.

He banged again. The cabin was small, and he was making an ungodly racket. He would take that as a no, Louis was not home.

Bass raced down the steps and ducked under the house, making for the dock behind the cabin. A glint of aluminum caught his eye. Praise the Lord. Lou's boat was here.

"C'mon!" he called to his teammates. "And bring the gear!"

Everyone piled out of the SUV, grabbed gear and came on the run as he felt around above the door to a small boathouse for the spare key Lou hid up on the ledge. His fingertips touched metal. Bingo.

He stepped into the low skiff and started throwing off mooring lines as the others piled into the boat and efficiently distributed the weight of themselves and the gear to keep the boat evenly loaded and its center of weight low in the water. Bass cranked up the powerful outboard motor, and it rumbled to life hungrily.

"Lemme drive," he told Perriman. "I know these waters like the back of my hand, and I can run fast in them at night."

Mick threw off the last line and stepped into the skiff, and Bass gunned the motor. The lightweight boat leaped away from the dock and accelerated like a bat out of hell. It should. Lou had been known to run drugs in from the Gulf of Mexico to dealers in the bayou in his younger days. He'd developed a taste for fast boats that didn't look like much but were beasts in the water. And this one was no exception.

The front end of the skiff lifted up out of the water as the propeller dug in and flung the craft forward. In seconds, they were skimming along the still canal water at close to sixty miles per hour.

He headed in the general direction of the van's last position, some five miles ahead of them. Bass was just starting to contemplate if he should slow down and transition to the much smaller, but silent, bass fishing motor, when Perriman called in his ear, "A boat's approaching."

Bass maneuvered quickly over to the edge of the

canal, tucking the fishing boat under a bunch of over-hanging branches and cut the big engine.

Everyone in the boat had to practically lie down flat to avoid getting an eye poked out. He deployed the trawling motor without turning it on and held on to the nearest stout branch, praying the passengers in the big, loud boat about to roar past them wouldn't notice them.

The passing speedboat's wake rocked them violently, and Bass hung on tight lest he get tossed overboard. The vessel's running lights retreated rapidly and rounded a bend ahead.

He immediately pushed off, using the branches to propel Louis's bass boat out into deeper water where the propellers wouldn't foul in the weeds and muck near the bank.

They cruised forward at only a few miles per hour toward the bend ahead. They were running completely dark, now. Mick and Ford had removed the bulbs from the boat's sockets for running lights, and while they'd been parked in the bushes, everybody had grabbed handfuls of grass and hacked off branches with their field knives. They used the plant matter to obscure the profile of the boat and cover up its shiny hull.

Looking like a floating beaver hut, they rounded the corner.

Perhaps a quarter mile ahead of them, a large, expen-sive powerboat was moored. As Bass peered ahead over the prow of his own vessel, he saw two figures climb aboard the boat. And one of them only topped five feet tall by a few inches.

His heart leaped in recognition and then immediately plummeted to the soggy floor of the boat. Carrie was getting into that monster boat with a killer. In no sce-nario he could possibly think of was that a good thing.

Perriman held up a closed fist, signaling Bass to stop the boat. He did, cutting the motor and letting Lou's bass boat drift forward slowly. The silence was heavy and unnatural and made the skin on the back of his neck crawl. The bayou should be a deafening cacophony of insects and critters at this time of night.

The powerboat roared to life and everyone ducked, expecting the boat to come back toward them. But instead, it raced away from them, on down the canal. Where was it headed?

He cranked up the main engine and gave chase, but that speedboat was going to outdistance him easily. And without the GPS tracking unit in the van, he had no way to follow her. Bass swore violently.

"What about her cell phone?" Trina asked. "Does she still have it on her?"

"Only one way to find out," Perriman replied. Bass listened in agony as his boss put in a call to SEAL ops to ask them to ping Carrie's cell phone. Bass fed his boss the phone number.

"They've got a signal," Perriman announced.

Bass sagged in relief.

"It's intermittent, though. Lousy cell tower coverage out here."

Bass could have told them that.

Perriman fed a set of GPS coordinates to Trina, who showed the map to Bass. The speedboat was headed toward open water. There wasn't much down that way but an abandoned oil refinery and some floating docks where ocean trawlers delivered their catch to shallow draft boats who hauled the catch inland.

"Why does Grange want Carrie instead of Hubbard?" Perriman speculated. "The old guy's semi-famous. Could be worth a little ransom. But her? She's a nobody."

Bass ground his back molars together while Ford and Trina exchanged a loaded look. Ford muttered, "Spoken like a man who's never been in love."

"My love life has nothing to do with this," Perriman snapped.

Trina popped back. "It's your lack of a love life that's under discussion. Carrie is the most important person in the world if Bass cares about her."

All eyes turned on him, and Bass scowled, not liking being the center of his teammates' attention.

"Grange and Carrie have some past history together. She called the cops on him a long time ago, and he went to prison as a result."

That silenced everybody. He didn't need to tell them that Grange would torture Carrie at best and kill her at worst.

The wind whipped past, spray slashing at his skin. They ran the canal at the boat's top speed for about fifteen minutes before Trina yelled, "Ops says Carrie's signal has stopped moving!"

"How far ahead is she?"

"About a mile!"

Bass cut the engine and shifted over to the bass motor. They glided forward silently for a couple of minutes, and then Trina murmured, "Her tracker's on the move again. She's moving away from the water slowly, like she's on foot, apparently."

They spied a ramshackle boathouse with a boardwalk leading from the structure to solid ground some hundred feet inland.

They had to assume someone was inside the boathouse until they cleared it. Hating to lose the time, Bass nonetheless steadied the bass boat against the outer wall of the building while Trina, Ford and Mick crept inside to clear it. In about sixty seconds, they declared it empty but for the speedboat Carrie had arrived in.

Quietly, Perriman ordered Ford to disable the engine. He lifted the engine cowl and removed a wiring harness. Good choice. The engine wouldn't run without it, but if the SEALs wanted to render the boat operational again, the wires could be replaced quickly.

Perriman pulled out a set of infrared goggles and scanned the thick undergrowth around them. "No humans or habitations within a hundred meters. Let's move out."

Thank God. Bass's need to be with Carrie and make sure she was safe was almost choking him.

"Bass, take point, but be careful. Take your time. Mick, behind him to help track. Trina and Ford, next. I've got the rear."

Bass nodded, silently acknowledging the wisdom of Perriman's warning. He scooped up his assault rifle, unlocked the safety, and headed down the boardwalk, moving with catlike stealth. No need to stomp down the thing and announce to everyone in the neighborhood that the cavalry had arrived. On elephants.

He tested each board for soundness and squeak as he put his weight on it. The SEALs behind him would step exactly where he had, ensuring silence for all. He moved swiftly, nonetheless, not liking how exposed they were silhouetted atop the boardwalk.

He was relieved to step ashore. The ground gave way spongily beneath his boot but took his weight with a faint squishing sound. He hoped this island got higher and drier soon, or they were gonna leave big ole' footprints all over the place, announcing their presence. Of course, there would be only one set of prints since everyone would step in his boot impressions. Still. Folks in these parts were hunters, and even kids could spot and track human footprints.

Speaking of which, he moved far enough ashore that everyone could get off the dock and acclimate themselves to the mushy terrain. He stopped and pulled out a dimmed, tight beam flashlight with a green filter. It was ideal for tracking because it highlighted shapes and shadows. He flashed it in an arc in front of him. Mick touched his sleeve and pointed off to the right just as Bass spotted the tracks too. Four sets of fresh human prints, one set noticeably smaller and shallower than the others.

"There's an oil refinery off that way about a half mile. Good-sized facility."

"Active?" Perriman asked.

"It was abandoned a few years back. To my knowledge it's not in operation."

Trina murmured, "I'll have Ops send us a schematic while we move."

Bass moved off in the direction of the footprints while Mick hand-signaled to the rest of the team that they had a live trail.

Bass paused to look for threads that would tell him what she was wearing and what color and texture of fibers to be on the lookout for going forward. He spied a bit of cotton lint. It appeared white in his night vision goggles but could be any light color. Looked like it came from a sweatshirt. He passed the speck of lint to Mick, who examined it briefly and then nodded. They moved on. Tracking considerably slowed the team's forward speed, but they still moved fairly quickly through the brush and trees.

Bass jolted as something slithered away from his feet. He paused to let a large, black cottonmouth snake vacate the trail. He'd outfitted everyone in the team with knee-high rubber shin guards for exactly this reason. A snake could strike at any of them and not penetrate the tough leg coverings. He signaled over his shoulder to Mick that he'd spotted a snake.

The Aussie nodded, no doubt understanding the warning. Where there was one snake, there were always others. And out here, there could be nests of dozens or hundreds of others. Rattlesnakes were the worst about nesting, and they were plentiful around here.

Unfortunately, it wasn't cold enough tonight for the local reptiles to be inactive. At least Carrie's footprints were moving away from the shore and prime alligator territory.

Mick touched Bass's sleeve and pointed out another speck of cotton lint on a bramble at about shoulder height for Carrie. His pulse jumped. She'd been here recently. She just had to hang in there a little longer, and then he would save her.

She must be terrified. God knew, he was scared to death. And he knew these woods top to bottom. On top of that, he was most at home in the dark. The wilder the terrain, the better for him and his teammates. But Carrie was no SEAL. She had to be out of her mind with fear.

The footprints he followed started to have a tiny bit of standing water in them. Which meant they were fresh enough not to have drained back into the ground, yet. He pointed out the water to Mick, who signaled back to the others to be on high alert.

A faint swish of cloth behind him was all the indication he got that the rest of the team had brought their weapons up into firing position. From here on out, they would be operating hot. Anything or anyone who moved in a hostile manner toward them was dead.

He took a deep, cleansing breath and released it slowly, forcing himself to drop into the calm state of hair-trigger readiness that was the SEAL's trademark.

Hang on, Carrie. I'm almost there.

Chapter 14

Carrie swatted at a bug and stumbled again, the soft ground giving way beneath even her slight weight. She moved away from her armed escort a bit, testing how far from him Grange's man was willing to let her stray.

Lonnie was walking ahead of her, leaving his flunkies to herd her along.

She ducked under a tree branch and straightened, only to run facefirst into what felt like a spiderweb across her whole face. She jumped, flailing her arms in front of her frantically, batting away the sticky silk, which seemed determined to wrap entirely around her head.

"What the—" the guy in behind her complained. "Stop that!"

Carrie jumped left, banging into the guard walking beside her. She shuddered and brushed off her entire body urgently. "Spiderweb," she gasped.

"Kee-rist, this place is a hellhole," the guy behind her grumbled. "I'll take New York City any day over this godforsaken jungle."

The other guard agreed fervently. They were both big, beefy men, but not diamond hard and battle honed the way Bass was. Please God, let him have gotten her phone message by now. Surely he would come after her.

For once, his possessiveness and tendency to over-react to any perceived threats in her direction was a boon. Although how he was going to find her out here in the literal middle of actual nowhere, she hadn't the slightest idea.

No wonder the New Orleans police hadn't caught the slightest whiff in the past week of Uncle Gary's loca-tion if he was hidden out here. There might as well not be any other human beings on the planet, given how isolated this place was.

Panic surged into her throat for about the hundredth time, and she forced it down yet again. But each time it came back, her control of it slipped a little bit more. Soon, it was going to get the best of her, and she was going to fall apart. And then not only would she be dead, but Uncle Gary would be, too.

"How much further?" she asked no one in particular.

"Shut up," Lonnie snapped.

She looked questioningly at the guy beside her, and he shrugged.

From behind her, the second guard complained, "I didn't think it was this long a walk."

"Quit whining," Lonnie snapped. "We're almost there."

Hah. So much for telling her nothing. She'd counted almost a thousand steps, which put them around a half mile inland, if her count was correct. As best she could tell, they were moving south and east. But that was assuming she hadn't gotten herself all turned around during the winding ride to the boathouse earlier.

At any rate, she had a rough direction of travel for herself and Gary when they made their escape. If he was still alive. And if he was ambulatory. And—biggest if of all—if they got a chance to make a break for it.

Perhaps three more miserable, sticky, bug-infested minutes passed, and a tiny speck of light became visible beneath the trees ahead.

She'd never been so relieved to see even the tiniest hint of civilization that the light represented. They walked a few more minutes, and the underbrush gave way to a wide-open area paved with weedy old gravel. Two huge cylinders announced this place to be an oil refinery or something similar.

The light was one of those fluorescent affairs that people mounted on barns and that came on automatically at night. It hummed loudly, casting blue light across the refinery yard.

Rust and decay were everywhere. The place must be abandoned. Drat. No workers to recruit to help her.

Lonnie pushed open a gate made of aluminum poles and hurricane fencing and strode toward what looked like a small office. Its walls were wood, gray and weathered, nailed vertically. The roof was made of rusty corrugated metal.

As prison-like as it looked, she was ready to have walls and a roof around her, no matter how crude, as long as they held back the insects and night creatures.

Lonnie threw open the door and waved her inside. She looked around the main room eagerly and frowned. "Where's Gary?"

"Oh, you thought we were bringing you to him?" Lonnie laughed, an ugly sound.

"That was our deal. Take me hostage and you have to let him go."

"I don't have to do anything I don't want to." He devolved into calling her various names and casting slurs at her, but she tuned them out.

Was Gary somewhere else in this large facility? Lonnie wasn't a local. Surely he didn't have multiple hideouts out here in the bayou. Gary must be nearby. If she shouted, would he hear her? Shout back?

One of the guards opened a cooler in the corner and pulled out three bottles of beer, which he shared with Lonnie and the other guard.

Frankly, she found it a bit insulting that they thought they could drink booze while guarding her. Did they really think she was that meek and helpless? She'd successfully evaded Lonnie for years, and the only reason he'd caught up with her now was because he'd dragged her uncle into this mess.

But hey. If they wanted to get sloshed before Bass got here, all the better. She moved cautiously around the small room, trying not to draw attention to herself. She checked out the windows, noting the simple locks and low sills.

"Is there a functional toilet in this building?" she asked.

One of the guards led her down a short hallway to a grungy bathroom that hadn't seen a good cleaning since the building was new. It had a small window, high up, but she thought she could fit through it if she could reach it.

Making a disgusted face, she asked, "Do you guys

have a sponge and some scouring powder? No way am I using this without disinfecting it."

"I dunno. Look under the sink," the guy said, unconcerned.

She opened the decrepit cabinet doors and spotted a toilet brush and what turned out to be a fossilized cardboard tube of scouring powder that had turned into a solid block. "I can work with this," she declared. "Do you have a table knife or a fork I can use to chip off some of the powder?"

The guard disappeared down the hall, and she took a quick moment to check out the lock on the window. It looked broken, and the screen over it barely clung to the window frame.

The guy came back with a plastic spoon, and she rolled her eyes. As a weapon, it was pitiful, but still, it was better than nothing. She scraped at the hardened powder and managed to loosen enough of the stuff to give the sink a vigorous scrub with the toilet brush. She moved over to the toilet and gave it the same treatment. Rust stained the porcelain and made it look awful, but at least it was reasonably sanitary, now.

"Satisfied, Your Highness?" the guard asked.

"Toilet paper?" she responded tartly.

Muttering under his breath, the guy left again and came back in a minute with a handful of tissues. The guy handed it over with rolled eyes and, as she stared him down, backed out of the bathroom to give her privacy. "Two minutes," he warned her.

Whatever. She wasn't breaking out of here until Gary joined her, anyway. Even if her old friend, an overwhelming urge to run, was making her jumpy as heck.

Where was Bass? Did he know she was gone yet? He must be furious with her for leaving without him.

But it wasn't as if she had any choice. She had to take the offer to save her uncle. Gary hadn't done anything to merit Lonnie Grange's ire, other than be related to her by blood.

Lonnie hadn't changed one bit. The garlic smell of his breath. The yellowing of his teeth from smoking. The truculent arrogance. The way he'd gelled his hair to disguise how it was thinning.

One thing had changed, though. She was determined to fight him to the bitter end, this time around.

Blessedly, she remembered nothing of his attack on her. The bastard had drugged her and snuck into her bedroom when she'd been spending the night with Shelly. She'd woken up sore and naked the next morning and put two and two together. But even hypnosis had failed to recover any memory of the actual attack. Which honestly was fine with her.

Just living with the knowledge that it had happened had been almost more than she could deal with. It had taken years for her to make peace with the fact that she hadn't been a tease or done anything at all to deserve what Lonnie had done to her. He was a criminal, and she the victim of a violent crime. End of discussion.

If Gary wasn't here, she might even entertain the idea of getting even with Lonnie somehow. She could think of a few pertinent body parts of his that she would love to maim or sever.

Memories of Shelly and her mother, both outgoing, fun people and how the light had gone out of both of them while living with Lonnie passed through her mind. He'd been rich, and Mrs. Baker had been lured by the promise of financial security at long last for herself and her daughter. She'd never dreamed what the price of it would be.

The old fear came flooding back, certainty that Lonnie would kill her, too, given the chance.

Of course, he'd conveniently been in Miami and loaded up with airtight alibis for the time in and around Shelly and Mrs. B's disappearance. The crime had never been pinned on him, but Carrie had no doubts. He'd had his thugs kill them both.

Had one of the men in the main room killed her best friend? Her breathing accelerated and her chest tightened until she thought she might faint.

What had she done? She'd voluntarily handed herself over to the very people who'd killed Shelly! She'd been so focused on getting Gary back, on running away from Bass, on fleeing his offer of safety and permanence—which was nothing more than smoke and mirrors at the end of the day—that she had run right into the arms of killers.

She was an idiot.

She deserved to die. For real.

A fine sheen of sweat broke out on her forehead, although whether it was from her silent panic attack or the muggy humidity hanging in the air, she couldn't tell.

She had to get away from here. Go back to New Orleans. Find Bass. Lead him back here. She'd suffered from temporary insanity in thinking she could handle this herself. As usual, she'd acted first and got around to thinking a distant second.

A fist pounded on the door. "Open up or I'm coming in!"

She flung open the door and followed the guard back into the office. Lonnie was gone. "Where'd Lonnie go?" she asked.

"None of your damned business."

She sat in the chair one of the guards pushed in her

direction but not before pulling it over to one side a bit, placing it squarely in front of a window. If Bass found this place, he ought to be able to spot her now.

Surely, someone would find her eventually. The way Bass described it, these waters were far from deserted and a lot of people lived and fished in the low country. Someone would spot her and say something to someone else. It wasn't great as escape plans went, but it was better than nothing.

She had no idea what time it was and didn't want to pull out her cell phone to check. They hadn't confiscated it from her, and she planned to keep it that way. When she'd gone to the bathroom earlier, she'd tucked it inside her bra where the guards were less likely to find it if they frisked her. Her cleavage wasn't anything to write home about, but it was substantial enough to cover up the presence of her cell phone.

All she had to do was stay calm, be patient and wait for her captors to make a mistake. And then she would find Gary and run like the wind.

Bass spotted an opening in the trees first. Then a petroleum storage tank. He slowed to an even stealthier pace and crept forward step by cautious step.

The team stopped, crouching at the edge of the clearing about twenty yards from a hurricane fence surrounding the facility.

Perriman used infrared optical devices to determine that three heat signatures were clustered in an office building. No one else was visible. But it was a big place with plenty of spots to hide behind thick metal that would mask heat signatures.

Perriman murmured, "Trina, Ford, set up a couple of shooting positions to cover all possible approaches to that office. Mick, I need you to scout the area. Bass, start working your way up to the office. If you can't look in directly, get me an audio feed."

Bass nodded and moved out on his belly, low-crawling toward the fence, rifle across his forearms, using clumps of weeds for cover. *Hang on, baby. I'm coming.*

He'd barely made it to the fence when Mick breathed, "Problem. I've got a tanker truck full of liquid oxygen parked behind the office."

Bass froze. A bullet into a tanker of LOX would cause an explosion big enough to fry the office building and anyone in it.

"Can we move the truck?" Perriman asked.

Ford interjected, "It's going to have GPS in it. Move a truck full of hazardous materials, and it'll trigger alarms. We'll have the sheriff out here in no time."

Perriman replied, "I can call the sheriff. Tell him to keep his men away."

Bass muttered low, "As soon as you call him, he'll tell all his guys a bunch of SEALs are out here pulling off a rescue. All his deputies will show up, along with any civilians who happen to have their police band radios on. We'll have a damned audience for this op."

Perriman responded, "Can you disable the GPS, Mick?"

"Yeah, sure. It'll just take some—" He broke off abruptly, and Bass went on full alert.

What had the Aussie seen that made him go dead quiet? Bass peered off to the left behind a bunch of pipes and fittings that had been the last place he glimpsed Mick.

At first, he saw nothing. But then he spied a light flaring briefly in the window of a large, run-down building that could have been a storage area or some sort of factory. That light would not be Mick. Someone else was out here.

Behind him, Bass felt as much as saw Ford, Trina and Perriman disperse, melting in the night as they moved around the perimeter of the refinery. It was a big place and was going to take them a while to reconnoiter.

They couldn't realistically move in to rescue Carrie until they identified all the hostiles and had some idea of what kind of firepower they were up against. Not to mention, Gary Hubbard could be out here, somewhere.

Bass's money was on that big building to be where Carrie's uncle was being held.

Swearing under his breath at the delay, Bass continued to move toward his primary objective, that small office structure. He stopped to peer at it through his spotter's scope and saw Carrie immediately, sitting in the window like she was waiting for him.

His heart leaped with joy and relief. She was alive, and apparently unharmed. Thank God. He actually felt weak with relief.

It was a struggle to keep moving at the speed of a glacier, but he finally made it to the side wall of the office and parked underneath the very window Carrie was sitting beside. He heard two men talking inside, arguing about football teams and brands of beer. Which was to say, they were relaxed and showed no signs of being aware that a SEAL team was moving in on them.

Various clicks over his earbud over the next few minutes indicated that the others were still working at clearing the sprawling facility. Carefully, he snaked a tiny camera on a flexible rod over the edge of the windowsill, parking it inconspicuously in the corner of the window.

Carrie's face leaped into view as he peered down

into a black bag containing a three-inch wide monitor for the camera. He'd never been so glad to see someone in his life as he was to see her, uninjured, albeit looking afraid.

Both of the guards were looking away from her, and Carrie was looking straight at the window. He risked moving the camera a little bit. She blinked and stared right at the lens. He moved it again. She nodded infinitesimally, and her mouth curved up into the faintest of smiles.

She wasn't out of the woods by a long shot, but at least she knew she wasn't alone now.

Mick came up on the radio, murmuring, "GPS is disabled. But this puppy's full up with liquid oxygen. One hit, and it's a fireball."

Ford replied, which meant Perriman must be someplace sensitive at the moment. "We'll have to move that truck. The civilians in the office will have no idea to avoid striking that entire tanker."

"It's gonna make a mighty roar when I start up the tractor trailer," Mick warned.

Ford said aloud exactly what Bass was thinking. "We'll move it simultaneous to making our assault on Carrie's guards. Speaking of which, how many hostiles are with her, Bass?"

He clicked his microphone twice.

"Copy. Two hostiles," Ford replied. "How about you, Frosty? How many hostiles have you spotted?"

Two clicks came in reply. There was a pause, and then one more click from Perriman. Ford followed up quickly. "Do you have eyes on Hubbard?"

One click.

That meant yes. One click for yes and two for no.

"Is he alive?" Ford asked.

No clicks at all.

"You don't know his status?" Ford murmured.

One click.

Bass swore mentally. If Gary wasn't ambulatory, they would have to allocate more force to liberating him and less to freeing Carrie. It was child's play for five SEALs to shoot four civilians. However, that liquid oxygen tanker was a wild card, and it was illegal for American military members to kill American citizens, particularly on American soil in an unsanctioned op like this.

Dropping four armed men without killing them—now that was a trick. They would have to close in to hand-to-hand range and drop Lonnie Grange and his men the old-fashioned way. Thank goodness he'd helped train Trina in close combat tactics. He knew full-well her capabilities, and she wouldn't have any trouble taking out Lonnie or one of his men.

At length, Perriman came back up in Bass's ear. Obviously, he'd backed away from wherever Gary was being held so he could talk with his team.

"Mick. Get inside the truck and be ready to hot-wire it and move it on my command. Ford, I need you with me to drop Lonnie, who's over in this building, and pull out Gary. Trina, join Bass. You two have the guards on Carrie. We all go at once."

Bass was tempted to demand to switch places with Ford so he could be the one to take out the bastard who'd made Carrie's life a living hell for all these years. But when it came to a choice between saving Carrie and getting revenge on some thug, Carrie was a thousand times more important to him. He sat tight on the other side of the wall from her.

Trina was almost on top of him before Bass spotted

her. She came around the back of the office building
with admirable stealth.

He passed the camera monitor to her, and she put
the black bag to her eye to get the layout of the room.
A big, old desk stood in the far corner of the space, and
several chairs stood in front of it. One of the guards sat
directly in front of the door, and the other close to the
back wall, not far from Carrie.

He pointed at his chest and then at the back end of the
room. Trina pointed at her chest and toward the door.
She then hand-signaled that she would go in through the
front door and that he should go in through the window.

He nodded his understanding and craned his neck to
stare up at the window. It consisted of two glass panes,
bottom and top. He would fit through the lower opening but would have to dive and roll to get through it.
Which was okay. The roll would carry him across the
room almost to the guard he was assigned to.

"Call when you're in position, Mick," Perriman whispered. "Everyone else, click in."

Meaning click when they were in position to attack.
Each of them had a discrete Morse-code sequence
which they used to identify themselves one by one.
Trina clicked first, then Bass. It took about two more
minutes for Ford to click in. Then, last but not least, Perriman clicked in. Now it was a waiting game for Mick
to get inside the truck, tear open the dashboard and pull
all the right wires. As soon as the Aussie touched the
correct leads together, the truck would start.

"Ready, steady," Mick reported in a whisper. "Make
the call, Frosty."

Perriman gave all of them a moment to collect themselves, to review in their heads what they were about
to do.

Trina stood up and moved over to the corner of the building. She would swing around to the side and burst in from the front while he jumped up, knocked out the window glass, and dived past Carrie.

Breathe. Exhale. Relax. No emotion. Just reflex and reaction from here on out.

"Go," Perriman bit out.

Trina spun away from Bass as a big, noisy engine rumbled to life. Bass jumped up and used the butt of his rifle to smash out the window glass. He paused just long enough to run the rifle stock around the edge of the window frame fast, knocking out jagged shards of glass that could snag his shirt and hang him up.

He caught a glimpse of Carrie's face reacting in shock as he leaped through the window and rolled practically on top of her feet. His guy had jumped up in the interim and was staring out the far window, presumably at the truck starting to pull away from the office.

And the bastard had a pistol in his hand, pointed outside.

Aww, hell.

Bass came to his feet and rammed his shoulder into the guard's back, praying he knocked the guy's aim off target.

The pistol fired four shots in fast succession—bastard had the thing on full-auto—blasting out the window glass and sending bullets out into the night, directly toward the damn truckload of liquid oxygen, but then Bass had him around the throat.

Bass yelled in his throat mic, "Gunshots incoming, Mick! Get out!"

Bass twisted away from the window, dragging the guard by the throat, choking the sonofabitch for all he was worth. It would take a good thirty seconds for the guy to fully black out, and the guard clawed at Bass's forearm violently. Thank God for his SEAL-issue, micro-armor shirt.

And then everything happened in slow motion. Carrie leaped to her feet, presumably to help him.

Trina's guy writhed in her grasp, and somehow managed to get a revolver out of his belt.

Carrie opened her mouth to scream, and the revolver fired wildly.

Then the mother of all explosions happened outside. Something hot ripped into Bass's flesh, knocking his arm away from the guard's throat, and then he was flying through the air.

The hard ground came up to meet him, slamming into him with the force of a freight train. And then the world went black.

Chapter 15

Carrie saw the guard by the door pull out a gun and in-stinctively dived for cover, screaming at Bass to be careful.

A blinding flash of brilliant light and a massive, deafening wall of noise smashed into her. The desk went flying, and she went flying with it. She hit the ground in a ball, and the heavy wooden desk landed all around her, her body tucked neatly in the leg space between the banks of drawers to either side of her. For once in her life, being small had been a boon.

She tried to shove the desk off, but it didn't budge. Awkwardly, she turned around and pushed with both feet against the underside of the desktop. It moved slightly, and a shower of dust and debris rained down on her. She should have heard that stuff falling, but it hadn't made any sound.

In fact, she only registered utter silence. Confused, she clapped her hands together. Nothing. Ohmigosh.

Was she deaf? Had the explosion shattered her eardrums?

She pushed again on the desk, and a ringing noise started inside her head. It was almost more painful and loud than the original explosion. Her head started to hurt as if she had a massive, all-over migraine, and she paused to rest.

She pushed again with her legs, and the desk shifted a little more. Then, all of a sudden, it lifted away from her, and a dusty-faced Perriman stared down at her. His lips moved, and it looked as if he asked if she was all right. She pointed at her ears and shook her head to indicate that she couldn't hear.

He nodded and flashed her an okay hand signal. It was okay that she was deaf? Or did that merely mean he understood her?

She mouthed, "Where's Bass?"

Perriman reached under the desk and pulled on both her arms, dragging her free of what turned out to be the blasted remains of the office building. It had been reduced to a pile of kindling and twisted metal. Carefully, she picked her way clear of it.

Again, she asked, "Where's Bass?" She could be whispering or shouting. She had no idea.

Perriman mouthed, "I don't know."

Oh, God. She turned to the debris pile that another man dressed like Perriman and a woman were picking through frantically. She joined in the search, shoving aside debris in wild panic.

He had to be okay. He had come for her. Saved her. Put his life on the line for her, the big, stupid, lovable jerk!

Bass had been just to the left of her when the explosion happened. She went back to the desk and started to work her way back toward the center of the blast. In about thirty seconds, she spotted something black. Fabric.

She shouted, "Over here!" and vaguely heard her voice inside her skull. Okay. Not permanently deaf, then.

The others joined her immediately, and the four of them tore at the pile. She'd found Bass's leg.

Please God, let it still be attached to his body and let him be alive!

The three others worked together to lift away a section of wall, and Carrie spied Bass's torso. Afraid like she'd never been afraid before, she grabbed his leg and gave a mighty heave. Where she got the superhuman strength to drag him clear while the others held the piece of debris off him, she hadn't the faintest idea. But drag him she did. All two-hundred-plus pounds of solid muscle.

He was unconscious. The others dropped the panel and knelt around him. The woman pushed Carrie aside unceremoniously while one of the other men felt for a pulse under Bass's chin and Perriman ran his hands over Bass's body. Must be looking for injuries.

Perriman found something because, all of a sudden, the woman was sprinting away and then sprinting back with a backpack. She dropped it on the ground, and the men used bulky scissors to cut away Bass's shirt.

Carrie glimpsed a black, ragged hole in Bass's right shoulder with something black oozing from it. Oh, God. Had he been punctured by a piece of flying debris?

Vaguely, she heard Perriman snapping orders. The others started handing him medical supplies. She watched in horror as Perriman stuffed something that looked like a balloon into the hole and then blew hard on a tube attached to it. Then gauze was being slapped over the wound, tape slapped over that, and Bass turned over on his side. The hole on the back of his shoulder was much bigger and gushing what had to be blood.

Carrie pressed her hands to her mouth and prayed for all she was worth. She couldn't lose him now. Not when she'd just found him!

She heard a voice as if from a distance and looked up. It was the woman, shouting in her ear, "Don't faint!"

Carrie nodded resolutely. She wouldn't faint. Not while Bass needed her.

Perriman grabbed Carrie's hand and slapped it over the wound on the front of his shoulder, pressing down hard on a hunk of gauze. She nodded, understanding that she should keep pressure on the wound.

Then they were stuffing another balloon thing into the rear wound and inflating it. She gathered that it was meant to slow internal bleeding. More gauze, more tape, and Perriman put Carrie's other hand over the whole mess again.

A few seconds passed, and then the woman took over pressing on Bass's shoulder wounds and nodded for Carrie to look at something across the refinery.

Out of a big building on the far side of the facility, two figures came outside slowly. One leaned heavily on the other. The faint starlight glinted off the leaning one's silver hair—

Uncle Gary!

He was dirty, disheveled, growing a scruffy beard, and had lost weight. But it was definitely him.

She bolted across the big yard, dodging debris from the explosion and flung herself at her uncle, tears streaming down her face.

"Thank God you're safe!" she sobbed. "I love you, Uncle Gary!"

"I'm safe thanks to you and your friends," he said in her ear.

Hey, she heard that!

"I never broke, baby. I never told them who you are. Never told them you were who they were looking for." And then Gary was crying too, clinging to her as tightly as she clung to him.

The reunion was poignant and sweet, but she had somewhere else she urgently had to be. "I love you, Gary, but I have to go check on Bass."

"On who? There's a fish out here?"

She lost the rest of his words as she turned and ran back to Bastien's side.

A discussion was underway over a radio about how to get Bass out to medical care the fastest. A helicopter from New Orleans would take a half hour or more to get here. There was a hospital in Morgan City, but by the time they carried Bass back to the boat, drove him to land, met up with an ambulance, and transported him, it could take as long or longer.

Perriman ordered, "Send a chopper. Tell it to fly like a bat out of hell. And make sure they've got units of blood onboard. My guy's bleeding heavily."

Carrie almost wished her hearing hadn't started to come back as Perriman described Bass's gunshot wound in gory medical detail.

Bass started to cough, and the sound was juicy. Bubbles of blood formed on his lips.

No, no, no, no, no. She couldn't lose him.

Carrie crouched down beside him. "Don't you die on me!"

Perriman touched her shoulder, and she turned to

him, frantic. He explained gently, "He's bleeding internally. It's filling his lung. He may not last until help gets here."

"What blood type is Bass?" she demanded.

"AB negative."

"I'm AB negative!" she cried. "Take a pint from me. Take two! And help him breathe, for God's sake! I can't stand here and watch him suffocate!"

"Technically, he'll drown," Perriman commented. "Help me sit him up, Ford. Trina, set up an arm-to-arm transfusion from Carrie to Bass. We'll hold off doing it as long as we can, but if Carrie wants to give him blood, I'm not going to stop her."

Good call. She would open a vein herself if she had to in order to save Bass.

He breathed a little easier once he was upright, and his eyes fluttered slightly.

"Don't you die on me!" she repeated.

"Don't have. To shout," he sighed.

She couldn't tell if she was shouting or not, and she didn't much care. As long as he heard her.

"I love you, Bass. You can't die. You hear me?"

Trina commented dryly, "Most of southern Louisiana hears you."

Carrie shrugged and kept right on shouting. "Stay with me, Bass. Fight to live. If I don't get to run away from you, you don't get to run away from me!"

He smiled up at her, a pale ghost of his usual bright smile, and then his eyes drifted closed once more.

"Wake up, Bass!"

Perriman looked up at her as she bent down over Bass. "He's unconscious. It's best this way. He shouldn't suffer."

"He's. Not. Going. To. Die."

"I like the way you think, young lady. Keep thinking that way."

She nodded resolutely.

Ford, monitoring a blood pressure cuff on Bass's arm murmured, "His pressure's starting to drop."

Perriman said tersely, "Now, Trina. Start the transfusion from Carrie to Bass. Keep the flow slow. We need to make this blood last as long as possible because it's the only matching blood we've got until that helicopter gets here. Keep watching his vitals, Ford."

Carrie held her breath, praying like crazy. "C'mon, Bass," she cried. "C'mon! Wake up!"

Ford muttered, "Pressure's stabilized. It's low as hell, but he's still with us."

Over the next several minutes, blood trickled from Carrie's arm through a thin rubber tube into Bass's.

"That's about a pint," the woman called Trina announced.

Carrie reached out fast to block her from removing the needle from her arm. "I can give him more," she insisted.

"A little. But we're not bleeding you out to save Bass. He'd kill us if we let anything happen to you." Trina leaned close to murmur, "He loves you, you know."

Carrie was starting to feel a little light-headed. Surely she hadn't heard Trina correctly.

In the distance, Carrie thought she heard the thwocking sound of a helicopter. Please, please, let her be hearing that correctly.

The SEAL named Ford glanced at his watch. "Twenty minutes flat. Impressive. They must have firewalled the engines and oversped everything to get here this fast."

"Damn straight they did," Perriman muttered. "Where's Mick?"

"He's alive, dazed, but mostly unhurt," Trina said. "I told him to lie down and rest while you guys worked on Bass's wounds. Bass warned him in time to get out of the truck."

"Saved my life, he did," an Australian-accented voice came out of the dark.

"I want you on that helicopter, too," Perriman ordered. "You were way close to that truck when it blew."

The Aussie protested, "I'm not the one hollering fit to wake the dead. Carrie needs the ride back to town more than I do. Besides, we've got a little cleanup to do around here."

And that was the first moment it had dawned on Carrie to wonder, "What happened to Lonnie?"

The SEALs traded looks over her head. Perriman said evenly, "He won't be a problem to you any longer."

"Is he dead?" she demanded. "He is, isn't he?"

"I can neither confirm nor deny that," Perriman answered. "Ford, Trina, go feed the alligators."

It took her a moment. But then it hit her. They were going to dispose of Lonnie's body where alligators would eliminate any evidence of what had happened tonight.

"What about his men?" she asked.

"We didn't kill any of them. If they survived the blast, they're welcome to find their way out of here. It's not like they'll go to the authorities to report us. And frankly, after tonight, I'm confident they'll never want to tangle with any of us again."

That caused a chuckle all around.

The thwocking sound was loud, even to her impaired hearing, and a violent blast of down-drafting air announced the arrival of the medevac copter. Paramedics rushed over to them, pushing a wheeled gurney with them.

Everything happened quickly, then. Bass was lifted onto the gurney, an IV attached to the needle already taped in his vein from the first transfusion, and then she was being hustled alongside the running medics and shoved into the chopper. Hands strapped her into a seat, and then they were soaring skyward.

The medics worked urgently over Bass, and she tried to take up as little space as possible, staying out of their way while they fought to save Bass's life. They emptied three bags of blood into him during the ride. That couldn't be good.

The ride seemed to take forever, but eventually, the helicopter bumped onto a hard surface, and there was another rush of people and gurneys and running across a roof to an elevator.

She was pulled away from Bass and pushed into an examining room while Bass was rushed on down the hallway into surgery.

And then the waiting began.

She barely paid attention when a doctor came in to examine her ears and declared her eardrums intact. He assured her that her hearing would return to normal shortly, warning her that she might experience some ringing in her ears for several days. The decision was made to admit her for observation to make sure she wasn't suffering from a concussion. She could live with that.

At some point, Cole Perriman poked his head into her room to tell her that Gary had also been admitted, suffering mainly from dehydration and a bit of malnourishment, but that he would be fine.

"How's Bass?" she asked urgently.

"Still in surgery."

Ford, Trina and Mick joined Perriman, holding a silent vigil for Bass in her room. They didn't speak much, they just sat in the shadows like patient ghosts, waiting in utter stillness.

As for her, she couldn't seem to be still. Nothing was ever going to be right again if Bass didn't make it.

How could she ever have considered leaving him? She'd seen him and his companions commit violence tonight. They'd rescued her uncle and saved her life. And frankly, she couldn't work up a whole lot of dismay or even disapproval that they'd done it. They were, indeed, the good guys.

Now, if only she got a chance to tell Bass that.

And to tell him she loved him.

Chapter 16

Bass woke up slowly. He registered a nurse in surgical scrubs hovering over him, and then he drifted off. Sometime later he came to again, this time in a dimly lit hospital room. He was no stranger to those. After all, he'd been a SEAL for a long time. His right arm and shoulder were heavily bandaged and throbbed distantly. Wow. They had him on the good drugs.

A small shadow moved in a chair by the window.

"Carrie?" His voice came out a whispered croak.

She was up and out of the chair instantly, rushing to his side. She perched on the edge of the bed beside him and he held out his good arm to her.

She accepted the offer immediately and cuddled carefully against his side. "How do you feel?"

"Good. Drugged."

He felt her smile against the side of his neck. "You gave us a bit of a scare last night."

"Last night?"

"You were in surgery for six hours, and you slept all day today. It's night again."

"My arm?"

"They saved it. They had to do a complete reconstruction of your shoulder, though. They think you'll regain full use of your hand over time."

He frowned, his brain still foggy. "Over time? How much time?"

"They couldn't say. Months. Maybe longer."

"Oh." He turned that idea over in his brain. "Am I done as a SEAL?"

"Commander Perriman says you can train SEALs as long as you can walk, talk, and, umm, use the restroom by yourself."

Bass grinned. Those would not have been Perriman's exact words, but he got the gist. His smile faded. So. He was done in the field, but he could stay on board as a trainer only.

A month ago, that would have been a gigantic tragedy to him. Maybe it was the painkillers, but he didn't find himself overly concerned about it now. He still had his police work, and he could keep his toes in the SEAL world by training the next generation of SEALs.

He looked down at Carrie, her head resting against his good shoulder. "I'm just glad you're safe."

"Me, too."

"How's your uncle?"

"Resting comfortably downstairs. He was dehydrated, malnourished, and in need of some antibiotics to clear up a sinus infection he picked up, but he's otherwise unharmed and charming the socks off his nurses."

Good. That was good. The details of the mission were starting to come back to him now. "Mick?"

"Fine. Your warning allowed him to jump out of the truck and run before it blew."

"Grange?"

"I believed the technical term for him is gator bait."

"Indeed?" He nodded, satisfied to hear that news. Then he grinned. "Look at you talking all southern-like."

She raised herself up to smile down at him.

"Oh, I just remembered something!" he exclaimed. "It's gonna make you happy."

"What's that?"

"Your friend, Shelly, and her mom? They're not dead. They went into witness protection after they testified against Lonnie Grange. They're alive."

Joy exploded across Carrie's face, and his heart warmed to be the one to put that expression there. "Can I see them?"

"Maybe. We'll have to file a request through channels, and it'll have to get passed to them, and then arrangements made for you to meet them without blowing their covers. But eventually, I expect you can see them both."

She stared down at him for a long time, relief and gratitude swimming in her gaze. At length, she murmured, "You did it, Bass. You kept your promise and took care of Lonnie for me. He'll never bother me again."

He smiled up at her and used his left hand to push a stray lock of hair back from her face and tuck it behind her ear. "I'm glad. And you can stop running now…if you want."

She nodded soberly. "About that. I have a confession to make."

His heart clenched in trepidation. Here it came. She

was going to dump him and be on her way, off to the next ghost story, the next anonymous town.

"The night Lonnie called and made me go to him…" She paused, seeming to struggle for words. "I was running away. I was on my way out of town and never coming back."

Pain that had nothing to do with his recent surgery twisted in his gut. "Why?"

"I was afraid. Afraid of Lonnie. Afraid I wasn't strong enough to stand up to him. Afraid of you."

"Of me?"

He struggled to sit up, but stabbing pain in his shoulder forced him back down to the pillows.

Carrie looked him square in the eye. "Yes. I was afraid of you. Of how you make me feel. I've never felt like this about anybody before. You made me consider stopping running for the first time. And that terrified me."

"What about now, with Grange out of the picture?"

Silence drew out between them as she searched his eyes, and he prayed she found what she was looking for.

She answered slowly, "I'll always run, Bass."

His heart plummeted to the floor. Just kill him now. He didn't want to live without her. He *couldn't* live without her. But neither would he force her to stay.

She continued in a rush, "But not away. I'll run to you. Every time. No matter how far away I go, I'll always come back to you. You're my anchor. The only home I'll ever want or need."

His heart started to beat again, and hope burst to life inside him. "You're sure?"

"Positive. If you'll have me."

A smile broke across his face. "If I'll have you? Woman, I don't want anyone but you!"

"You're sure?" she asked in a small voice.

His smile widened. Filled his whole face. His whole being. "I'm positive. You just run right into these arms, and I'll catch you every time."

Right then and there, Carrie leaned down and whispered in his ear the four words that made him know, without a shadow of a doubt, that this time she was here to stay. "I love you, Bass."

"And I love you, Carrie."

They stared at each other in wonder that, through all they'd been through, all the doubts and suspicions and obstacles, they'd found each other.

"Marriage?" he asked.

"Definitely."

"Kids?"

"Lots."

"When?" he inquired.

"Immediately."

"Done."

And with that, she climbed into his arms, exactly where she belonged.

Forever.

* * * * *

Don't miss the rest of the thrilling
Code: Warrior Seals miniseries:

Undercover With A Seal
Her Secret Spy
Her Mission With A Seal

Available now from Harlequin Romantic Suspense!

Get 4 FREE REWARDS!

We'll send you 2 FREE Books plus 2 FREE Mystery Gifts.

Harlequin® Romantic Suspense books feature heart-racing sensuality and the promise of a sweeping romance set against the backdrop of suspense.

FREE
Value Over
$20

Ian heard Petra's scream and his blood turned cold. He leaped from the floor and sprinted out the door.

The walkway was empty. Petra was gone—vanished. The echo of her shriek had already faded.

He turned in a quick circle, his eyes taking in everything at once. He saw them—a set of hands clutching the bottom rung of the railing. Petra. Her knuckles were white.

He dived forward and grasped her wrists. "I've got you," he said. "But don't let go."

Petra stared up at him. Her face was chalky and her skin was damp with perspiration. His hands slid. He clasped tighter, his fingers biting into her arm. One shoe slipped from her foot, silently somersaulting through the air before landing with a thump in the courtyard below.

"Ian," she gasped. Her hands slid until just her fingers were hooked over the metal rung. "I can't hold on much longer."

A sharp crack broke the afternoon quiet. It registered as a gunshot and Ian flattened completely.

Just as quickly, he realized that the noise hadn't come from a firearm, but someplace just as deadly. One of three bolts that held the section of railing in place had cracked.

If one of the other bolts broke, the whole section would topple, sending Petra to the courtyard twenty feet below. Then again, maybe that was the best way to save her life.

"Look at me," Ian said to her. She lifted her wide eyes to his. "I have an idea. It's a long shot, but the only shot I have."

Her face went gray. "Okay," she said. "I trust you."

"I'm going to let go of your arms," he said.

Petra began to shake her head. "No, Ian. Don't. This railing's weak. It could fall at any minute."

He ignored the fear in her voice and the dread in her expression. "That's what I'm counting on. I'm going to kick the other bolts loose."

"You're going to what?"

"You have to hold on to the railing and I'll lower it down. At the end, you'll have to drop, but it'll only be a few feet."

"What if you can't hold on to the railing?"

That was the real question, wasn't it? Ian refused to fail. The alternative would be devastating to Petra—to him. "I won't let you get hurt," he vowed.

Petra bit her bottom lip. Their eyes met. "There's no other way, is there?"

Ian shook his head. "Hold on," he warned, "and don't let go until I tell you."

"Got it," she said.

Ian paused, his hands on her wrists. He wanted to tell her more, say something. But what? The moment was too important to waste on words.

"Don't let go," he said again.

Find out if Petra falls in
Rocky Mountain Valor *by Jennifer D. Bokal,*
available September 2018 wherever
Harlequin® Romantic Suspense books
and ebooks are sold.

www.Harlequin.com

HRSEXP0818

Need an adrenaline rush from nail-biting tales
(and irresistible males)?

Check out **Harlequin® Intrigue®**
and **Harlequin® Romantic Suspense** books!

New books available every month!

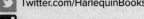
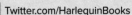
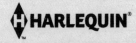